THE SHADOWED WAY

A NOVEL

LEGACY'S ROAD
BOOK TWO

M. DANIEL SMITH

This story is dedicated to my family, all. My father, a man of honor and capability to manage problems with a calm and knowing mood. My mother, a wise woman who shares her empathy with everyone she meets. To my two older sisters, who, though of the same blood, are as different in their approach to life as the sisters in this novel, loving their brothers who adore them both. To my brother, youngest in age but towering over us all. A man with an innate knowledge of the world about him. And to all the other members of my family clan, blood related or not, each with their own stories to tell—thank you for sharing them with me over the years.

And finally—to my beautiful, vivacious fiancé Yvonne. You are truly my muse—a generous, emotionally open, and earnest woman bringing light into my life. I am blessed that you've agreed to us being joined as husband and wife.

CHAPTER ONE

BRISTOL, ENGLAND
EARLY SUMMER, 1760

Pipe-smoke scented the air of Richard's study with a mix of oaky sweet tars and redolent oils, a rich blend of Turkish and Virginia colony tobacco leaves. Harold leaned back in a chair near the window, a vacant expression on his face. His father, sitting behind his desk with pipe clasped in a scarred hand, searched Harold's eyes, measuring the change in him. He finally nodded, breaking the silence, his words edged with sorrow. "You have met the beast."

Harold lowered his eyes and stared at the scar on his left hand where the outside finger had been lost to a musket ball, leaving a gouge torn along his upper ribs and shoulder. "It has made a feast of me. Body—and soul." His voice was whisper thin. "As you prophesied."

Richard shrugged, then tapped the bowl of his pipe against a clay container, emptying it of charred residue. He offered it to Harold, who refused with a wave of his injured hand. His father slipped it away in a waistcoat pocket, then nodded. "It was not too much of a meal provided it. Precious few managing to escape its bite—especially when leading from the front. Which, if certain tales related by spurious pamphleteers were written true—you did, the entire time you were there."

Harold angled his head, the light streaming through the study window highlighting thin wrinkles pinching the edge of his eyes. "You —read them?"

"As did we all." Richard considered his son. "You saw the crowds yourself. Heard your moniker echoing in the air, with everyone in a frenzy as they shouted it. Red Fox. Red—" He stopped, seeing a grimace of pain slip across his son's face. "I'm sorry. Spoke without consideration of how you might feel—receiving acclaim for dark deeds needing to be done."

He leaned forward, hand outstretched, though he was sitting too far away to touch Harold's. "Your uncle and I kept abreast of what you accomplished, albeit two months or more after the actions described in broadsheets. Poured over the lurid descriptions of your many victories —along with the loss you suffered—your injuries described in painful detail."

Harold turned away, shoulders heaving, hands clenched as everything he'd felt, experienced, and buried away over the past two years rose to the surface, fully exposed in the presence of the only person who could understand what he was feeling. Had been feeling, ever since placing the final rock atop his mentor and friend, left lying in eternal rest thousands of leagues to the west. The press of a warm hand on the back of his neck broke the dam, Harold turning into his father's body, his grief spilling from him in silent, heart-wrenching sobs. He clung to the man he'd never been able to reach out to before, tossing aside stiff lipped English mores as he shared his love for, and pain from, the loss of those he'd stood alongside while facing down the beast of war.

As his son began to unwind the gnarled threads of his bittersweet memories, Richard listened without comment, recalling moments of his own spent facing certain death, the echoes of his comrade's voices as they fought and fell beside him swirling through his mind.

Harold's mother, standing on the other side of the study door, leaned her head against it, listening as her son slowly revealed his journey through the shadows of war with shuddering gasps and long, drawn out pauses. Holding her hands clenched over her heart, she ached to go to him. To go to them both. Then she straightened up, wiped her eyes, and walked away.

Richard went over to his desk and opened a drawer, removing a bottle and two tumblers, pouring each half-full of whiskey. "They will come for you. Have already started the chase—in using your visage for their own propaganda." He handed his son a glass. "Here's a bit of—"

"Mother's milk—I know." Harold nodded his thanks, taking a healthy sip, savoring the deep-bodied flavor before swallowing, the warmth of it spreading throughout his chest, helping him recover from the memories of those he'd lost, each a dagger to his heart. "My second—Sergeant Major Scott—Robert—he always said that after every action, while offering me his flask." Harold paused, staring at the whiskey in his glass. "Until the last one."

Richard studied his son, unable to find any sign of the son he'd shared drinks with at a local pub in what seemed to have been only a handful of days ago. A man now, full grown, appearing to be of middle age, his face lined from the pain of grievous wounds suffered over the two years and more he'd been away. "Was in the same position myself—more than once. Offering liquid comfort to young officers, new to the game. More than a fair share of them slipping through my grasp over my years of service." He smiled as he lifted his scarred hand. "The lack of two fingers—not helping me keep a tight enough of them."

Harold leaned back, buoyed in spirit from sharing a connection with a fellow member of the fraternity of war. "I was fortunate—to be placed under his tutelage. Of both his and General MacLean's, the two of them having served together long before they arrived in the colonies. Back when Aidyn—when the General was no different than I was. New to the, as you named it—to the grind." Harold shook his head, lips pressed tight. "As you tried to warn me about, in telling the truth of it."

Richard shrugged, then refilled and lit his pipe, eyeing his son through a trail of smoke rising from the bowl. "Destiny finds a man—one way or another. The few who manage to meet it with some measure of success often left suffering the most for gain in notoriety. Paying for it with the loss of those who helped them rise through the ranks—both friend and foe."

Harold looked up, finding his father's eyes. "And you believe me to be one of them—a man of destiny?"

"A named man often becomes a reflection of himself as seen in other people's eyes. I served alongside a few of them in my time. All—with feet of clay, though marked by an awareness outside of themselves. Allowing something—unseen—to move through them. At times." Richard leaned back, a soft smile hazing the edges of his weathered face. "I was honored to stand in their shadow back then—as I am honored to stand in yours, this day."

Harold blushed, embarrassed by the look of respect in his father's eyes, resisting any alteration in their relationship. "I'm not—"

"You are, Harry, despite any protestation made against it. I recognized it in you long ago, seeing it for the first time, out back in the yard. Saw it in your eyes when you looked up at me in anger, slowly turning to awareness as you—as you saw the truth of what I was trying to show you."

Harold looked down at the glass clasped in his hands, the dark surface of the whiskey reflecting the memory of the day in mention, a few hours after his younger brother was laid to rest. Himself, left alone, standing out in the back yard staring at the sandbox where the two of them had spent hours recreating battles. His mind numbed by grief, unable to fathom ever being able to do so again, alone. Lead-metal figurines left standing where Jackie had placed them before chills and a fever had forced him from the battlefield.

⸕⸕⸕

The sun was a smear of a dull circle hiding behind a thin curtain of gray clouds. Rain, intermittent throughout the day, had not yet been fully delivered, leaving Harold standing outside the family manor, studying the interior of a wood-framed rectangle resting on the ground. His eyes were narrowed in concentration as he stared at a line of British troops formed into a solid wall of hand-painted red and white figures, facing a horde of enemy soldiers represented by a mix of acorns and pebbles, posed in a semi-circular arc, pinched between two mounds of earth piled at one side of the sandbox. The battle lines as shown had come from a drawing in his newest book of military campaigns: a birthday gift from his uncle Thomas, frowned upon by his father, though grudgingly consented to after a pleading look from his mother.

"God's eye." The gravel thick voice of his father calling out from behind startled Harold. "The view—from on high, with everything seen clear and true. Same as was written down in the books you and Jack—" There was a slight pause, his father's voice softening a bit as he continued. "The same ones you were always studying. The author's drawings showing the field of battle as described, based on after action reports—with no regard for the viewpoint of the men, standing the line."

Harold started to turn around, unable to complete the motion, his neck held in his father's firm grip, forced to the wet ground, the iron-forged hand sliding down and pressing on his shoulders until he was fully prone, head arched back, jaw jammed in the sand of the box, his throat squeezed against the edge of the thick wooden frame. Harold struggled to free himself, unable to find a reason for his father's harsh behavior, his eyes stinging with tears from the undeserved punishment.

A hiss from his father's lips, close to Harold's ear was frightening. "This is what the plan of battle looks like—when seen from a soldier's perspective. Low to the ground—the enemy hidden behind folds in the earth. Unseen. Their voices heard—felt—in here." A solid thump hit him between his shoulder blades, resonating throughout his chest as Harold heaved, trying to free himself from the painful assault.

"Sit up." Released, Harold complied, his hands shaking in anger, tears in his eyes, forbidden to flow by his firm will. His lips were pressed thin by repressed fury as he watched his father kneel beside him, careless of the wet grass and its potential to stain his best pair of pants. Harold noted the wince of pain on his father's face as he bent his knees. "The men—line soldiers—those who churn the ground into muck at the General's whim and wish—have only the view just shown you. One with a man standing to either side, the terrain in unseen detail before them. No lofty perch on horse, eye to glass for them. Left having to wait, watching for the first sign of movement. Their bowels loose—breath short—hands trembling as they cling to their muskets."

"You were here." Harold tilted his head, gazing at his father. "I mean *there*, on the ground—" Harold pointed. "With them."

His father nodded. "I was. And it's not as the words in your books describe it. Each group of soldiers—left standing on their own island, surround by the chaos that comes along with killing. Currents of unbelievable rage carrying reason away. Training—hundreds upon hundreds of hours—the only thing keeping men standing the line. Firing—reloading—firing again—and then again, until released by the order to rush forward—thrusting with bayonet, over and over again without thinking. Until finally—it ends."

"In victory for us. For England. For the King!" Harold looked at his father, the man's eyes locked to a point far beyond the horizon, blinking slowly. "Right—Father?" The old soldier nodded, wiping his brow, the ends of his fingers dragging tears away as he did so.

"Yes, Harry. For England—and the King." Richard held up his hand, waiting for his son to stand, then help him to regain his feet. "I did not mean to interrupt your recreation of the battle. I only wished to impart an—alternate point of reference. One not found in the books you and—and our Jack were always pouring through."

Harold gazed at the battle scene his brother had laid out, noting the precise placement of each soldier, just in front of the imprint of his chin, embedded in the sand. He knew he would never see it the same way again, his mind forced open to a deeper appreciation of what his father had been through and managed to survive. At a cost of more than two fingers, having lost some unseen part of himself somewhere deep inside his pain twisted body. A loss still with him to this very day.

⸎⸎⸎

"They will come for me—as you said." Harold raised his glass, taking a long sip, fighting an urge to drain it, and then the bottle as well. He looked over at his father, who watched in silent appreciation. Harold forced a tight grin. "I know it will happen—know it's already started, seeing the throng of people waiting at the docks. Felt it—from the man sitting in the carriage beside me, his mind whirring away as if a clockwork, considering when and how hard to press the lever—with myself the fulcrum to his ambition."

"That would have been a member of the consortium who made their approach to me. Men with black-stained fingers. Dangerous men, Harry—holding the power of peoples rapt attention, hanging onto every word in print."

Harold nodded. "Words wielded for bad or good effect, depending on one's viewpoint, based on their political inclination and degree of personal morality—entwined."

"Your head is in their noose." Harold's father shrugged. "The price of trumpeting your success, well-earned though it was, a bill they will soon want payment of." He paused, eyeing his son carefully. "Would you go back and change it—any of it—the decisions made, or actions taken?"

Harold shrugged. "Maybe. A few. None that helped aid our campaign against the French. But as to spending more time with, and a greater effort made for ensuring the welfare of those I became close to —then yes. I'd go back and not waste a single moment in letting them know how much I cared for them. How much I came to love them —all."

Richard nodded. "It's an ache we both bear, having lived with our heads pressed against the earth. The future—a misty field in morning fog at the best of times. A tempest whirlwind of earth, bodies, feces, and blood—when things go south. Our eyes blinded by fear, anger, and loss."

Harold raised his glass, then drained it, setting it down on a small table. He leaned forward; hands clasped between his knees. "So—what is your advice as to what comes next? I'd hoped to have an opportunity to encourage negotiations between colonies, crown, and native groups. To speak on behalf of an increase in trade of goods. Partaking of mate- rials in ripe abundance in the colonies. More than enough for all. Hoping to use my title and the fame assigned for what it is I want to accomplish." Harold paused. "I'd welcome your views, based on your experience—to help me form a plan of action."

"A war of a different sort, as it were." Richard nodded, emptying his glass with a careless shrug of head and hand. He wiped his lips as he stood up, helping his son to his feet.

Harold grabbed his father's arm, the whiskey having gone to his head, causing him to stumble. He let go and straightened up, his voice overly loud in the hushed confines of the study. "To victory of right—over greed. Sense—over sedition. Morality—over—over might!"

Richard smiled. "How about we aim for a first step made, without you falling flat on your face—the drink having floated your thoughts. Go—and lay yourself down while I consider the planning of this mission in greater detail."

Harold's mother opened her son's bedroom door and slipped inside, carrying a large mug of cold tea. She walked over and placed it on a small table between his bed and the window, leaving it there for when he woke up. Taking his shirt, left draped over the back of a chair, Eira held it up, wondering when her boy had grown large enough to fill out its wide shoulders, as if a transformation made in the shadows. Able to accept it now, with Harold home and in one piece, more or less, his smile distant but still there, tucked away in the corners of his mouth.

Harold stirred, throwing his left arm back in a restless toss, exposing the scars on his wounded side. Eira muffled a gasp of shock, her fingers pressed to her lips as she stared at the large, bone-white patches of skin on her son's upper chest and side, revealing the horrible damage he'd suffered. A wave of pain rose from her womb in a cold fist, squeezing her heart, her mother's soul tormented at not having been there to soothe him, to wash the sweat from his fevered brow with cool water, leaving behind a trail of her warm tears. Her knees trembled beneath the weight of harm seen done to her boy, coming to rest on her shoulders as if it were her own to bear, her child lying before her as if a precious painting, the canvas rent by a clumsy stoke of butcher's blade, sewn back together with clumsy fingers, leaving ghastly tears upon his flesh.

Harold opened his eyes and smiled, feeling young once more, if only for a moment stolen from time, his features quickly settling back into a practiced routine of tight grimace then release as he stretched his arms, yawning. "A bit too much—as Gran Da used to say—of *Agua Vitea*. The water of life, imbibed."

Eira pulled a ready smile from where all mothers hide them, slipping it across freckle dusted cheeks beneath deep-blue eyes and hair the color of spun gold, trimmed in white along the edges of her forehead. She hid her pain, not wanting to add to the burden her son carried. "Not so much of it in ye, as your Da. But true enow—with its curse of a headache caused." She reached down and picked up the cup. "I've brought cold tea for you, if you're in need of it."

Harold hand was a serpent's strike, taking it from her and bringing it to his lips, drinking noisily, thin rivulets streaming from the corners of his mouth, landing on his chest. "So good. So thirsty —no doubt due to all the childish tears, shed on Father's chest." He sat up and wiped a hand across his bare skin, then took his short from his mother, noting the line of her sight. He slipped it on as quickly as he could to try and soothe the look of concern in her eyes. "It was a ball—a musket ball—from one of my own soldiers. Took my finger off, then knocked me flat. The shot made in error, coming from a young man new to sentry duty. Caused by my having come upon him out of the dark, as if an apparition. Unexpected and —unidentified."

Eira smiled. "We need not speak of it again. You're home safe, and I'm finally able to draw a full breath once more."

Harold buttoned his shirt, head down, easing circles of carved ivory through needled slits in the thin fabric. "I know you heard what was said, earlier—in Father's study—your head pressed to the other side of the door." It was not a question, Harold's eyes soft as he reached for his mother's hand, squeezing gently. "I'm glad you did. Would not have been able to say those things to your face. I could never paint such a look of sadness on your lips. Hard enough for me now, seeing it in your eyes."

Eira released herself from his grasp, turning and throwing open the curtains, letting the early afternoon light into the room. "Get yourself dressed and come down to the kitchen. You must be famished."

"The mid-day meal you provided was more—"

"Mid-day, yesterday, Harry. You've slept the night through, and more."

Harold cocked his head, his hair hanging over one shoulder, dark as midnight, like his father's. His face still much too thin, appearing to him in the mirror as if a reflection of his mother's father, the past two years having scrubbed away the softness of his cheeks. "Really? I had no idea of having needed it—the rest. Though I didn't sleep well on the voyage back. Spent my nights walking the deck, keeping watch from the bow." He shook his head, giving his mother a warm smile. "Like Grand Da always did, going outside the wee croft house in the highlands in the early morning and staring up at the mountain. Jackie and I would watch from our bed, yawning, rubbing our eyes, wondering what he was looking at."

Eira nodded. "Speaking of my Da—I've booked a carriage to go and see him, near as he is to a final climb to the top of the mountain." She gave Harold a searching look. "Would you like to go with me?"

"I am, as the General—as my friend and former commander Aidyn told me when we parted, free to pursue a life of luxury, having been granted a colonel's pension. With an additional stipend attached for wounds suffered in service to the King."

Eira stared at her son. "I didn't—I mean, your father and I didn't know. A colonel? We understood you to be a lieutenant."

"There is a story behind it, as with most things waiting to be told. One I will be happy to share with you both—once we have buried the carcass." Eira arched her reddish-blond eyebrows in confusion. Harold grinned. "Of the beast I'm about to consume in its entirety—once it's been cooked, carved, and plated."

The dishes were cleared away, with a full-bodied red wine used to dampen his mother's reactions as Harold wove his tale, detailing as much as he felt could be shared in her company. His father listened without interruption, filling in the spaces between occasional pauses in his son's voice with thoughtful nods. When Harold told of his mentor's passing, his parents exchanged a knowing glance, and then another when he mentioned having drawn the cameo likeness of the girl named Sinclair.

Harold, his voice steady, paid homage to his mentor, friend and boon companion. Then he told them of Meghan and her passing, having to stand up and go to the window, arms crossed on his chest, his cheeks wet with tears. When he'd finished and dried his eyes, he returned to the table, draining the rest of his wine as he looked down.

Richard was the first to speak. "Few words indeed, used to account for endless hours of a life—lived in full. It's why we are compelled to carry the memories of those we've come to love, so as to mark their passage into, then through our lives." Harold and his mother exchanged a glance of their own, never before having heard Richard wax poetic, the taciturn man seldom using two words where one would suffice. He nodded as he tapped the bowl of his pipe into a clay jar on the table, then stood up, begging his leave to attend to bills of lading waiting for him in his study.

Eira reached across the table and took Harold's hand. "Thank you for sharing. I feel I have come to know those you've spoken of as if part of my own family. Happy they were there for you when in need of comforting. Sorry for their loss—such a brutal life, at times, for those standing so close to the edge of—of civilization."

"There's no boundary to be found there, Mother. No edge to it at all. There is a vast nation of civilized people who've long been in residence there, between the edge of the eastern ocean and whatever lies beyond. We're the ones who've continuously encroached on their lands, accepting offers of hospitality and trade—returning disease and broken promises in exchange. We have behaved in our finer moments as if a large, overly friendly dog—with mud-stained paws. As if ravenous beasts with slavering jaws—in darker times, led by snakes with false smiles and twisted words, encouraging tribe to fight against tribe. Father—against son. Until blood on both sides is made to run like water, along the red path of war.

Eira stared at her son, uncertain as to his meaning, unable to marry the image of the boy Harold had been to the man he'd now become. "Surely there is more than enough land—for all?"

"A piece of it can be enough for most people, Mother. All of it—

never enough for some. Those are the ones I need go up against in order to protect the rest."

"To protect your friend—the Indian girl. A'neewa."

"To protect those who are natives, Mother. A'neewa and all her people, including those of the other native tribes. To help them secure an independent state, or territory. Left to live in as they see fit. Allied to England, in word and deed with generations of young warriors eager to help defend our—defend their cause and ours. Brave men helping to expand our military forces, sent to every corner of the world. Joining us—eager to prove their valor in battle. A fair exchange for self-government granted. Their blood, if you will, in exchange for enhanced trade with us."

"It sounds—horrible, in hearing it stated so—so—"

"Bluntly?"

"Yes, Harold. I've never heard such thoughts coming from you. Not from the son I—"

"Watched sail away? Tucked into a shadow at the dock, hat and veil on your head and tears in your eyes. As if you could hide yourself from me. As if I would not find your face in the milling crowd. Along with Father's, too—each of you there without the other knowing."

Harold stood up and came over, pulling his mother to her feet, holding her, his chin resting atop her shoulder. "I see it all so clearly. Always have, no matter the moment. I knew you understood my need to leave, though you were unable to accept the reason behind my decision." He leaned back, finding her eyes, seeing her for the woman she was, while loving the mother she'd always been. Harold was happy to go with her, to make his own goodbye to her father, his Gran Da. To pay homage to the elderly man who'd lent himself in full to two young boys in restless itch, eager to take from him all the attention he had to offer. Without apology offered or regret felt at the theft of his time and energy, spent on their behalf.

Eira smiled, reaching up to smooth her son's hair back, her fingers touching the side of Harold's face. "You've always been different. Much more so than our sweet Jackie ever was. Not as bright a light as he—but willing to spend so much of your time with him. Always patient with him." She leaned in, rising to her toes in order to kiss his cheek. "You were born with a wider view of things, though able to narrow your vision and look deep into them as well. It's why you managed to survive—and are standing here now, having rediscovered —no, having fully revealed yourself. The lessons learned—painful ones, at times. The rewards—equally as painful. But I can see they are cherished memories, too. And will be with you throughout the rest of your life."

Eira released herself from his arms, leaving him to the warmth of the dining room and fireplace, coals glowing red against the press of the cool evening air.

The family warehouse was dark, its cavernous interior holding rows of shelving containing a huge volume of bundled materials, along with stacked kegs and large oak barrels, lying on their sides. Two large doors, closed against the afternoon air, were locked from inside with thick wooden crossbars. Harold and his uncle Thomas stood on an upper platform at the top a narrow stairway, staring into the shadowed recess of the interior that represent his father's half of the family business, with three small temporary storage buildings located at the near end of a long finger pier a hundred paces away, belonging to his uncle.

Harold had been asked by his father to meet with Thomas in order to go over a manifest list. He'd agreed, aware the manifest was more of a ruse, allowing his uncle an opportunity to speak in private with him. A meeting Harold had been looking forward to, with his uncle always willing to listen and then share his thoughts, feelings, and ideas.

Thomas waved his hand, pointing into the interior of the large building. "Then we agree that we're in complete accord with the city assessors report." Harold nodded, following Thomas as he turned and led him through a doorway, ending up in Richard's office. His uncle sat down behind the desk, taking notice of a leather valise lying on the floor, one he'd gifted to Harry when he'd shipped out to the colonies, two years ago. Thomas aware now, based on the deep lines etched in his nephew's face, that the months between his departure and return had aged him greatly.

"My thanks, Harry—for you're coming here today. I appreciate your willingness to help—as always."

"My pleasure, Uncle." Harold crossed to a seat on the opposite side of his father's desk. He pulled the valise over and undid two leather straps, pulling out four journals filled with notes, observations, drawings and other information, a record of his experiences while waging war in the vast wilderness surround of the American colonies. He placed them on the desk, his uncle eying them as if they were bags of coin. "It's all in there, Uncle Thomas. Every thought, feeling, and emotion—written down when and where they occurred, or soon after—given time and energy enough to do so."

Harold paused, closing his eyes and sighing, remembering back to when he'd been another man, living another life in a richly colored and vibrant land. One he was still tethered to by a headstone in a family plot, bearing the name of a woman he'd been willing to die for, and with. And another stone, placed in the ground between the thick roots of a sentinel oak, honoring a man standing a lonely watch over a wide valley bordered by a twisting ribbon of gleaming water.

Harold opened his eyes, then slid the journals across the table. "I want to share these with you. As repayment of the gift of them to me—used to help keep the memories alive of people as close to me as my own flesh and blood. Memories of those I served with. All the people I came to love—some of them lost to me." He paused, taking a deep breath, exhaling slowly. "Allowing me the honor of holding their stories in trust, to be shared and reflected on by—whoever reads these. You—being the first, if so inclined. And one day my children—should I be granted opportunity to have them."

Thomas touched the stack, his fingers trembling. "I—am bowed down by your willingness to share these." He paused, glancing up at Harold. "My brother—has he had time enough to go through them all?"

Harold shook his head slightly, his eyes fixed on his uncle's. "He's not been offered them."

Thomas reached out, caressing the leather surface of the top one, noting the damaged cover. "Are you certain I should be the first? Perhaps better to wait and share them with him, when he's ready."

"My father has his own memories of what he suffered through." Harold leaned back, folding his hands in his lap. "You provided the pages to be filled in. They are now provided you to read—to learn what your nephew has done and been made party to, since last you saw him standing on a dock, the gift of the valise and journals in hand." He paused. "The honor now falling to you. The burden of it—as well."

Thomas gazed back, his eyes gleaming. "I don't know what to say, Harry. Don't know—"

"Then best to say nothing. Just read, so we can speak of it another day. All of it." Harold felt a calmness settle over him, seeing the other man clearly as if a veil had suddenly been removed from between them. "As if—father to son. As if Jackie and I were your very own."

Thomas leaned back, a look of shock on his face, gone pale in the flickering light from two wall sconces. "You—mustn't say that, Harold! You're wrong—to suggest such a thing."

"My father's wounds—the scars on his lower body. His stiffness when standing, and time needed to—relieve himself. The look of pain on his face every waking moment, with every step he takes. All the worse when on horseback, his body tense, trying to hide it." Harold paused a moment, his face relaxing into a contemplative gaze. "As well the look in my mother's eyes whenever you visit. Fading away when you leave—or whenever my dear aunt enters."

Thomas looked down at the journals. He swallowed, took a deep breath and released it. "How long—how long have you known?"

"For certain?" Harold shrugged. "Just now, from the look on your face when I offered you my personal history. Could see the truth of it in your eyes. A different look than that of my father's. Which he is— and will always be."

Thomas clasped his hands in front of him, his voice soft. "It was both his and your mother's proposal."

Harold nodded. "I realize that. My mother's no—well, the arrangement most certainly would have been a difficult one. For all."

"Your father—" Thomas looked away, his voice filled with grief. "Somehow Richard bore it—in wanting heirs. Someone of his own blood—to share what the two of us were building."

"You loved her. You've always loved her."

"No." Thomas shook his head. "Not like that. I would never—"

"You do, Uncle. I recognize the look—having worn it myself." Harold nodded at the journals. "It's all in there. My having sworn my love to a woman still in love with another man. A good man. Unable to let him go, though he was long dead. Herself wishing to be with him, again. Loving the thought of me as husband, but not able to accept the ring, wedding, and promise of home and hearth. Aware she could never bear our children. Too brutal a reminder to her of what had been wrenched from her. Torn from her body. From her heart—and soul."

Thomas looked at the journals, biting his lower lip. "I am almost afraid to look. To see it revealed. A common pain—for us all."

"It's not all we share, Uncle—though I understand and appreciate your feelings." Harold shrugged. "Perhaps this revelation will allow for more open discussions of other things. Where your issuance of insightful advice can be offered openly, between a doting uncle and his appreciative nephew—which we are. Still."

"Yes, Harry. Of course. Nothing's changed on that account." Thomas hesitated a moment, staring back. "I've always wanted only the best for you. For you and—for Jackie." Tears began to flow at the mention of his name, Thomas bowing his head, his narrow shoulders trembling, his thin hands drawn into fists, resting on top of the desk.

Harold smiled. "Jackie had your looks. Your hands, ears, as well as your intellect, greater than my own and that of my father's. An equal match to your own—the chess matches between the two of you things of beauty and finesse."

Thomas reached up, wiping his tears away. He looked at Harold with a soft expression. "You, with your father's mind and eyes. The two of you always looking for and finding a strategic maneuver to employ. Seeing everything. Missing nothing. As if you were able to read other men's thoughts."

"Until the one time—when I didn't." Harold looked down, his hands twisting in his lap. "Leading good men to their deaths. Leading one—dearer to me than all the rest, to his. Nearly ending with my own."

Thomas pulled the small pile of books closer, resting his hand on top of them. "Revealed in here?"

Harold nodded, his eyes half-closed, fatigue pulling at his shoulders and upper eyelids as thoughts crowded in, prying at doors he'd resisted opening, banging on them now. He stood up and stared at the books lying beneath his uncle's hand. "We'll speak again, Uncle—when you deliver these back to me. At a corner table in a public house, tankard of ale in hand, sitting in the shadows toasting to our common pain."

CHAPTER TWO
SCOTTISH HIGHLANDS
SUMMER, 1760

The scent of hay mixed with the earthy odor from a long-haired highland bull compelled Harold to close his eyes, drinking in the heated reek and sweet-grass scents welling up from a stall in his Grand Da's stable. He started to turn, feeling his brother standing there beside him. Stopping, letting a wave of loss wash through him, having learned to accept the cleansing effect. Then he squared his shoulders, prepared to face the beard-framed scowl of his grandfather.

"There's a shovel in lean with your name on it. Stall could use a mucking out, if'n ye have wits enow to manage it being done."

Harold's grandfather came out from behind the front end of a large Scottish bull, both of them shaggy in appearance; the smaller one in crooked stoop with spindly arms and legs. The vision of his Gran Da was a shock to Harold's eyes, one he quickly recovered from, grabbing the shovel with one hand, giving the older man a hug around his much too thin chest before settling into the messy work.

𖤓𖤓𖤓

The urine stained floor of the stall was covered in a layer of fresh hay, strewn about. The thick blanket of animal waste had been hauled away to an open shed where air could circulate, helping to convert the odorous mass into a rich mulch to be spread on three small gardens, arrayed in neat lines along the sunniest side of a narrow valley floor.

The farm was an ancient family croft that fronted a steep rise of snow-dusted mountains. A nearby peak, several hours hard climb away, looked down on the small field-stone house where his grandfather lived in self-administered isolation. Staying there alone, tending his crops and a single, well-aged bull. Both of them irascible of mood and cantankerous toward family and strangers alike. Barely able to tolerate one another, an even match of dour moods.

Harold found his grandfather to still be strong in mind and speech, much the same as he'd ever been when his mother would bring him and his brother in visits made to her family's highland estate. Their arrival followed by a steep climb to a small stone croft tucked away in the southern range of Scottish mountains overlooking the border shared with England. Both brothers engaging in a footrace each time, eager to be the first to receive a cussing out for one imagined trespass or another as soon as they piled into the yard of the ancient croft. The elderly man's words still rung in Harold's memory, as well the image of Jackie's face, beaming, relishing the oft repeated verbal tongue lashing.

"Why ye hae nawt but broomsticks for legs, the lot of ya. You'll be in climb of the mountain each day, come rain, shine, or hail be damned! Building calves ta shame those weak-kneed, bandy-legged bastards living below. Might as well be Irish, for all they care in the doing of an honest day's work."

There would be a pile of kilts and other kit in Scott Clan tartan waiting for them, fashioned in a pattern of red and green, supplied each time they arrived. Changed into, along with sturdy leather boots sized from a pile of hand-me-downs, the clothing donated from a host of male relatives living in the lower valley.

The days spent with their grandfather were filled with hours of back-breaking work and endless drudge, long days spent in a constant climb to gather and lug down stones or wood from the high forests, with meals but twice a day. Sleep would often find them with spoons in their bowls, heads resting on the table. Carried off to bed, their kilts hung on wooden pegs, waiting for them at the rise of sun. Their only recompense: stories shared in odd moments of quiet repose, their Gran Da's words vividly describing men in battle, with the chaos and whirl of long bladed claymores drawn in their imaginations, along with tales of murder, betrayal, mayhem, and the loss of men in clan tartan. Standing side by each in victory, or back-to-back in a final stand. Dying with prideful sneers and ripe disdain for the damnable English dogs who cut them down or strung them up.

Harold smiled, remembering how Jackie had adored their Gran Da, giving the scarred warrior his full attention, never interrupting, hanging on his every word. A memory that tugged at his heart, still, wishing his father had allowed Jackson to be buried here in the manor plot, near as possible to, as Jackie always called it, his most favorite place in the entire world.

He reached up, wiping away a tear with his free hand, the other holding a shovel, heading uphill through a cleft in valley wall to a small mill spring, where grain from clan fields below had once been ground into flour on an ancient millstone. He knew it would most likely need attending to, silt filtering in from the side of a spring in the mountain's flank, the paddle wheel always in bind.

"You're more a man full grown than last time I laid eyes on ya. Bit more weathered in ya hide, as well. The bite from a musket ball in ya side, spied while ya was flailing away in the stall."

"One of English manufacture. A soldier on my own side placing it there."

"Happens when shit is being slung to all sides, like the tail of a cow at milking." The old man narrowed his eyes. "See ya tried to catch it first." He pointed with his whiskered chin at Harold's hand, the outside finger missing.

"Was waving to get the sentry's attention. Foolish move, left paying a hard price for the lesson learned."

Harold's Gran Da shrugged, changing the subject. "Watched you wallowing in the outlet of the spring, clearing it of three years or more of silt. Your calves look halfway decent—for someone spending their time in the low-lands."

"Then you'll not be having me run up the mountain—this time home?"

His grandfather stared at him, then shrugged. "Figure you'll do what needs being done. Reckon if there's something waiting for you up there, you've mind and sense enow to go look for it." He paused, his blue eyes faded, turning to gaze up at the heights. "But I won't be the one to send you there."

Harold nodded, finishing his plate of fresh greens and well-aged meat, boiled from a dry husk to wet. Tough, salty, but able to fill the ache of a stomach in need of a hearty meal. The taste and texture nudged recall of meals shared in huddles with soldiers around fires, doing the same.

⁂

The morning broke with a wash of bright sunlight, raising a drift of mist from the side of hills. Harold had risen early, eager to welcome the birth of a new day. He was moving in a full stride along the top of a ridgeline bordering the narrow valley centered by the small croft house. The top of the mountain loomed above a narrow brook flowing from spring-fed pools and snow-melt waters, starting just above a line of stunted trees where the woods ended, and the real climbing would begin.

Harold remembered how each visit had presented him and his brother with the challenge of going as high as they could, struggling with the thin air and steep slopes, needing to stop to recover their strength, though they'd somehow managed to make it up each time, before their month-long visits came to an end. Telling young Jackie, it was only a matter of will, seeing it through, spurring them upwards, aware their grandfather was watching from below for them to appear on the summit ridge. Once there, they would turn and wave, having reached the rock cairn built by the old man years ago as a marker for them, touching it together, before heading back down.

Harold bowed his head as he made the solitary trek, hearing the ghost of his brother's voice in the keening of the wind, and croak of a raven's call. Along with the familiar gasps of breath, his lungs complaining, calves aching from months having passed since exertions made in the elevations of the mountains in western Pennsylvania. He finally was forced to a stop, hands on his hips, head back as he opened his throat to the crisp air, remembering the first time he'd made the climb all the way to the top with Jackie, who'd just turned ten.

"Are you quitting?" Jackie stood a few steps below his brother, his breathing steady, eyes gleaming in satisfaction as he watched his older brother struggling to catch his breath.

Harold frowned. "I've the bloody pack to carry—Shadow."

"Gran Da evening the odds a bit. You're older—and stronger. Only fair you carry the water, and the food."

"Along with cloaks, in case the weather turns and closes in. By the way—your sword tip is touching the soil. Bad form that—a punishable offense."

Jackie raised the tip of his carved wooden sword, his eyes cutting to one side, looking back toward the house far below, hoping his grandfather hadn't seen. "You won't tell him—Gran Da?"

Harold grinned, then reached out, tousling his younger brother's hair. "Of course not. When have I ever let you down, brother-of-mine?"

Jackie's face lit up in a smile. "Never have, and never will, War Chief Harold—of Clan Scott." He stepped back, raising his wooden sword, presented him by their grandfather, carved while awaiting the arrival of his two Scottish grandsons, their English father be damned! "Engarde, Chieftain—I am making my claim to the title!"

They met wooden blade to blade, going back and forth until Jackson pressed too hard, striking Harold on the cheek, opening a welt that started to drip beads of blood. The younger boy lowered his sword, a look of shock in his eyes as he watched his brother wipe the blood away with a finger. He stared in silence as Harold reached out and rubbed it on the edge of his blade, held in a trembling hand.

"First blood goes to you, warrior of Clan Knutt."

Jackson's eyes widened. "Gran Da wouldn't like you saying that."

Harold shook his head, wiping blood from his cheek, a firm expression on his lips. "Gran Da be damned! We are of our father's blood—as much his own. Best remember that, Jackson Knutt. It's our name and birthright, given. With the right to wear it with pride. You know as well as I the origin of it—a royal lineage stretching all the way back to C'nut himself. First king to rule all of Britannia."

Jackson stared back. "Agreed to—in principle. But Father is there —" He pointed with his sword in the general direction of England. "And Gran Da is down there." The sword swung in a line, pointing toward the wee croft house, far below.

"Damn good point, Shadow." Harold raised his sword tip, thrusting it into the air, the light beginning to dim beneath a layer of gray clouds shifting in from the east. "To Clan Scott!"

⸙⸙⸙

The crest of the rock-topped mountain beckoned through an icy mist, starting to turn to snow. They were close enough to the cairn to coax one more effort from tired legs protesting the toll paid in strained muscles and throats rubbed raw from shuddering breaths.

"Almost—there—Shadow. Take my hand." Harold, feeling as if some external force was drawing him up the final stretch of a steep, loosely formed gravel slope, was determined to make it this time, weather or weariness be damned. Jackie took his hand, then sagged, his reserves of energy spent, with nowhere left in his thin body to pull it from. Harold gathered him up, placing him on his back, arms under his legs, carrying him uphill until he came to a stop, leaning against the pile of heavy rocks.

Harold knew his grandfather could not see them there, clear weather or no, the line of sight impeded by a shoulder of granite ridge below. He smiled, kissing the stone, then turned to go. His brother's voice called to him, a whisper in his ear.

"We made it—you and I."

"Aye, Jackson, son of Knutt, and heir to the Clan Scott. We did. Together. Just like I promised you we would."

"Like you—promised."

"Aye, Jackie. As I told you long ago—where I go, you're free to follow. Always."

The cairn was still intact, though several small stones had fallen away from one side, put back in place by Harold, his fingers stiff from the brush of the raw wind. The sun was out, though the thin air was unable to trap its heat, left to bleed away along the sweeping shoulder of weather scattered stones.

Harold slid down and leaned back, his legs drawn up, hands clasped around his knees, feeling the abject loneliness of being without. Without his brother. Without Robert. Without Meghan and A'neewa, who he swore he still feel the energy from, somewhere over the far horizon to the west. He wondered if she ever thought of him, or if she'd turned her head from the life they'd once shared, moving on and letting go of such foolish things.

He sighed, knowing it was time to release the accumulated pain, ending the process begun with his father, finishing it here, alone. The stones seemed to be warming against his back, as if from a wave of energy coursing from within them, helping to heal his wounds.

Harold closed his eyes, softly shedding tears of sorrow, knowing hard work lay ahead of him, sensing the danger lurking alongside the path he must take, walking into shadows where a single misstep would spill him onto a hard and unforgiving ground. One lying far below, and thousands of leagues away.

"You reached it." His grandfather's faded blue eyes reflected the afternoon light. He angled his head, squinting as he measured Harold with a steady gaze.

"The cairn you built—yes." Harold nodded, his body drained of energy from the climb and outpouring of his emotions.

"Nae, lad. Was never a cairn, but a crypt—for a good man helped up there from this very spot. A hole in his side from a British musket ball, same as your own. Got him above the ridge, carrying him on my back as a storm started blowing in, hiding us from pursuit. Then placed him where the bastards would 'na find him. God-cursed lowlanders!" The old man turned and spit on the ground. "Like yourself did, first time you and Jackson made the climb with him on your back. Same as me, other than the burying part, though the laddie did cause me a wee bit of worry—what with the cough he took on and was hard put to be rid of."

Harold stared. "You—followed us?"

"Aye. Of course. Every time you made the climb. Your Ma with a blade to my throat if'n anything ever happened to ya."

"It was the climb that day—that led him to his death." Harold lowered his eyes, staring at the ground. "The thin air—it weakened his lungs."

"You'll be burying that thought, or feel my fist in your throat, you will!" His grandfather came over, taking Harold's coat in his thin hands. "Was no such thing, you daft fool!" He paused, reaching up and giving Harold's face a gentle cuff. "Our Jackson was the luckiest one of us all, having you as brother to him. He lived his entire life, short as it was, hanging on every breath you took. Found his joy in each hug you gave him, though you never learned the doing of that from your own Da—or myself either." The old man stepped back and gazed up at the mountain. "Your brother stood on your shoulders trying to touch the sun, with the stars and moon thrown in as well. Was no fault of yours—the fever taking him."

Harold turned his head and joined his grandfather in looking up at the mountain, recognizing the truth in his grandfather's words as he recalled the first climb all the way to the top, on through to having left his brother behind on the final day of his life. Remembering the look of pain in the younger boy's eyes, measured against the look of satisfaction in Jackie's light colored eyes whenever he won at chess, or how he looked up at him that final time, lying in bed with the sound of bugles sounding in his fevered mind.

Harold nodded, understanding life was its own reward with each day met. With every moment in pass. Each beat of heart and suck of air a precious gift shared with family and friends well met, then let go of, all. "Thank you, Gran Da. For teaching me another lesson I needed to learn."

"But not the last one I'm needing to teach you."

"No?" Harold stared at the old man.

"The bull has gone and shite the stall near full again."

Harold nodded, then made his way over to the barn, head raised, finding a measure of peace at the thought of mucking it out.

The weight of Harold's bag settled in on his shoulder. His kilt was back on a peg in the croft house wall, belonging to the bear of a man his Grad Da had once been. The old man came up, his steps halting, hands shaking as he reached out and touched Harold on the shoulder.

"You'll be needing to come back and see me, laddie—long after I'm bones 'neath a pile of rocks in the far end of the pasture."

Harold pointed with his chin toward the mountain. "I could always come back and carry you up there."

His grandfather shook his head, a cackle slipping from his pale lips. "Nae. The top of its too damn cold for my blood. Haven't had the stomach for it since—well, you know the story told. I'll be satisfied, in resting over there." He pointed in the general vicinity of the end of the field of grass. "Where the bastard bull can come plaster my rocks with shite." He chortled, then started coughing, needing a moment to gather himself. Then he sighed, looking at Harold. "Your Ma—did she ever tell you of my gift?"

Harold shook his head. "No. But I'm not wanting anything from you, other than your-"

"Not that kind, you daft fool! The gift of sight—the ken of things —unseen."

Harold stared back, then shook his head. "No. She never has."

His grandfather shrugged. "Your Ma—she's a feisty lass, at times. Suits her, being with a man who's strong enough to abide it, without losing sight of her spirit. Her Scott spirit." He stared at Harold, his eyes rheumy with age. "She inherited most of my stubbornness, along with all my backbone and grit. And she'll end up with the manor house and lands, along with this place, belonging to her Ma. Handed from mother to daughter of the Scott clan from as far back as any can recall." He paused, drawing in a breath, then spitting on the ground. "The gift I'm speaking of is one of visions, seen clear. Where I'm not on the ground, but in a hover in the air, seeing all with my knowing what needs doing—most times. A gift you have as well, based on what your mother shared in visits made over the past few years. Passed on to you through her, along with the others mentioned. The stubbornness and—"

He started coughing again, raising his hand, stopping Harold from reaching out as he placed a square of linen to his mouth, tinged with blood when he removed it. "You know what I mean. And you've a good measure of your Da mixed in too, much as it pains me to admit it. Hidden away somewhere inside ya, in how you measure things with care, balancing all sides against the middle."

Harold held his thoughts, waiting for the old man to finish. When his grandfather remained silent, he dared a reply. "Thought you—were not enamored with my father."

"Is that your high and mighty education speaking?"

Harold grinned. "Thought you hated my father."

"Did—and still do. For his being English. Not for how he's always loved my wee lassie, much as any man ever could, and in having gifted me two fine grandsons. Nae, I've nothing but respect for him in doing that." The old man sighed. "I just couldn't see past the English side of things, seeing's how they—well, we've had talk enow of all that. Let us leave it where it lies. You have the truth of it from me. Do with it what you will."

"Thank you, Gran-"

"Not finished yet, lad. I need to bring you back 'round to the matter of the gift. Need you to know and to trust what I'm gonna tell ya." He waited for a nod, then wiped his lips with the cloth. "You will need to bring them here—yourself with a bonny wife and children in hand, to protect them from what will be heading your way, should you stay to your path. You'll need bring them here, then leave—wiping away your trail like I did for him as lies up yonder." The old man motioned toward the heights. "It will be a parting made in sorrow, for I'm not knowing if you'll be coming back. Your woman—she will need be bound tight to our kin, who will shelter her, making certain she and your children will thrive." Harold kept his lips pressed tight, sensing the same wash of energy move through him as earlier, when leaning against the crypt.

"Do you hear me, boy?"

Harold hung his head, his voice a whisper. "I will be forced to—leave them behind?"

"Aye. No choice for the man you became as soon as you stepped foot into lands across the ocean, setting yourself on your path. No way off it now, yourself on the journey you were born into the making of." The wrinkled-face seer smiled, his thin lips widening, a twinkle in his eyes. "So—raise your head and face it like a true grandson of mine, and not some weak-kneed—"

"Low-lander." Harold looked up, knowing how much he'd miss his Grad Da, aware he'd never see him standing upright again. The old man's grin spread, his light-blue eyes catching and holding a beam of sunlight, piercing the thin clouds racing by overhead.

"Aye, laddie. Like one of those poor bastards—living down below."

CHAPTER THREE

BRISTOL

LATE SUMMER, 1760

The knock on the door of the inn he was staying at caught Harold in the middle of his morning shave. He hesitated to answer it, thinking it was the middle-aged maid having returned again, assigned to the care of his room at the inn during his stay. Harold smiled, ready to turn her away with a shake of his head before she could start in about how a man with his reputation should be married, offered to introduce him to several young ladies of her acquaintance, all women of high moral standards. Each time she'd tried to corner him, he'd managing to side-step the repeated offer without cause of too much vexation: his need for female energy met with frequent visits made to his uncle's estate just outside the city of Bristol, enjoying the company of his aunt their three young daughters, only the eldest one of age.

He crossed the floor and opened the door, stepping back in surprise finding Nathan standing there, his hand raised to knock again, sporting an oversized mustache above his upper lip, along with a thick beard.

"Colonel Knutt! I have finally managed to track you down. A heroic task—with you having dropped out of the social scene, shortly after we last shared a meal."

"Nathan." Harold flashed a warm smile, though the expression in his eyes remained wary. "A surprise. Both in your arrival at my door, as well the—display on your chin and upper lip." He paused, a wide grin spreading across his face. "Worn as a disguise, no doubt—keeping you safe from a jealous husband. Or perhaps a—spurned lover?"

Nathan grinned. "Is naught but an affectation—though I will admit one grown in support of my pursuit of a lady with an eye for the like. And yes, it does offer me some small measure of disinterest by keen-eyed observers stationed at the docks in Bristol, as well as others, scattered throughout the realm."

Harold went back to his depilatory efforts, using a straight-edged razor to remove all traces of facial hair, listening with half-an-ear as Nathan regaled him with the latest in gossip as if they had parted company only yesterday. Once Harold wiped the remnants of lather from his skin and finished buttoning up a clean short, the publisher got to the point, shifting verbal directions with practiced ease.

"I find myself in need of your services, paid for handsomely, of course. Though you do not seem to be in any hurry to spend your well-deserved allowance from our good King George." Nathan paused. "I understand you have not yet found a property to your liking in the countryside, hereabouts. Perhaps you are considering a return to the colonies? Philadelphia is a prime place for investment. I know several men dealing in properties who would-"

"Services?" Harold focused his eyes on Nathan's, his expression tightening.

Nathan didn't blink: a speech already prepared with the fuse lit. "A meeting, needing but half a day—or perhaps a full day of your esteemed presence required—at the most." He nodded with a satisfied look, as if having presented Harold the opportunity of a lifetime, a beaming smile on his wide-cheeked face, although Harold noted a glint of something harder hiding in the corners of his dark eyes.

"With whom—and to what end?"

"Men. Friends of mine." Nathan hesitated. "Some of them, at least. Others—less so, although of like mind and similar vocation. Gazetteers all, the term they prefer." He stopped, taking in a breath, stroking a finger along the line of his moustache.

"The purpose, Nathan? And try to anticipate my next question, helping to reduce the ebb and slow flow of your getting to the point."

"Yes. The sooner we're finished, the more time allowed for dinner and drinks. I quite agree, Colonel."

Harold sighed. "It's Harold—to you, Nathan. As I've stated countless times before and during our crossing of the Atlantic together."

"Harold." Nathan narrowed his eyes, considering for a moment before reaching up to remove his powdered wig: the jovial tone of his voice let slip away as he relaxed into a slouch. "I sometimes forget the man you are at heart, my friend—seeing you as the man who served with such distinction in the war. There being too few like you in number, I fear, posed against the relentless tide of men like me—who are far too common. I would do well to remember that, treating you with respect deserved due to your service offered—and sacrifices borne."

"I'm near to tears, Nathan. Please—do get to your point."

"The coalition I belong too, made up of numerous men involved in informational exchange on all sides of political and—moral considerations, wish to enlist your name and reputation in—" Nathan raised one hand, wig clutched in his thick fingers, staying Harold's shake of head in instant rebuke of the offer, half-made. "Please, Harold—if I might be allowed to finish, if only to get the sour taste of this vile invitation I've been tasked to make out of my mouth." Harold leaned back, arms crossed on his chest, waiting as Nathan regathered himself. "To enlist your name and associated reputation in helping to establish a momentum of public opinion designed to reduce the increase of tensions now that our King and—misguided heads of commerce have begun tightening the screws, demanding full remittance of the funds expended in securing lands west of the colonies for the empire."

Harold gazed at Nathan. "That is—truly amazing."

"I thought you might appreciate my presentation, knowing how you feel about such matters. Of mutual interest to us all, based on our conversations while at sea."

Harold shook his head, arms still crossed on his chest. "Not at the message, Nathan. I'm in awe that you were able to get it out with but a single breath."

Nathan lips formed into a pout, his hand dropping to his side, the wig dangling from his fingers. "You do not agree—as to the validity of the cause?"

Harold shook his head, going over to the curtained window, looking down, watching people passing below. "It is a three-legged stool in balance, not two."

"You fear the French will reapply themselves, forcing themselves back into the fray? They are as bankrupt as is the Crown—and short of warm bodies to absorb lead propelled by powder that no one has monies enough left in their royal coffers to buy."

"Native lands, Nathan, as I have always made mention of. There needs to be a nation formed of tribal states, if you will—left in control of their natural borders throughout the entire watershed of Ohio Basin, to north and south."

Nathan frowned, shaking his head. "You would still propose ceding them control of the river system connecting the territories of New France in the south to those in the north. From head to tail, as it were."

"Protecting our interests, by providing guarantee of theirs. Promises made and kept, honoring our promises."

Nathan went over and looked at the bed, glancing at Harold who nodded. Sitting down, he rubbed his bald pate, then placed his fingers on his chin, stroking his upper lip. Harold finished dressing then looked over at Nathan, watching as the other man working through the benefits and potential drawbacks of Harold's plan.

"It is damnably simple, brilliant in design. And—unworkable in the world we woke into this morn, and will, with God's grace, go to sleep in later tonight, or in the early hours of tomorrow, depending on how the evening plays out."

Harold nodded. "I concede it will be a difficult proposition to put forth, hoping to get a fair hearing—but it is the proper path to take and will provide far more benefits than—"

"I have worked it out, Harold—in concept." Nathan pursed his lips. "I'm not as simple minded as I pretend to be."

Harold smiled. "Have never thought that of you, my friend."

Nathan tightened his expression. "It stresses me to no end in knowing I have put my small fortune and life at risk in attempting to manipulate the opinions of powerful men, hoping to align them with the—least unfavorable elements of your plan. Though I will say it again—it is not workable. Your Indian—sorry, your native friend, the intrepid A'neewa, will most likely be left to suffer, along with her people. As too the colonists—once their fruitless rebellion begins."

Harold sighed. "You see no hope of avoiding it?"

Nathan shook his head. "Not unless you—" He paused, giving Harold a cold stare. "Not unless you are prepared to throw yourself and your considerable reputation into the mix, seeking a political position from which to pontificate, under guise of support for King and Country, with swivel made to fair treatment of our colonies—and the native peoples—once you are firmly ensconced. Then, and only then—can the public's opinion be made to follow such a fanciful diversion—if properly framed by pamphleteers in unison on both sides of the coin in play. A bit of bread and circuses for the mob, as it were."

Harold shook his head. "Again, your ability to orate without stopping to draw breath beguiles the mind." He sighed, then stepped over and placed a hand on his friend's thick shoulder. "I appreciate your efforts made on my behalf—but I will not seek a position in government. There must be another way. Perhaps if I speak with those who are resistant to-"

Nathan tightened his stare. "I had not thought you simple, Harold. There is no other choice. None. Not if you want this idea of yours to survive to birth and—hopefully—beyond."

Harold looked at Nathan. "You think it could work?"

Nathan smiled, shaking his head. "No. But watching you turn yourself inside out trying to maintain a smile when amongst the wolves, knowing you are tempted to reach out and snap their necks between your able fingers—it might, just might be worth the effort and risk on my part to support you." Nathan bounced up off the bed, resetting his wig, his eyes blazing with new ideas.

"As well mine." Harold's voice was soft.

"What's that?" Nathan glanced over, having gone over to stand in front of the mirror. "Oh, yes. Of course. Your risk, too. Quite right." He finished a final readjustment to his wig, gave a slow caress to his moustache, then turned and faced Harold. "So—we are now on to good food, strong drink—and the company of wanton women?"

"The first two, agreed, now you've managed to reset the dead animal upon your head, and made an attempt at taming the other, perched on your upper lip."

"I can help you to find her. It is what we—my companions and I— what we do." Nathan spooned pudding into his mouth, followed by a large bite of cake, closing his eyes as he swallowed, savoring the mix of flavors. "And, once the lady you seek is found—you will file papers for the seat left vacant in the House of Commons."

Harold pulled back slightly, sitting across from Nathan at an out of the way table, watching as he consumed the last course of an expansive meal. "You are—that certain of finding her?" He paused. "Making sure it is done without a direct approach? I will not have her bothered, if found."

Nathan raised one hand, eyeing a dribble of pudding dangling from the tip of one finger. "If she is in England proper, then she is as good as yours." He dipped his finger into his mouth, noting the flare of light in Harold's eyes. "To be approached by you alone, Harold—with no opinion offered as to the nature of your designs, if any, toward the lady in question." Nathan paused. "Her name?" Then he placed another forkful of cake in his mouth as he waited for Harold's response.

Harold sighed, his hands clenched on top of the dining table. "I have only her first name. The rest of it—unknown. Her last name was Scott, at birth, though I believe it may have been changed when she turned seven years of age." He paused, knowing the task of locating one person among countless thousands would most likely not succeed. "She is named Sinclair—and would be in her early twenties by now." He watched as Nathan's eyes widened slightly, anxious to find Robert's daughter so he could present the letter written to her. To let her know how her father, at the end of each day, would bring the cameo bearing her likeness into the firelight, his thumb caressing her image. "I see by your reaction it is an impossible task."

Nathan, thrust out his hand, taking Harold's. "It is—a difficult task put before me, but not impossible, my friend. And once the lady—Lady Sinclair's whereabouts have been discovered, I will provide the documentation needed for you to secure election to the open seat. Then each of us will do all we are capable of in support of the rights of the many—over the inherent power of the few."

❊❊❊

The public house was crowded with people moving in and out, several large cargo ships having just arrived from the American colonies, loaded with goods. Merchants stopped by for a tankard of liquid refreshment, their heads bent, scanning ship manifests to compare goods on hand against current prices, trying their best to accurately judge which way the numbers might go. Leaving after a round or two. Some of the more influential among them occasionally invited to enter a private room, held in reserve by a person of high birth, though not ennobled.

The needs of those invited in were seen to by the owner of the house: a greasy man with narrow forehead, dark eyes and nervous hands, constantly wiping his apron as if trying to remove an invisible stain. He was currently standing in a restless hover at the entrance of the room, bowing to a corpulent man sitting at the head of a large table. The owner kept nodding his head, anxious to accommodate the other's every request, causing the obese man to frown, finding the nervous mannerisms of the sweaty man grating, to a fault.

His name was Alfred, Earl of Camborne, a prominent member of the House of Lords. He sniffed, then lifted the tip of one finger, signaling the owner to approach, lowering it as the man drew near, halting him in his tracks. "My friend and I will have another bottle—of the same label, though a year older—assuming you have it on hand."

The thin man bowed his way out of the room, then broke into a run for the cellar, apron in flutter, scurrying away as if a rat chased by a dog. He had a wide range of vintages tucked below, specific to the large man's taste. The Earl was a frequent visitor, often in company with other titled men, along with those whose identities were unknown, silent men, the scent of power hanging in the air as they entered the private room. His hands trembled as he reached for a bottle, checking the label, sighing with relief. Nervous each time the Earl convened a meeting, the group he belonged to rumored to be in league with the seedy underbelly of London, but a few leagues away. He left the cellar, nodding his head at his wife as he entered the kitchen to open the bottle and let it breath, her voice haranguing him as he passed by, reminding him to present the bill at the end of the meal. A considerable debt having been accrued over the past few meetings, and long overdue.

Nathan was tense, having watched the sorry affair play out, witness to it many times before, though always from the other side of the door. Made to maintain a station suited to his position, at a table in the great room without. On call as needed. Bidden entry now. Invited to sit at the same table where men of quiet wealth usually sat, some in powdered wigs with heavily bejeweled fingers. Others in dark clothing with sullen pose. All with purses hanging from their belts. All perfectly safe to wander the streets near the docks as they wished, under the eyes of unnamed men. Serious in posture and purpose, their tools of choice honed to a razors edge. A deadly presence that assured the usual collection of cut-throats, pick-a-purse waifs, and bully boys would stay tucked away in the shadows.

"The owner is an—interesting sort."

Alfred pursed his lips as he surveyed the table. "He suits me, having everything near to hand required to satisfy my—every need." Picking up a cloth napkin, he dabbed his thick lips. Puffy, a dusky-rose in color, much too full to be considered masculine. Too thin to fit a more feminine describe, left somewhere in between, as too his reputation for being entertained by young children, girl or boy.

The over-stuffed man reached for a small, silver bell, shaking it: the clear notes providing immediate arrival of a large platter filled with fresh rolls, selections of thinly sliced meats, and an assortment of cheeses, with cups of various sauces arranged around its edge, there for dipping of bread. The heavy platter placed on one end of the table by a thick bodied woman with strong arms. Alfred waving a finger in a small circle, sending her away, watching as she walked over to the door with a measured pace, hesitating for a moment before pulling it closed behind her, causing Alfred's eyes to narrow. "His wife, on the other hand—is a burden to my emotions."

Nathan was feeling discomforted, unable to relax in the presence of the Earl, just the two of them, his first time invited in and told to sit down. "You wanted to discuss-" He clamped his lips shut, lowering his eyes, noting the other man's instant look of reproach.

"My good friend—you have only just now arrived on this side of things. Are you in such a hurry to a return to your usual position—on the other side of the door?" Alfred sniffed, lifting one hand, considering the perfect sheen of his polished nails. "And with your signature barely dry on the parchment."

"My apologies—in overstepping. Was driven by my eagerness to reveal recent success, prompting the—" Nathan paused, wondering if he would earn another rebuke, the Earl allowing the slightest of a nod, indicating he should continue. "He has agreed to do it."

The other man raised an eyebrow. "What leverage did you apply so as to overcome his initial reluctance to re-enter the—fray? Given, as I was led to understand—by your personal assessment, I would add, that he would not be so persuaded."

"A trivial matter, of no real import. He wanted to locate a child, to present a letter written to her by a father, deceased in actions in the colonies. A man who was a—mentor to him." Nathan was careful to center his expression, his words tossed out with a causal tone. "I agreed to help him, of course. Putting it to members of my fellow group of pamphleteers, on this side of the watery divide, to seek said child forthwith."

Alfred half-closed his eyes, pupils squeezed from sight behind fat-thickened lids, a slim gleam of satisfaction barely able to shine through. He reached out, piling cheese and meat onto bread, dipping it into one of the bowls of sauce, holding it there for a moment, waiting for the liquid to be fully absorbed, then quickly folding it into his mouth. Not a single drop was allowed to fall, keeping the surface of his immaculate silk jacket, unstained.

Nathan joined him, refusing to release a bead of sweat rising from beneath the edge of his wig, denying it access to his forehead. His stomach lurched, knowing he'd told but half the truth, having chosen to keep any further information close to hand. The details of his conversation with Harold would remain hidden for now. Dangerous, if he were caught out in his attempt to deceive. Necessary, in order to placate what remained of his weakening morals and a growing attachment to the young war hero, when hearing Lady Sinclair Haversham's name fall from his lips.

"All I know is her first name. Sinclair. Her surname, or rather that of her father—is Scott."

"Master Sergeant Robert Scott. Yes. I placed his name in type myself, many times, over the past few years, his notoriety in rise alongside your own. A great loss, indeed. A man of distinction. And a dear friend to you. I can see it reflected in your eyes."

Nathan let his voice continue to roam unattended as he covered his startled reaction to hearing the name Sinclair used as a proper name. More commonly used as a surname. Rarer still when applied to a woman, with only one person coming to mind it could belong to. A young woman of the same age, adopted daughter to Lord Haversham, inheriting the estate of the deceased member of the House of Lords. With herself, well known to high society, though she had never been inclined to enter into it. A sweet enough young rose, waiting to be plucked by a daring hand, though with a reputation earned of having sharp thorns and a cutting wit, honed to perfection by her adoptive father, a man known for cunning and penetrating vision, no doubt having passed the trait down to her, along with his immeasurable wealth and vast holdings.

"It will take some time. So—you will need be patient. In the meanwhile, we shall begin preparing you for what is to come once we've announced your political ambitions to the public. A man will need to be assigned you as—an advisor, helping guide you through the somewhat tangled and tiresome process."

"How long?" Harold leaned forward, his hands clenched in his lap.

"Within the week, I'd say. I have several people in mind. Good men —of impeccable backgrounds."

"The girl, Nathan." Harold's eyes reflected his tense tone of voice. "How long to *find* her?"

Nathan stared at Harold, the wheels of his ever-active mind in turn, imagining their pairing, should biology provide for it. Two like minds, each with a callous disposition when it came to meaningless titles, ignoring the use of the leverage coming along with them. He shuddered, considering the forces he might be about to release in slipping two such naive innocents into a stockyard filled with stoic-faced, extremely dangerous men. Shadowy giants, striding the globe in grasp of everything, everywhere, at all times. Their world a playground, adorned with kings, armies, and commerce, seen as pieces to be moved about the board. "Soon, Harold. I promise. Soon."

❦ ❦ ❦

The owner returned with slip of paper dangling from his fingers. The cost of their meal and libations, marked upon it in a scrawled hand. Alfred did not bother looking at it. He used the tip of one finger to dislodge a small sliver of meat, swallowing it, burping, then reaching down to pat his plump belly. The material covering it was stretched tight, without a single wrinkle to be seen.

"Send a man around to my manor. Leave it with my steward. In the meantime—I require something more. A sweet dessert, I think."

"We have fresh pastries, from a shoppe just down the road. An assortment of-"

"A more pleasing type of dessert. One with a warm, compressive texture." Alfred noted the hesitant look on the owner's face. He sighed, heavily. "Your daughter. The middle one, this time. See she is washed and that her hands are well scrubbed." He paused. "As well, her mouth. And do have her chew a sprig of mint, if you have any." He looked over at Nathan, eyebrows raised in question. "Yourself?" Nathan shook his head, waiting for Alfred's nod of dismissal. "And a small capon. Whole, uncut." When the other man nodded, his hands performing their usual dance on his apron, Alfred hardened his voice.

"Now. And take the paper with you, adding to it the fee for the — additional service. And do not return — until summoned by the bell."

Alfred sighed, stretching, his pudgy arms outthrust like a child looking for a hug. He nattered on for a while, discussing items of gossip, asking Nathan his opinion as to their truth. Nathan responded with one eye on the door, standing up and excusing himself as it started to open. He walked toward the doorway, hands clasped in front, considering the step he'd recently taken. Choosing to move further into the bowels of a world-wide cabal. Wondering now how he would be able to square his own ambition, fueled by greed and lust for true power, with that of his genuine concern for the young war hero, whose toe would soon be caught in the grip of an implacable force. As was his own.

He neared the doorway, moving aside as a small girl stepped through, no more than eight years old to his discerning eye. She clenched the knob of the heavy door, looking up at him as he moved by. Nathan turned around, watching as she closed the door with a solemn, resigned look on her face, one that tore his heart in two.

CHAPTER FOUR

BRISTOL

AUTUMN, 1760

The address on the paper in Harold's hand matched that of a large building standing in the heart of Bath. His ride there by coach from Bristol had been made without event: the one-hundred furlongs covered in less than half a day. The establishment appeared to be a place of residence for dozens of people, though the front of it was not identified as an inn or public house. A bustle of people passed in and out, making their way through a single large door, left in a constant swing on its thick metal hinges.

Harold's legs were trembling, as if facing the advance of white-garbed troops coming on in a steady march across a field of battle. He steeled himself, his hand raised, reaching for the metal knocker. The door fell open before he could grasp it, a young woman's face framed by dark curls standing before him, her silver-gray eyes widening in surprise as he tried to pull back, the knuckles of his fingers brushing against a thick brocade in the center of her chest, leaving them both in a moment of shocked pause until the ringing of a church bell announced the mid-day hour had just arrived, breaking the spell.

Harold felt the blood drain from his face, mortified at having almost landed an unintended blow. The young lady, one hand raised, clutching at her chest, stared back, looking resplendent in a dark green dress with charcoal colored trim.

"I apologize—for my having—for having startled you, Miss. I only meant to—to announce myself." Harold bowed his head slightly, swallowing his nervousness. "I am Harold Knutt, of Bristol."

"It is of no concern, sir." The woman smiled, her balance regained. "Tis a coincidence of timing—and nothing more." She stepped back slightly, then raised her hand. "I am Lady Sinclair Haversham, of— many places. One of them here, for this day."

Harold eyes widened slightly as he took her hand, releasing it with regret, her skin warm to the touch. He bowed his head. "My pleasure, Lady Sinclair Haversham—of many places. Including here, for this day."

Sinclair placed her hand on the edge of doorway and stepped back, inviting Harold to step inside. The building entrance led into a wide hallway with doors on either side, small groups of people moving between them, a wash of scattered voices spilling along both sides. "You are seeking someone, Mister—" Sinclair paused, sudden awareness dawning on her narrow face. "Colonel Harold Knutt?"

Harold flushed, wishing to have met as strangers. "I am—though now retired. No longer in active service."

"You fought in the western regions of Pennsylvania colony. Against the French." Sinclair paused, considering him for a long moment, leaving Harold to press ahead. "I had the great honor of serving alongside the man who was your father, my Lady. Sergeant Major Scott— Robert Scott, killed while doing his duty. The finest soldier—the finest man I have ever known."

Sinclair angled her head, the curls of her long hair shivering down the front of her dress. "You have come here then to make yourself known to me. To present your condolences, though there is little need of it. My father has always been but a faint memory, let fade." She blushed. "I apologize, Colonel—Harold Knutt. I am afraid you have made the journey here in vain, in wishing to offer—" Sinclair raised her eyebrows, a look of concern coming over her delicate features. "How—how were you able to—"

"I have friends, or more accurately, acquaintances—able to locate—"

"You had people—hunt me down?" Sinclair's eyes narrowed in anger as she stepped forward, starting to pull the heavy door closed behind her.

"Only so that I could give you this!" Harold shoved an envelope with his letter inside toward her, almost hitting her in the chest again. He withdrew his hand, his face a match in color to her own.

The door was yanked open, Sinclair forced to release her hold of it. "Our Lady—Miss Sinclair has a suitor, girlies!" A large-bosomed woman of middle age waddled through the doorway, the rasping croak of her voice one a crow would give both its wings to own. She shoved past Sinclair, presenting her hand, eyes locked on Harold's, waiting for a kiss on her dimpled knuckles.

Harold bowed his head and complied, then straightened up, noting Sinclair's softened posture, though her cheeks were still flushed. His heart skipped several beats as he took in her image in full, unable to look away until the large woman nodded, reaching for his arm.

"Do come inside, more fully, Mister—?"

Harold started to make his introduction, stopped by Sinclair as she took him by the hand and pulled him around the wide girth of the grinning woman, guiding him down a hallway, then stepping into a small side room. She closed the door and leaned against it, hands at her side, preventing the other woman from following them in. "He's only a messenger, Millie—not here as a guest."

The older woman made her verbal protestations known from the opposite side of the door, then wandered off on a new adventure, leaving the two of them staring at each other. Sinclair was the first to smile. "It is as if a farce, penned by the great Bard himself."

"I humbly beg your pardon, Lady Sinclair Haversham—for my poor choice in approach. I should have used an intermediary to-"

"I should very much like to see that, Colonel Knutt. A humble begging, as it were, from an officer—a famous officer at that. Please, sir—you have the floor."

Harold reached up, rubbing the side of his head, a lock of hair slipping free from the tie fastened about his thick ponytail. He started to tuck it back in, failing miserably, more spilling free until the twist of black leather gave up, falling to the wooden floor. Sinclair reached down, retrieving it, allowing Harold a view of the top of her full breasts as she did so. He averted his eyes, the image stirring him, adding to his sense of discomfort with his mentor's visage in his mind's eyes, wearing a dark scowl.

Sinclair touched him on his shoulder, turning him about. "Let me help to gather it up." She had things put right in a flash of thin hands, then touched his shoulder, encouraging him to turn back around. She gently touched his cheek before stepping back. Harold bowed, having regained a small measure of composure, settling into a practiced display of military courtesy shown officers of higher rank.

"I humbly beg your pardon, Lady Sinclair Haversham—for my poor manners in choosing to contact you directly to present a letter your father asked me to write, then deliver to you on his behalf. His final request—as it were."

"A Colonel—attending to a Master Sergeant's request—as a personal favor. Has the staid English military hierarchy been made to reverse itself over in the colonies? Perhaps it is due to the influence of the word independence being bandied about, by criers of news in the street? Publications being made of speeches by passionate men of notoriety, circulated amongst a restless citizenry, rumors spreading to this side of the world calling for rebellion."

Harold shook his head. "I am only here as a favor sworn to between two men, Lady Sinclair—"

"Please, Mister Knutt. Or Harold, if you'll allow a—less formal address to be used. I would prefer being called Sinclair, since we are alone, with such nonsense as titles unnecessary here, out of sight—and earshot."

Harold considered a moment, then nodded. "As you wish. Sinclair." He lowered his voice, looking down as he continued. "Your father, Robert—he was as close to me as my own. Closer, perhaps, in the bond of trust formed between those who have saved each other's lives on—" Harold stopped, clenching his jaw. "I apologize again, Lady—Sinclair."

Sinclair stepped back and motioned toward a small settee in front of a large window in one corner of the room. "We will dispense with formality, seeing you are a man of good reputation, known throughout England as the Red Fox." She paused, seeing a look on Harold's face of genuine pain. "Please, Harold." She took his hand, leading him across the room. "Come sit by the window and we will start over—each of us allowed a fresh start."

Once they were seated, Sinclair reached out, touching Harold on his wrist. "My father asked you to do him a favor, and you have complied—willingly I take it, from your description of the relationship you shared with him."

"Yes, very much so. I was beyond willing to provide your father my support, done as a last favor before he—I mean to say—" Harold hesitated, looking directly into Sinclair's eyes. "Though you made a claim of there being no closeness to have existed between you—I find myself reluctant to tell it to you true, lest I disturb your sensibilities."

"The truth is all I require from or ask of you." Sinclair leaned back, the diffuse light through the window highlighting her smooth skin. "I assure you I am not made of glass. Your words, as plainspoken as you would make them—will not break me."

"Your father was pinned through by an arrow from a native ally of the French. Passing from his lower back into his upper shoulder, puncturing his lung. Dying—slowly, in order that I might live. Not that it would have mattered in the end, his having hastened his own end, hoping to allow me an opportunity to elude capture and, what seemed at the time, to be certain death."

Sinclair waited, appearing unaffected, her touch on his wrist encouraging him to continue. Harold finished describing the details of what had occurred that day, ending with them having reached the sentinel oak, the story pouring out as if water from a spring-fed pool. When Harold was finished, Sinclair reached and touched the letter in his hand.

"These—are his words? His—final words?"

Harold nodded. "Blended with a few of mine, at his request. Reading them back to him as he labored to breath. They—" He hesitated, looking away, a sea of memories rising within, needing a moment to allow them to settle. "They seemed to satisfy him, knowing they were an accurate reflection of the feelings carried for you in his heart."

Harold offered her the pages, but Sinclair placing her fingers around his and gently squeezed.

"They are his words—and yours. I would hear them read aloud if you are—willing to oblige." Harold gave her a look that revealed his reluctance to agree, Sinclair aware she was asking more from him emotionally than he might wish to reveal in mixed company. She was about to withdraw her request, when Harold began to speak without needing to look at the pages torn from his journal, held in his trembling hand. While he did, tears fell from his cheeks, staining them as Sinclair sighed, feeling his pain. When he came to the end of her father's sad story, he turned and looked away, without adding any further details as to what had happened that day, though Sinclair sensed there was more to the story left hovering in the shadows of his soft-edged words.

"I thank you, Harold—for all you did on my father's behalf. And just now, for me—someone who is but a stranger to you."

"No, Sinclair." He turned and looked at her. "You have never been a stranger. Not to me. Your father sharing every memory, every feeling felt for you, throughout our time together."

"Why you were able to write what is in there—" Sinclair nodded. "At the beginning of the letter and again—at the end."

Harold nodded, folding the pages, placing them beside him. "I came to know you as if part of my own family—as is the way with soldiers huddled around campfires, or on shared sentry duty late into the night. We all have need to speak of the world we've left behind—in order to remind ourselves there is a purpose to the insanity of conflict, based on civilized rules. As if death has any concern as to the fair treatment of men standing shoulder pressed to shoulder, in line. The end of a person's life balanced on the toss of the die, bad luck, fate, or-"

"Destiny?" Sinclair leaned forward, her eyes on Harold's.

"Yes. As some might subscribe it to be. Your father—holding strong feelings toward you that only increased the longer between his last meeting with you—unto the day he passed."

Sinclair leaned forward. "I wish I could return those feelings, Harold. Truly—I do. But—I have no memories of him—or if I do, they are buried beneath all the things my—" Sinclair held her tongue, hands pulled into her lap, leaving her thoughts unsaid.

Harold gave her a considered gaze, then leaned back slightly, lowering his voice. "If I may—the necklace you wear about your neck —holding a silver locket—with a cameo of your likeness inside?"

Sinclair's eyes widened in surprise, her fingers going to the slight bulge beneath the cloth of her dress. "How—how could you possibly know that? It was a present—from my mother."

"It was a gift of love—from your father. A perfect match to the one he was holding when he released his final breath, his thumb gently caressing the worn lines of your face. Something he did every morning and evening—before and after every battle, as if a talisman to protect him. Each day that he survived bringing him one step closer to his eventual return to England. To find his daughter—hoping to see you once again."

Sinclair's beautiful eyes filled to overflowing with tears as she pulled the locket from beneath her bodice, pressing it open, her thumb resting on the carved image. "I—am undone by this news. I never knew. Never imagined he would—that he could—that such feelings might have existed within him. My mother—telling me—lying to me, over and again—saying that he'd abandoned us."

It was Harold's turn to touch her arm. "I mean no distress to be caused you, in delivering those words. Nor would your father want you left feeling out of sorts by them."

Sinclair shook her head. "I asked for the truth—and you have delivered it nobly. I am appreciative of your willingness to share your feelings so openly. And so honestly. A trait not uncommon in men with warm hearts, as I had opportunity to discover in watching them being torn to pieces by my mother—though that is of little concern to this moment between us, remaining my own burden to carry."

She straightened up. "I owe you an opportunity to meet anew. Not as a messenger fulfilling a sworn vow—but as someone sharing something of great importance. Memories of my father. Yours, clearly stated and wonderfully defined. Mine—hazed by time and distance, seen from a young child's perspective, tainted by lies told true." Sinclair gave Harold a warm smile. "So, if you are of a mind to do so, please return again when you are able—and we shall try this, again."

Harold rose to his feet. He took her hand, kissing the back of it gently, then turned to go. Sinclair's voice caught him as he reached the door. "And do not delay in doing so, Colonel Knutt." She waited until the door closed behind him, then stood up and looked at her reflection in the window, smoothing her hair. When she went to open the door, Harold was standing there, his hand poised as if to knock.

"Allow me to introduce myself, Lady Sinclair Haversham. I was — I *am* a friend of your fathers and would like to invite you to join me for a meal at the fine establishment across the street — with Miss Millie as our escort — should you prefer a chaperone."

The older woman stood behind Harold, in full beam, a crooked grin on her wide-cheeked face. Sinclair smiled. "Whatever took you so long, Colonel Knutt? I'm *quite* famished and would welcome the opportunity to remedy such. And — as to our lovely Miss Millie — she can go and *stuff* herself with *sausages* for all I care."

⸸⸸⸸

The kitchen was a blend of the scent of fresh baked bread and the savory aroma of meat pies, stirring Harold's appetite. His stomach growled as he prowled the edges of the heated room, kept at bay from the still warm loaves by the rap of a wooden spoon across his knuckles.

Eira gave her son a practiced glare. "You'll be waiting on your Da, young man."

"He'll be another ringing of the bells or more, before we see him home."

"Never-the-less, you'll be waiting 'til then."

Harold came over, hands raised in surrender, circling his mother's age-thickened waist with his arms, dancing with her in a smooth swirl about the kitchen floor, his smile bright enough to light the room, without need of opening the windows, spilling the heat from the kitchen.

Eira removed his hands, standing back. "You're in fine fettle. No doubt due to the young lady you've been chasing after."

Harold snagged up a small loaf, knowing it was meant for him, all crust and baked dark brown. His mother smiled as he bit into it, recalling her two boys circling the large butcher's block as if a flock of crows, descending on a field of ripened corn.

"What makes you—think such a—thing as that?" Harold finished a large mouthful of the warm bread, swallowing it down with swigs of cold tea.

"The deep ruts made between here and Bath by your horse, kept in a constant gallop." Eira shook her head. "Poor thing, made to pay with sore hooves for your lack of patience—or restraint."

Harold grinned. "My experiences overseas taught me that when the moment presents itself, one must advance quickly—the advantage gained."

His mother gave her son a sharp look. "Are you planning to make a conquest of this lady?"

Harold smiled, ignoring her concern. "My aim is to form a mutually agreeable alliance—once the swirl of the dust 'tween here and there has had a chance to settle."

"And her parents? Are they not concerned by your vigorous approach?"

"*Both* of her fathers—one her *own* blood, Robert—and another, who forged a deep filial bond with her, are gone. Along with her mother, though I am cloudy as to the details—dying of a flux, I think."

Eira's hands tightened on the front of the apron she was wearing. "Poor thing. And she is of an age to attend to her own affairs?"

"A year ago, Mother. But do not *fash* yourself. She is strong and independent in mind—and spirit. Not in need of motherly concern as to—"

"You will take me to see her, the next time you go. By carriage— nae by horse. I will prepare a basket. Tomorrow, I think. Yes. We'll leave and take the rest of the bread and pies. Go—make the arrangements needed this very day."

⚘ ⚘ ⚘

"Here? Alone in a rooming house of—public abode? Poor thing. She should not be reduced to such a state as this, having suffered the loss of her entire family."

Harold raised his eyebrows in exasperation, having been unable to dissuade his mother from her mission of mercy. "She not only *lives* here, Mother, but is the —"

"The door, son —when you can manage it."

Harold reached to open it, Millie overflowing the entrance, her hands filled with a large basket, more than a match in size to the one he was carrying, brought at his mother's insistence.

"Harold! It's so good to *see* you again. Just going out to deliver this food to the family you met, your last time here. Such sweet things." Millie paused, noting Harold's mother. "And who have we here? Another soul in need of a warm bed and a decent meal?" She handed her basket to Harold, reaching with a firm arm, pulling his mother into the plump cushion of her massive chest. Sinclair arrived in the nick of time, performing an extraction, preventing potential asphyxiation.

"Millie! How many times have —" Sinclair stepped back, registering the shocked look on the face of the woman standing at Harold's side. "You —you must be Harold's mother. He's told me so much about you." She reached out, taking Eira's hand. "My name is Sinclair. Please —do come inside."

Harold received a cutting glance from a pair of narrowed, light-gray eyes and ducked his head, aware of the inevitable blame that would be assigned to him for not having warned Sinclair in advance.

⸙⸙⸙

"More tea, Mrs. Knutt?" Sinclair poised a teapot above a cup, placed in front of Harold's mother.

"Thank you, Sinclair. And please —call me by my Christian name, Eira." Harold's mother waited until Sinclair stepped back, then held the teacup to her nose, inhaling deeply. "It is a *wonderful* brew. A mix of leaves, I think."

"Black and green varieties. Though a bit heavier on the green, for today."

"My husband —Richard —he prefers the black, due to its lower cost. While I am of the other persuasion." Eira paused, a gentle smile on her lips. "Interesting, don't you think, the choices one makes in selection of a favorite libation, occupation—or host of other things catching their interest?"

Harold sipped his tea, listening as the two women made small talk. He smiled, satisfied the impromptu meeting would work out to the benefit of his blossoming relationship with Sinclair.

Eira cut him a sideways glance. "Harold—you should have spoken to your father and I of your interest in Miss Sinclair. We would be pleased to invite her for a visit, if she is of a mind to do so." She leaned forward, facing Sinclair, lowering her voice. "My son is not accustomed to social niceties, having had his nose buried in books over the greater part of his youth, including his years spent away at school, matriculating at Marischal. In Scotland."

"I was not always with a nose in a book, Mother. I had other interests as well." Harold tried to hide a sudden blush as the memory of his nose buried in the inviting bosom of the daughter of one of his instructors flashed through his mind.

"True. I completely forgot about the hours you spent playing with your little dolls."

"Figurines, Mother. Of military formations—used in studies made of tactics—"

Eira raised a hand, waving it in his direction, her eyes on Sinclair. "Be a dear, Harry—and go fetch my shawl from the carriage. I seem to have forgotten it there."

Harold looked from his mother to Sinclair, who returned a slight smile, one eyebrow in full cock. "Of course, Mother. I'll be right back." As he made his way to the door, Eira called out. "And do go across the street and find some of this delightful green tea to take back with us. I believe I saw a coffeehouse thereabouts." Harold offered a grumbled reply, then left.

Once he was gone, Sinclair gave Eira a lukewarm smile. "You have questions regarding my living in a place such as this. To the point of considering if it is merely a front—for an entirely different sort of establishment."

Eira hesitated, uncertain as to her footing, the younger woman exuding an energy that bordered on serene, appearing not the least offended by the subtle jabs pointed her way. "I would never consider, let alone suggest such-"

Sinclair interrupted. "My mother—was a woman of repute." She took a sip of tea, allowing the remark to hang in the air. "Not any of it good, mind you—with her going about the business of marrying the two of us into positions of wealth—many times over. She was betrothed to a succession of good and—gentle—men, deserving a better fate then found in taking her hand in matrimony. All but one left broken shells of their former selves, having been offered and gratefully accepting me as a loving daughter—taken from them, along with a substantial amount of their monies with I—the Judas lamb—lead them to their emotional slaughter."

Sinclair paused, gauging Eira's reaction, a dark shadow, reflecting nothing back. "Until—when I was of age—my mother having made her way to the top of societies rigid levels, she offered me up to a Lord. To be adopted as his heir." She paused once again, taking another sip of tea, Harold's mother as silent as before. "Her plan worked—to a point—leaving me to inherit all. But not her. She was—outmaneuvered, paid off and sent packing. Lord Habersham, a gentle and loving man who would fight for what he believed in like a—" Sinclair paused once again, her eyes glazed with unshed tears. "Like a great, silver-maned lion—fighting for fair treatment of all, high born or low."

Sinclair stood up and went over to a cupboard, retrieving a glass bottle filled with amber liquid, and two glasses. "I was given liberal use of his fortune before he passed. Then was left having to fight tooth and fingernail for his estate, after he was gone. But I succeeded in the end. A slew of legal maneuvers used to acquire control of his wealth, helping to turn buildings such as this one into shelters for women in need of a helping hand. To improve their lot in life through education and training for suitable vocation. An outcome I am happy to provide to them, working with women like my erstwhile friend, and adopted aunt—Millie. Our doors open to those able to meet and follow but two simple rules.

Eira leaned back, having reassessed the young woman standing on the opposite side of the table. "And those would be—?"

"No lies—and no men, other than children—brought through the door. Ever."

Eira stared into the cup of tea she was holding, enjoying the warmth that had seeped into her palms, easing a nagging ache. "And what of my son? Is he not a violation of your second rule?"

Sinclair grinned, her eyes lighting up with delight. "My house. My rules—when it comes to his visits—made in daylight and of short duration. Our time together mostly spent at the local university, perusing leather bound books filled with truths, half-truths—and damnable lies, as my father would always say. Your son and I searching out the former, as if pearls hidden in a sea of—as I've heard on occasion muttered between your son's clenched teeth—the shite of a *braw* bull!"

Harold came rushing through the door with Eira's shawl, dropping it into her lap, placing a packet of black tea on the table beside her. Then he eyed both women, trying to gauge their mood. "Thank you, son." Eira paused. "And what of the green tea—were they not able to provide any?" Her voice betrayed not one hint as to the direction of the emotional wind in the room, leaving Harold to sigh, heavily, wishing he'd not displayed his improved mood in front of her the previous day. He exited the room again, shoulders sagging. Once he was gone, Eira looked at Sinclair, then placed her tea cup on the table.

"That looks to be a bottle of Agua Vitae? Is the source Irish—or Scottish?"

Sinclair gave her a sly smile. "Scottish, of course—like your own heritage. Your son having overfilled my ears with your family's history."

Eira nodded. "Would that he had done the same with me, in return. Though I am not disappointed in having learned your story—first hand." Sinclair nodded, then un-stoppered the bottle, pouring a healthy amount into each glass, knowing she would gladly accept Harold's mother's invitation to visit, once offered.

CHAPTER FIVE

BRISTOL

EARLY AUTUMN, 1760

Harold's father pulled on the reins of his horse, a large, thick bodied black stallion with silver mane and tail. It came to a stop and pawed the ground, wanting to run, its breath fogging the morning air as it teeth gnawed at the bit. "He needs the exercise—but I'm not able to sit the saddle long enough to satisfy the beastie." Richard looked over at his son. "Are you willing to do the honors?"

Harold dismounted from his mare, then helped his father do the same. Leaping into the saddle of the black, he gathered the reins and turned it into the field of his new home: a small manor a handful of furlongs from that of his uncle's. He looked back, smiling at Thomas, a shorter version of his father, slimmer in build though age was thickening his waist due to a lack of activity in the out-of-doors. "Are you up for a race, Uncle Thomas?"

The other man shook his head. "No. I'm in agreement with your father. You go chase fame and glory while we rest here—swapping comments on how fine a rider you are—or only think yourself to be."

Harold was off in a blur, his heels pressed against the side of the stallion, rising out of the saddle and leaning forward, his hands loose on the reins, voice urging the horse into a full gallop, its tail straight out, neck stretched ahead with flared nostrils as animal and rider raced away.

"His form is—perfect!" Thomas shook his head. "Wasted in the infantry. The Calvary—now that's where he would have shined."

Richard shrugged, rubbing at his lower abdomen, trying to ease a lingering ache. "He did well enough, ground-bound and out in front. Different war there, Thomas. Different terrain—and different type of enemy, as well."

"True. And I meant no diminishment of his many victories, Richard. His accomplishments, if only half of what's been written is true—remarkable. You should be very proud."

Richard frowned. "Prouder—if I'd been able to stop him joining up."

Thomas stared at his older brother. "You—can't mean that."

"I can and do." Richard looked at his brother, seeing the shadow of Jackson lurking in his features: the two men as closely knit as had been their own two sons. "Would have done so many things, in looking back—differently, in the raising of them. Been less—"

"Stubborn? Hard-headed? Irascible? Ignorant to their—"

Richard cut him off with a grin. "I'm too lame to gallop the steed this day, brother. Though not too lame to give you a thrashing."

Thomas nodded. "I do see the path you're left to walk, Richard. Our Harry is ripe with reputation and ready for the plucking, with others no doubt queuing up to use him to their own ends. But that is through no fault of yours. Harry is—has always been his own man, from early on. Left standing slightly apart from the rest of us—other than his mother." Thomas paused, his eyes tracking Harold and the stallion as they slipped in and out of view on the other side of a line of trees. "Harold seems a better version, now—of the man you've always striven to be. No offense intended."

Richard scuffed the wet grass with the toe of one boot. "None taken, brother. I willingly concede the point." He looked across the field, eyes narrowed in critical judgment, then he shook his head. "He does ride damnably well." The horse was in a wide, looping turn, still at full stride, guided in graceful swerves between stands of trees. Harold, staying in line with its outstretched neck, continuing to urge it on, encouraging it. "But I fear he'll not be able to outrun those looking for him to lead their movement."

Thomas stared at his older brother. "You have a—premonition of this?"

Richard spat on the ground. "I'm not his damn Gran Da! That—irascible old *bastard*. Nor his mother, sweet girl though she is, with her own curse of seeing visions, come true." He looked over at his younger brother, always near to hand, helping to balance out his own paternal failures. Allowing him the same privilege in return, with three young girls climbing into his lap during frequent visits, the pain caused him, balanced against the kisses and cuddles received. Both men had leaned on what the other had to offer to both families. His brother serving as guide to the boys when they needed advice and he was away, work pulling him to other ports of call for weeks of travel on end.

Richard sighed, knowing there was nothing he could do to get back those days, already spent. "I can smell it in the wind—the stench of greed from men seeking power. Or perhaps it is only an old man's fears, said aloud."

"I'm of an age with you, brother—and do not consider myself as old. Is only a father's fear, one shared in common in worry for our children, not that we'd ever share those feelings with them—keeping a stiff upper lip and all." Thomas paused, lowering his voice slightly. "Not like those of your acquaint, residing in northern climes, free enough with their feelings openly expressed in curses of anger, or joy—when deeply immersed in—well-lubricated stories." He grinned. "Perhaps you should try and be more like them—down to the wearing of a kilt, though your legs are no doubt too skinny to pull it off."

Richard gave his brother a practiced glare. "I warned you before—about a beating."

Thomas nodded, waving his hand as Harold came riding up, the horse in lather, its rider sitting upright with a gleam of pride on his lined, yet still youthful face. "Yes, brother." Thomas took in, then released a deep breath, overwhelmed with his feelings of pride toward Harold. "You most certainly did."

♆♆♆

The third pint went down easier than the first two, leaving Harold's face flushed, his voice rising in volume amongst the thick murmur of men at surrounding tables. His father and uncle were sitting across from him, tucked in one corner of the public house, listening to patrons sharing verbal jousts while discussing the latest political maneuverings, inflated in importance due to news of continued unrest in the American colonies.

"The price, Uncle—to be paid—will be worth the cost in time and attention spent—on what needs—what needs—doing." Harold covered his mouth, muffling the sound of a muted, wet burp.

Thomas glanced at his brother, noting a look of concern on his face. "It's certainly a possible consideration, Harry—in how best to approach meeting your goal. By choosing to stand up for your ideals on behalf of the common man. Politics an honorable vocation—if you choose it for yourself."

"It is a deal made with the devil, Uncle—one already done. A promise made—to—to one of many who wield the power of—of vox populi. And now—and now it is, it must be kept."

Richard reached across the table, the three of them sitting in the same public house he'd visited with his son before seeing him off to the colonies in what seemed a lifetime ago. "It is not a decision to be entered into lightly, Harry. There are many—"

"I've—given my word, Father. In return for what they offered me. The decision already made. Oars in motion. Tide—in rise—" Harold covered his mouth with a cupped hand as Thomas pulled him to his unsteady feet and escorted him through a side door of the tavern, opening into an alley where his nephew bent over, releasing a voluminous helping of ale onto the ground. When he straightened up, his face was red with shame as he wiped his lips, the cooler air helping to still the quivering in his stomach.

Thomas gave him a gentle pat on his shoulder, leaving him there, rejoining Richard, who'd chosen to remain inside. Once reseated, he looked at his brother, giving him a gentle smile. "It's a long road from the saying of something—to seeing it done. No doubt there will be a few twists in the path, along the way. Time enough to swing him 'round—while keeping a light touch on his reins."

Richard shook his head, frowning, his voice a low grumble. "He's too much of me in him and will not be dissuaded, now he's made his bed. It's his choice to lie in it, along with his intention to pursue some girl he's only just met—one he and his mother are always going on about." Richard stared into his tankard of ale. "She's to come for a visit —for a stay of a few days or so. Over my firmly voiced objections— Eira remaining deaf to my feelings on the matter."

"Welcome to my world, brother, with the odds stacked four to one against me." Thomas lifted his pint, touching it to Richard's with a metallic thud. "Why I'm here—drowning my false sorrows with you, along with the other members of our sorry club of love-worn men." Thomas stared at the ale, wishing it were wine. "Our Harold is in full blush, at the moment—but the scales will fall from his eyes, soon enough. You'll see." Then he lifted his mug. "To our children, may we never be wrong in loving them as we do. Each and every one."

A circle of men with beaming faces reflected back a false light, one Harold marked well, knowing them for the opportunists they were. Shakers and movers of the common man's opinions, wielding broad-sheets supporting like-minded men with ample bellies and over-stuffed cheeks, making them appear as if swine released from one wallow, heading to the next. Joined together this evening in a private room at a house of medium repute, surrounded by a flourish of low-cut clothing exposing feminine flesh, the gleam of candlelight on their upper breasts matched by the feral smiles of the assembled committee. One that had grandiose plans in mind for Colonel Harold Knutt, his name often in print, known to all as the English warrior, Red Fox.

Harold swallowed a sip of ale, keeping to a cautious pace while nodding at a thin man with thick glasses perched on a long, pock-scarred nose. He was handed a pile of documents, his signature needed to enter the race for a seat in the House of Commons. The flow of energy around him built in a steady rush, with a blizzard of broad-sheets already printed, covered in words announcing his entry into politics, extolling his service record and wounds suffered in support of crown, country, and colonies. The list of battles won, removed from mass distribution due to his direct intervention, as they were not his accomplishments, rightfully belonging to those who'd made their sacrifices in full measure.

There remained more than a handful of misinformed quotes and opinions inserted into stories written on behalf of Harold's candidacy for public office. Each one had provoked a dour expression on Harold's face, with pats of condolence on his shoulders from his father and uncle, their faces pinched with worried expressions. Along with a cocked eyebrow from Sinclair as she read through them, raised above a pair of perfectly shaped, light-gray eyes.

"You step beyond where I had imagined you capable of going, Harold. Writing of your memoirs—yes. Escorting me about the countryside while introducing me to family and friends—acceptable, as we are in court of one another. And should you choose to lie here, on this very stone in midst of a thick wood, staring at your toes for weeks on end— you would have my earnest support. But to reach for a position such as this promises to become, requiring a realignment of your morals in service to these—these men of questionable backgrounds and mean reputations—it leaves me to wonder if you're the person I thought you to be." Sinclair pursed her lips, leaving Harold to explain his decision to run for election to the House.

"I am still—and will always be my own man." Harold reached for her hands, denied them by Sinclair, who pulled them back against her waist. "Though I do not deny the charge—as leveled." Sinclair lowered her brow, eyes gleaming with anger. Harold continued, his voice even. "I will confess to selling a—small part of my soul—in exchange for efforts made to locate you. But as to my want of personal gain—or desire to join with men such as you describe—I am innocent of that crime, seeking the opposite of what they wish to see happen. I seek the seat as leverage of political standing in order to prevent, if possible, an excess of harm falling on our intrepid countrymen across the sea—as well as the native peoples, further west."

Sinclair lowered her eyes, her voice a whisper, hands hanging at her side. "I'm afraid I need all of your soul, Harold—if this delightful wooing is to continue. The same as has been freely offered you, in return." She looked up. "Nothing less—if we are to wed."

Harold stepped closer, taking her hands in his, squeezing them. "I'm speaking of blood, Sinclair—dripping from the forged barrels of cannons—and muskets by the thousands. Soldiers, in great number, sent overseas to spill the same from their veins. Off-loaded from transport ships, ordered into battle, spilling it upon the very ground I bled on!" He lowered his voice, tears in his eyes. "I'm trying to save both sides from a repeat of such—of such carnage as I was witness to. Having been the cause of it, at times—to my everlasting shame. It will be a waste of all I've pledged to and provided on the backs of men who stood the line with me. Your own father there alongside me, trying to preserve—to increase the warmth of our embrace of our colonial citizens, as well those who could be made allies, if left to rule their own lands as they see fit." He released her and stepped away, looking toward the east. "That is what I seek—what I hunger for. And if the price to fulfill that pledge means having to make a choice between pursuit of it and—" Harold paused, lowering his head.

"Yes?" Sinclair softened the former tone of her voice, her lips trembling as she waited for him to continue.

Harold turned around. "Of my having to let go of someone I have been in—fascination with—ever since seeing a cameo likeness of her beautiful face in a silver locket, come to life. Looking at me—here and now—while the faces of those of people I came to love, then lost—while they stare in quiet eyed judgment at the life I'm living, theirs at an end. My future—the very measure of my honor—based on decisions waiting to be written-"

Sinclair stepped over and rose to the tips of her toes, kissing him. Then she brushed his ear with her lips. "One." Harold pulled back, a confused expression on his face, hands clasped to her narrow waist, searching her eyes. "One—what?"

"Vote. Yours." Sinclair painted a wicked smile on her lips, her eyes bright with passion, her emotions stirred by his impassioned words.

"Go—and get the rest needed to win this seat. Then show the bastards what someone like you can do—once released upon a grander stage."

Sinclair took Harold by the hand, pulling him down onto a bed of thick moss carpeting the middle of a small glade, tucked away in the woods bordering his manor. An agreement was soon struck, one ensuring Sinclair an equal voice in how far Harold would allow himself to be led onto a narrow plank thrust over dangerous waters, with the surging currents of public opinion in constant heave, made to change on the whim of those with ink-stained hands.

⁂

"Colonel Knutt. There is a Colonel Sandersen here, waiting without and wishing to speak with you at your earliest convenience." The personal assistant assigned by Nathan to Harold waited for a reply. He was a thin slip of a man with narrow face and delicate features, his hands tipped with finely shaped fingers, wearing a powdered wig, perfectly coifed. His name was Charles Beamon, Esquire, late of London proper, assigned to help Harold during his run for a seat in the House of Commons. Available to stay on should the election be won. He'd arrived with a large valise, moving into a nearby boarding house just down the street, mere steps away from a small office lent to Harold by a group of well-heeled backers. Nathan had hired the young man to help manage the effort through election night, approaching with the speed of horses in a mad gallop, with the counting of votes less than three weeks away.

Harold sighed, lowering his eyes, staring at a desk overflowing with papers. "How do you find him to be, Charlie? Your opinion shot straight—without pausing to aim if you will."

"He appears to be the—opposite end of a horse, from whence the oats go in, sir. And again, it's Charles—not Charlie."

"Of course, Charles. My apologies. A hard habit to break, your joyful countenance always in suggest of a less formal address. It will not happen a third time today, I assure you." Harold paused, setting his shoulders, readying himself for an exchange of pleasantries with a man he thoroughly enjoyed the hating of.

Colonel Sanderson entered the office with a flurry of pomp, and little circumstance. His uniform was a radiant display of rows of brightly colored ribbons and polished medals, dangling in a shimmer of gold. He stopped, one hand on his hip, elbow angled, appearing as if a proud peacock posing in self-manufactured plumage. Harold supposed the awards had been pinned in place by superior officers in need of financial backing in order to retain ownership of their impoverished estates.

"You are out of uniform, once again—Colonel Knutt." The attempt at a light-hearted jape hit the floor with a dull thud, Sanderson unaware as he strode over to Harold's desk. "Though you are retired, so—no demerit assigned you. Still, it would behoove you to wear the colors proudly, lest people think you hold some measure of shame in regards with the work we did together to secure victory over the poxy French—and their savage brood of Indian allies."

"A damnable pleasure to see you again, Colonel Sandersen. Congratulations on your promotion having come through. No doubt hastened by your arrival in London—as you predicted."

"Yes. A terrible state of affairs, communications being what they are now-a-days, with six weeks or more in exchange of news on current affairs, when going from hither to yon." Sandersen paused, taking in the small office and former comrade in arms, standing on the opposite side of a non-descript desk, wearing a plain shirt, the sleeves unbuttoned, rolled up to mid forearm. "I have interrupted you at your rest. I apologize, having made clear to your man-servant I was here on urgent business—concerning important matters of State." Sandersen drew himself up into another practiced pose, head angled slightly up, as if posing for a portrait. "I am to be appointed to the House of Lords."

"Congratulations are in order, Colonel Sandersen. Or rather, Lord Sandersen—that being the requisite title for regal nod in your direction.: Harold paused. "Though it will be a burden—one of great responsibility."

"I have recently inherited the title, and yes—it is proving to be a difficult position." Sandersen waited, as if expecting additional acclaim.

"I'm—sorry." Harold watched as the pompous man narrowed his

eyes, seemingly confused by the offer of condolence. "For your loss, having heard you use the word—inherited."

Sandersen recovered quickly. "Quite right. Of course. A terrible thing—my father dying, leaving me to take control of his—of my estate. In need of constant oversight and review."

"As well your additional responsibilities—to the welfare of the realm."

"A great weight, indeed." Sandersen sighed, head lowered in a slight nod, then looking up, his expression brightening. "When you have secured your seat in Commons, we should make use of our close acquaint to further our mutual interests. A liaison, as it were, between comrades. Each of us according to our own societal level, of course—but acting in concert, our years of military service bonding us in a common cause."

"To the good of all men—entitled or not." Harold fought back his desire to toss the pop-in-jay out on his ear. "As our Charter so eloquently defines—to the greater good of all men in common."

Sandersen waved his hand. "Mere details, in need of working it all out at a later date. The moment before us one of great opportunity, with men such as ourselves about to take firm hold of the reins of power, wielding them to great effect."

Harold nodded as he came around the desk and placed his hand on Charles upper arm. "Allow me to introduce my friend and associate, Charles Beamon, Esquire. Assigned to me in my quest for political office. And please, there is no need of apology made for having mistaken him as my—man- servant." Harold ushered Charles over, bidding him to take Sandersen's hand, outstretched in greeting. "Bid welcome to my dear compatriot, Charles—a former soldier and future Lord. Another poor soul willing to serve the people of this great empire at great personal expense—of his valuable time. Daring to enter a particularly hellish environment, where one must step carefully, lest risk burning one's toes—as happened with me at the Big Burn. A good many common-day soldiers made to pay with their lives—for my mistake."

Sandersen narrowed his eyes further than normal, the pale orbs already in danger of touching, bringing a thin smile to Harold's lips when given a grudging nod of respect by the tall, gangly framed man. The Lord in waiting nodded. "If I recall correctly, my friend, the Red Fox—you did not made any other mistakes—over there or here, your reputation intact."

"You are too kind, Colonel. Too kind by half." Harold nodded at Charles. "If you would be so kind, my friend, as to take the Colonel's hat and coat to the outer room, returning with a bottle of—port?" Harold looked at Sandersen, receiving a slight nod. "Along with three glasses, as it promises to be another long day as I'm certain Colonel Sandersen has serious matters to discuss."

The visit by the faux Colonel wound its way through a maze of thinly veiled probes by Harold, eliciting as equal number of shifty responses by the other. The pompous prig of a man finally begging his leave due to pressing matters requiring his attention, exiting the small office none the wiser than when he'd arrived, with a superior look of supreme confidence on his face, unaware of having been led in circles by the tip of his overly long nose.

Charles closed the outer door behind the insufferable man, then stepped back inside the small office, shaking his head. Harold looked at him, grinning. "There's a horse outside wanting to have a word with you, Charlie. It seeks the satisfaction of a duel, to be fought between the two of you, its second to meet with me to discuss where and when it will be taking place. Your choice of weapons. I would suggest pistols, at dawn."

"I will proffer the animal an immediate apology—in writing, sir. Published, for all the horse world to see, begging forgiveness at my having compared its arse to that steaming pile of excrement!"

Harold handed him a glass of the port, watching as the man drained it with alacrity, having refused to do so when first offered one, having felt the nose-down stare of the uncouth officer who considered his joining the two of them in toast to be bad form. Bad form indeed.

Charles shivered in anger. "I do not know how you managed it, spending a single moment of time with the—with the likes of him while in the colonies, pistol near to hand, the entire wilderness to bury him in." He stared at Harold, shaking his perfectly coifed head. "In awe, Harold—simply in awe of your vast powers of restraint."

Harold shrugged. "Not worth the powder and ball, as soldiers often said of officers failing to meet the needs of the men in line. Nor risk of a noose." Harold pointed at the chair across the desk from where he was standing. "Would have your thoughts on his ill-handled offer to share influence, Charles, if you care to make a comparison with mine."

Charles shrugged, reaching for the near-empty bottle of port and drinking from it without need of a cup. "Please, sir—call me Charlie. And where am I to begin?" He began to list his opinions on a dozen thoughts centered on Colonel Sandersen's unscheduled visitation, made seeking a pledge of future alliance.

⚝⚝⚝

The rush in and out of young boys holding slips of paper in their hands was constant. Tally boards, fashioned of thin slabs of slate, marked, erased, then re-marked with chalk. Nathan sidled over to where Charles and Harold were in conversation, waited for an opening, bidding the two of them to join him.

"The count is four to one in our—in your favor. A one-sided victory in the offing. Congratulations, Representative Colonel Knutt—newly elected to the House of Commons."

Harold was silent for a moment, then nodded. "A victory for those backing my campaign as well. A matter now of ensuring my seat is firmly built, making certain it can bear the weight of so many— esteemed asses, eager to join mine in sitting in it."

Nathan winced, coming as close to blushing as was possible, his skin thickened by years of service to, and reward from, a vast coalition of political and commercial influencers. His hands, while not tied directly to them, were resting on the outmost strands of a vast spider's web, his place now assured, delivery having been made of a man he'd come to respect over the past half-year.

"It will not be as difficult a position as you have so solemnly projected in our labored conversations over the past few weeks. Come,

Harold—join in the fervent celebration amongst your friends and supporters, in surround." Nathan reached out, clasping the taller man by his shoulder. "Consider this as if the morning after your first grand adventure at the helm of troops in precarious waters, in need of your inspired leadership. The small force you led against the Français Armée Royale, standing in stiff opposition. You found your way to success then, against long odds. You will be certain to find your way through the pallid machinations of us lowly pamphleteers and those of the opposing party—winning over all of us to your side."

Harold gave Nathan a quiet look. "Leaving our relationship ever in a delicate hover."

Nathan frowned. "You'll have my backing, as always, even when it requires my having to serve both sides against my own interests. I assure you, Harold—it can—it will be managed."

"And when the bill for favors extended my way is presented—with interest accrued?"

Nathan smiled. "You will no doubt pull from your vast experience a ploy or two, putting the enemy to rout, no matter the color of their flag."

Harold sighed, loudly. Charlie reached out, handing him a glass of watered wine. "Go, Harold. Let them see your face and raise a cheer. Building esprit-de-corps with the public willing to hang their hopes and dreams on you. Tomorrow will be here soon enough, with the work begun of trying and set a' right the wayward ship of State."

CHAPTER SIX
BRISTOL
LATE AUTUMN, 1760

The bells were in a steady toll of solemn-toned notes. The King, George the Second, plucked from his throne by the same finger of death all men face, born high or low. The new King, young George the Third, would soon be seated in his stead. A new age begun, one filled with promise as bright as the rising sun in an azure sky.

Richard stood beside his son, each in silent contemplation of what the bells might portend for them. He was proud of Harold for having secured his seat, knowing he would serve his district, and the people of England on both sides of the watery divide, with integrity and every effort made to avoid the impending conflict. He also realized it would bode well for the family business, his brother having already fielded multiple overtures by those with an eye on tying themselves by a commercial association with the political influence of Harold and his peers.

Richard shivered, overcome with a sense of dread, the same felt when a fever had landed in his youngest son's eyes in the morning, left overly-bright in steady burn throughout the day, his life consumed by the midnight hour.

Harold broke the silent mood. "We are in a new day—at the dawn of a new age. I feel as if this is part of some greater plan. God's plan, if you will." He turned and looked at his father, noting the increased depth in the lines on his face, and sag of his jowls, having passed through middle-age at forty years of age and four. The burden of familial responsibility and efforts to obtain a measure of wealth that would ensure his family's future had leached the color from his hair and bushy eyebrows, replaced with a mix of gray and silver. His father's eyes looked back with an unsettled stare. Harold smiled. "Cheer up, Father. It's the King's funeral—not yours."

Richard started to reply when a scuff of shoe on a cobbled walk announced the imminent arrival of Sinclair. She appeared wearing a light-yellow dress with rose trim, carrying a tray laden down with teapot, cups, and fresh baked scones, along with a bowl of dark-red berry sauce for a topping. Eos, goddess of the dawn, Richard thought as he moved to help her, reaching for the tray with a broad smile, feeling as if the gods on Olympus had sent her to him and his son, to greet the day. He looked forward with great anticipation to escorting her down the aisle, beyond proud to have been asked to perform the deed by the bride herself, as soon as their engagement had been announced.

"My dear, you are, as always—resplendent, in both appearance and approach."

Sinclair bowed her head, releasing the tray to Richard's thick, war-scarred hands. She leaned forward, presenting her cheek for his kiss, her eyes cutting to Harold, who watched with a bemused smile on his face at his father's genial comments. "Your compliments are too kind by far, Richard—but welcome. You are a true gentleman, as would be your son, should he ever choose to reflect the tiniest morsel of his father's love for me as well."

Harold opened his mouth, then shut it quickly as his father spoke up. "He is struck dumb, my dear—as he should be. Both by your beauty and the aroma of the scones—the grumbling of his stomach a match and more to the tolling of the bells."

"And cakes—with lemon flavored icing! And sugar needing to be ordered in. And flour, as well, in fine grind." Eira was a flurry of high-toned words and dozens of ideas, the news of Harold and Sinclair's engagement stirring feelings she'd long kept buried. One of her three nieces was already married, and the other two of age. Their own mother having their personal affairs well in hand, measuring potential suitors with a discerning eye, making it clear she required no input from herself.

Harold shook his head. "Mother, there is time enough and more for such planning. The campaign of wooing only now having come to an end, with victory for both sides, due to my artful weaving of strategic ploys and rapid deployment."

"Was I forced you into a final battle." Sinclair stepped over, placing her hand on Eira's shoulder. "And please, dear mother to be—feel free to do all you deem necessary in plans for—" She tossed a glare in Harold's general direction. "In plans for my wedding and thus yours to help design down to the tiniest detail." She paused, giving Eira a kiss on her cheek. "I only ask that all bills be presented to my charge de affairs for handling—a non-negotiable clause in our agreement, allowing for as wonderful a wedding as can be provided via your capable and trusted advice."

Eira stood up, taking her daughter-to-be into her arms, tears streaming down her cheeks as she hugged her. "Agreed! I have—so many ideas, with so much to do. And so little time."

Harold interrupted. "It's to be near three months until the day, Mother. More than time enough-"

The two women turned and looked at him with mirrored glares, their hands on their hips. Harold raised his own in surrender as he stood up and made his escape, with one final scone snatched on his way out of the dining room.

A slender man of wiry build walked along a midnight dark street of London's waterfront with a casual stride. The hour was late, with no one else in view as he entered a back-water alley where few would dare pass on the brightest of sun-lit days. He moved with the coiled strength of a cougar on the prowl, ready to leap back and slash should any two-legged vermin appear from the shadowy recesses tucked along the passageway. None dared try their luck, anyone in lurk instantly recognizing him as an unnamed man, the lack of a moniker a distinction earned in the seedy underbelly of cities and towns throughout England, based on a reputation of dark deeds, done.

He was taller than the average male citizen of the capitol city and its outermost environs. Reedy in arm and legs, thin of chest with no spare weight carried about his frame. Unimposing, when leaning in a casual stance, arms crossed, scanning the faces of those passing by. More threatening in appearance when in furtive approach toward those who were delinquent in payments owed, information promised, or having failed to provide services already paid for. A final payment taken from them, left with their most precious cargo soaking through their clothing from punctured heart or slit of throat. A man to be avoided. One of dozens of like operatives belonging to a deadly organization. Hired by men wielding power from behind the facade of civilization's thin veneer.

He cut a probing glance behind as he reached the halfway point of the alley, knowing his trail had been unmarked by hooded eyes from the shadows. His instincts well-honed by years of struggling to survive along the grimy edge of waterfront docks, a deadly playground in his youth, composed of rat infested hide away holes, and slimy rock shelves perched above putrid canals. A safe place to lay his head at the end of a night spent pilfering of goods left under careless watch, awakening in late afternoon, having depended on intuition to keep him safe. Always alone, with no one else to trust.

He made one last look along the pinched slot between a huddle of wooden buildings, then slipped through a small doorway.

Lord Sandersen, newly approved by and accepted to the House of Lords, sat at a small desk inside an otherwise empty room. He looked up, his demeanor calm as he studied the man who'd come through the door, known to him as an uncouth courier, tasked with carrying monies and messages to and from men like himself. A removable asset, Sandersen thought, his lip rising in a sneer, feeling it to be beneath his station, tasked to work with men like these lurking in the shadows. Then he reminded himself it was a duty he need fulfill, having signed his name in red, opening the door to unlimited wealth and power.

"The funds are there. In the corner. Twice the normal rate, with expectation of additional effort made." Sandersen reached out, sliding an envelope across the surface of the desk. "This is to be delivered to — whatever address is named on the outside. Remaining sealed — the die pressed firmly."

"Bloody poser, you. Incapable of what needs doing. Why you hire of the likes of me." The man leaned in, his hands on the desktop, the light from a single candle revealing his face, covered in pockmarks with a spray of fine-lined scars on one cheek and the side of his soiled neck, the only identification of a man who'd lived his life between hard times and harder places. His voice was a gutter-scruff whisper, matching the reek of fish offal on his clothes and skin. "The payment is all I need from the likes of you — messenger!"

Sandersen sniffed in dismissal of the slight to his honor. "We are to meet again — a fortnight from now. You're to bring a report in full, handed to me. You may now take your leave." Dressed all in white, he smiled as he waited for the offensive tongued guttersnipe to leave.

The artful dodger snatched the paper, then the bag of coins, the door opened and closed in one swift motion, no sound made in his leaving. Once he was three streets along and two corners turned, he let go the over-played stoop and straightened to his full height, shedding his clothing as if a serpent peeling away old skin, leaving it behind in a noxious puddle on the curb. Then he whistled, a signal to a nearby coach, the driver clucking softly as the horse came awake and moved forward, coming to a stop beside the man. The driver leaned over, handing the naked man a bucket with a brush, then held out a towel and change of clothing, looking away as the silent man scrubbed himself clean. Once dressed and inside the coach, the poseur nodded at the only other occupant, then leaned back, a thin smile on his face, offset at one corner by scars earned long ago.

Nathan gave a polite nod, not bothering to greet the passenger by name, aware it would never be revealed to anyone, except during specific and fatal circumstances. The other man remained deathly silent, leaving Nathan to flirt with a pensive look as he forced himself to appear relaxed, a smile filling out the edges of his plump lips. "The hook is now cast. The man at the end of the rod—unaware. The fish in play, as it were. All going as planned, now that you've set in motion-"

"Please. Spare the cunning verbiage. Not interested in idle chatter —printer."

"You presume to guess as to my identity?" Nathan fought down a tremor in his voice, his nerves taut, the scent of his fear hanging in the confined space.

"I will presume less if you shorten your speech—wordsmith. The hour grows late, and you are in a risky position, choosing to hold the candle by its middle, with both ends set afire."

Nathan shrugged, conceding the point. "With the young King about to be enthroned, there will be money and blood in copious flow before the next phase will begin. Of innocents and the guilty, alike." Nathan pursed his lips. "But not his. Not a single hair to be set out of place by the least of a breeze. Is that understood?"

A sneer formed the other man's reply, his voice a cold whisper. "My ears work as well as yours. And as to spilling of blood—none are innocent. All of us guilty of original sin, are we not?"

"Most, perhaps. But not this man. Which is both a blessing and curse for him to bear."

The coach lurched as it rounded a corner, heading uphill to where a bastion of small houses and middling estates were located, forming the base of a pervasive shadow government of the English Realm, along with other likeminded men in similar perches throughout Europe, and beyond. Nathan rapped on the roof, signaling a halt.

"There will be additional work assigned you in two weeks' time, involving a mission of consequence, with—some measure of risk."

"There will need be two bags of similar weight and composition provided. And another—should the task require hiring of help."

"It will not be needed. The work is a matter of—furtive observation. The only risk, that of being seen, resulting in the target's curiosity being raised. He is a veteran, with more than a few campaigns behind him, along with a distinguished resume of military repute. He can be identified by the lack of two fingers on his left hand. He may prove to be—" The other man silenced Nathan with a cold stare, then touched a finger to the brim of a dark, slouch hat, leaving as silently as he'd arrived.

Nathan signaled with another rap of work-thickened knuckles, the coach brought to motion, the sudden lurch prepared for. He pressed his hands into the seat beside him, knowing the anonymous operative was right: that he was in turbulent waters well over his head, with two sides being played against the middle. Harold, in the center, needing to be protected at all costs, if possible. Nathan aware the caveat had to be made, in honest examination of the forces surrounding his own life, having placing his fate alongside that of the younger man.

He slipped a thin flask from his inner pocket, holding it up and making a singular toast, whispering in German, his native language. "Zum Scheitern oder Erfolg, die Anstrengung machte genug für gelobte Helden—in Sieg oder Verlust." He repeated it in English, honoring his friend who was facing an uncertain future. "To failure or success, the effort made enough for heroes praised—in victory or loss."

⁂

Charles considered the final draft of a proposed bill, readied for introduction. It was to be Harold's first effort, with overwhelming support lined up from both Bedfordite and Old Corps factions: two of the most important legs of the Whig party, currently holding sway in the House of Commons. The first group was under the leadership and guidance of William Pitt, Secretary of State and architect of the successful conclusion of the military victory in the war against the French in the colonies. The second was led under the healthy influence of Thomas Pelham-Holles, Duke of Newcastle, leaving the third leg of the party, the Patriots, a diminished group who would have mixed feelings about the bill, though any opposition on their part would be swept aside by numerous broadsheets pouring into the streets for public consumption and discuss.

Charles handed it to Harold, who took it as if it were a verminous rat. "It is a—fine piece of writing."

Harold frowned. "It's shite—and you know it." He slammed his hand on the desk in his small office, the same one where he'd waited out the results of the vote, six months earlier. It seemed time was spinning away from him with the wedding having taken place one month after the election. Two months later, he'd been given the news of an impending birth with a babe on the way, delivery expected in seven months' time. Sinclair was in radiant form and excellent health, having made plans for a lengthy retreat to his family's estate in the highlands of southern Scotland, well and away from the miasma of soot hanging in Bristol's air. He'd just returned from a journey there and back, made in a single, harried week. Returned to the House of Commons now, placating the men standing in the shadows behind him with strings tied to his hands, gently coaxing thus far, though firmly in control. He chafed at the thought. "It's meaningless drivel meant to inflate my reputation. To everyone's gain—except those most in need."

"First steps, Harry." Charles had let go all formality with his willful charge, months ago, bowing to the inevitable. He watched as Harold paced around the small room, his mood dark.

"I would as soon leave London behind, and hie to the hills." He paused, drawing his hands into fists at his side. "Damnable lowlanders, all."

Charlie shrugged. "Your son, or daughter—deserves a better life than that to be found in constant roam, just below the clouds. As too, your wife—with a solid reputation for the good work done in helping women back to their feet."

Harold gave Charlie a searching look. "You leverage your remarks based on my wife's fondness for you, knowing you are safe to strike me from behind." Then he smiled. "Just letting the wind spill from my sails, my friend, knowing I'm in safe harbor—with you at the helm."

Charlie nodded, sensing Harold's frustration. "Lady Sinclair Knutt will not deliver until well after the bill has been submitted and passed. You'll have time enough to return and continue your pacing there, in wait of the child." Charles went over to the desk and opened a drawer. "The springtime air will clear your head and dour mood, once you're away from the soot and night-soil scents of our fine capitol city." He reached out, handing Harold a quill and vial of ink. "Sign it—and be done with it. The public will raise a cheer for you heard back in Bristol. One that will reach into the wilds of Scotland as well, I'd wager."

"A wager from you will be a cold day in summer." Harold leaned down. "Dice or cards never to be found in your moral grip." He slowly affixed his signature in full, each loop and whorl in perfect symmetry. Then he blew on the ink and handed the proposed bill to Charles, feeling the smallest sliver of his soul detach, followed by a single drop of his honor, both falling to the floor.

CHAPTER SEVEN

SCOTTISH HIGHLANDS
CROFT HOUSE GLEN

SPRING, 1761

Sinclair approached the top of what Eira had promised would be the final hump in a sloping hill. Snow-capped mountains ringed a narrow valley with small structures strung through it, visible as the two of them cleared the final rise. Sinclair stood in awe, mouth open to the cold, dry air of the beautiful late-spring day. She drew in a deep breath, recovering from the steep climb. "Every color, shade, and texture of green—a varied palette, as if a dream come true." She turned and grasped Eira in a firm embrace, her belly pressed against the mother she'd claimed as her own. "Thank you for bringing me here." She pulled back slightly, tears in her eyes. "I—cannot express in words, how I feel. How—"

"Now, dinna fash yourself, Lass. Ye need not thank me, for the pleasure is mine. It does my heart good to know it will be in strong hands when I'm gone. Yours, if you're of a mind to accept it as a gift from one who sees you as a daughter—of her own blood. You having a share of the Scott clan, inserted somewhere into your Da's line—due to a chance meeting along the wandering line of the border between here and there."

Sinclair's eyes widened in surprise. "You can't mean that, Eira. This—" She turned to one side, her arm making a slow wave, taking in the small croft house and valley beyond. "This is a family holding, surely meant for Harold as your only heir."

"Nae. 'Tis always been in a woman's hands, passed from mother to daughter on down the line since—well, since the mountains rose from the hills. And the hills rose from out of the low lands. And the lowlands—which are the spawn of the devil himself, according to my Da —since the lowlands were birthed by the green-blue sea. With the good Lord choosing to put us Scott's as high above the bastards below as possible—nearer to his loving embrace."

Sinclair shook her head. "You're—serious."

"As birth, dear one." Eira reached out and placed her hand on Sinclair's firm belly. "It's a son you'll be having. I'm certain of it."

Sinclair stared. "You are?" She watched as Eira nodded, then winced. "Then he'll be born with shoes on his feet from the feel of it. He just kicked me in the ribs."

"He's nae kicking, Lass. It's a highland reel he's a' doing, in knowing his Ma is now joined to the land his kin sprung from."

"Are you absolutely certain?"

Eira gave her a quiet look. "Never more so, daughter-o-mine."

Sinclair threw her arms about Eira, the two women sharing the sun and green-colored surroundings with the child in a warm hug, between. She felt a sense of completeness, same as the one between herself and the babe. Then her shoulders began to shake, a long-buried heartache rising to the surface as she recalled the last time she'd seen her own mother, so many years ago.

Sinclair calmly studied the face of the be-wigged man standing behind a large wooden desk, instructed to call him father during the past few months. Her mother stood pinned in place beside her, delicate hands placed on her hips, clad in the latest finery, topped by a gleaming mound of perfectly coiffured hair. She wore a look of satisfaction on her face, eyes glowing in anticipation of another financial windfall, near to hand.

The tall, thick-bodied man opposite her stared back, then nodded, his expression passive. His voice, when he broke the silence, subdued. "You will—not be swayed from your decision to leave?"

Sinclair's mother shook her head, carefully, not wanting to disturb the placement of a small silk hat, copying the latest fashion of the aristocracy, perfectly balance on top of her beautiful hair. She bestowed her latest benefactor a thin smile, tiny fractures appearing in the light frosting of pale-white make-up covering her face, used to defy her age. Failing. Sinclair taking note of the pinched look in her mother's eyes as she turned them toward her.

"Sinclair and I will be leaving—once you have agreed to my terms. I'm certain you'll recover your balance quickly enough. A man of your reputation has to maintain an appearance of control in all aspects of his life. Your fellow Lords and ennobled friends will eagerly accept whatever tale you need tell them, as to our—"

"The child will remain with me. You—are free to go."

Sinclair stepped back slightly, hands clasped just above her abdomen as she'd been taught to do by her mother. In a dignified pose, her hair more plainly done, pinned in place with a thick fall of dark curls flowing around the sides of her face. Framing it, helping to elongate the squarish look of her firm chin, with a small cleft in its center. One perfectly captured in a cameo worn around her neck.

Her mother swiveled her head back around, gazing at the man, one of many made to suffer after a few months of emotional gain, followed by heart-breaking loss. Made partner to her ability to enchant men with witty remarks and a teasing smile. Along with a child of caring demeanor, returning their love for her as a daughter. Men of power, prominence, and wealth, eventually left with anguished looks in their eyes, and pain engraved on their faces and earnest hearts.

"You—are not serious."

"I am." The man looked at Sinclair with a gentle smile on his wide face. He beckoned her forward with an outstretched arm, watching as she moved toward the desk, stopping beside her mother. Then he reached into a drawer and pulled out a leather bag, letting it drop onto the surface of the desk with a heavy thud, filled with gold coins, their round edges jutting from beneath the thin leather skin. With a practiced twist of his fingers, he undid the tie at its top and removed a single disc, holding it out, the light from lamps stationed about the interior of his wood-paneled study reflecting from its polished surface. "Sinclair, my dear—take this from me." Once she had the coin in her small hand, he smiled. "Now turn and give it to your mother." Sinclair did so, reaching out, her mother snatching it away.

The man spoke again, his voice low in volume, but firm in tone. "This is for the purchase of the locket—hanging around your neck." Sinclair flinched, reaching to where it lay, hidden beneath a thin layer of cloth centered between budding breasts, as she was starting to come of age. "Not in purchase of it for me, child." He paused, giving her a loving smile. "For you."

"But I—I already own it. Given me, years ago by her." Sinclair looked at her mother, who was rubbing the coin between thumb and finger, as if eager to make the trade.

"It has never belonged to you, my dear. Only an accessory on loan against the day she would need return of it to pay one middling debt or another, if unable to find another mark—like me."

Sinclair's mother slipped the coin into a small purse she was carrying, then turned her attention back to the man, a quizzical look on her face. The bag of gold coins re-centered her gaze as she stared at it, estimating the number within.

"Take this." Another coin was removed and proffered, with enough value to provide for several months of reasonable living expenses. A half year, for most of the inhabitants of a nearby town, nestled about the edges of the man's large estate where Sinclair and her mother had been living the past few months. "This coin is to be used to purchase yourself—from her, leaving you free to decide your own path through life, as you are just now coming into the flower of it."

Sinclair's mother drew in her breath, raising her ample bosom. "You are mad, sir. Mad—if you think for one moment I'd countenance—"

The man pulled out another coin, then four more. He placed them in Sinclair's hand, their weight enough to settle it slightly as her fingers curled around their edges. She turned and held them out to her mother, staring into her eyes, almost of a level with her own. The coins were quickly added to the purse.

"Come, my child—and stand beside me." The man waited for her to move around the desk, then lifted the bag, staring at the woman. "Enough, in here—to give you another new start. Should last you long enough to find someone else to pillage. Heart, mind, soul—and savings. You need only walk away, leaving Sinclair with me to be raised in accordance with her—limitless capabilities. To be educated in the sciences. Trained in the ways of commerce. Made ready to inherit all I own. Wealth, land—my entire holdings, including this estate. Not my title, of course. But everything else—to be hers."

Sinclair looked up at him, understanding his words, uncertain as to the sudden change of the course of her life. One separated from that of her mother's, where she'd been offered up as adoring daughter to a host of good men. Left to watch in silence as her mother twisted her greedy fingers deep into their heartstrings, ripping them apart. Herself, made an unwilling accomplice to the crime. To the theft of their happiness, their faces falling into despair as they watched her leave, hand in hand with her mother. Their futures in ruin, left financially and emotionally bankrupt.

Her mother's voice snapped through the still air. "I—I will not agree to it! I demand you recompense me as directed—or I will claim you have abused her!"

There was a soft rap on the study door, opened by a short, thin man with white-dusted wig. He bowed his head toward Sinclair, then toward the man, ignoring her mother. "They have arrived, M'Lord. The constables you summoned—waiting just outside."

"Thank you, Martin. Bid them bide a while and offer refreshments. We will be done here shortly. One way—" The man looked at the woman. "Or another."

"Very good, M'Lord." The door closed with a soft thud, with Sinclair gazing at her mother, who seemed nervous.

"You sent for—the constables?"

The man smiled. "Did you think I would not have thoroughly investigated your background, before allowing you entry to my home—my life? Thrusting your daughter before you, attempting to leverage my genuine interest in providing for her wellbeing—for her future?" He raised his eyebrows, then shook his head. "I have met with those you have damaged. All assuring me that Sinclair is innocent of any claim to being a willing accomplice, herself as much a victim to your avarice as were they." He paused, placing his arm around Sinclair's shoulders. "You have a choice, Madam. Take the money—or join a group of lovely ladies whiling away their days turning hemp into rope at one of England's finest prisons. You certainly have the fingers for it, though the occasional accident might reduce the length—or number of them."

Sinclair watched her mother stared at the bag of coins, then at her, the tip of her tongue running along her upper lip, as if measuring the value of one against the other. Then she reached for the bag and spun around, leaving without a word, the two of them left standing in silence, each considering where they stood, now the deed was done.

The man was the first to move, reaching back with one arm, locating the edge of a settee, his knees shaking as he sat down and leaned back, his face pale, hands quivering.

"Are you okay?" Sinclair sat down beside him, taking one of his large hands in both of hers. "Shall I go and fetch Martin?"

He shook his head, then reached up, removing his wig. His own hair was thin, gray, damp with sweat, plastered to his scalp in tight curls. "I'll—be fine. Just need a moment to recover my—strength." He looked over, his pale blue eyes fully open, revealing twin pools of such love that Sinclair felt she might fall into them and never come up. "How are you doing, my child?" He studied her face carefully. "Do you wish to go—or will you stay, content to be my daughter and legal heir? Or I can see you placed with a fine family, one of means, who will love you as you deserve. As their child—and not a possession. As yourself."

Sinclair squeezed his hand, bringing it to her lips and kissing it, then placing it over her heart. "There were so many who looked at me —in the way you do now. Surrounding me with their love—always. Bringing balance to my mother's—indifference. All of them wanting to protect me, as best they could. Outplayed, each time—but not you." She took a deep breath, holding it a moment before letting it out, then nodded her head. "I will be a daughter to you—for being the man you are. Not a Lord—nor owner of a vast estate. If penniless and a pauper, it would be the same to me—Father. A title you've earned, many times over—leaving me humbled, and honored to be named Haversham."

"I—am undone. Beyond—words."

Sinclair lowered her head to his chest, listening to the steady beat of his large heart as she rode the movement of his breathing, feeling the loving stroke of his hand upon her head. Her eyes filled with tears, too long held onto, her chest heaving in soundless sobs of pain from years of loneliness, let to flow away. She circled his solid girth with her arms, clinging to him, knowing she would never let him go.

The sigh of wind against the outside corner of wall met with the overhang of the roof, creating a background moan echoing the gasp of two lovers in probe and caress of each other's bodies in passionate entwine. The noises came to a sweet balance, then drifted off into silence as a full moon filled the remote valley with silvered light.

Harold rolled onto his side, head cradled in his hand as he stared at Sinclair in the moonlight. "The bairn—you're certain there's no chance of—damage?"

Sinclair sat up, her enlarged breasts swaying. "Oh, my poor, sweet, delusional boy. No. You're large enow, but nowhere long enough to disturb our wee lad's slumber." She paused, a worried look on her face. "Though there is *some* risk to you, should he be provoked. I sense the wee laddie has a grip of iron—like his grandfather."

Harold reached out, tweaking one of her nipples, eliciting a yelp and firm slap on his upper leg. Sinclair placed her hands over her breasts as a barrier against further assault, Harold left trying to catch his breath as he took in the sight of her, poised in silvered radiance. "Lie back down, Lass. You'll catch cold—the air chill tonight from effect of the full moon."

"I like it." Sinclair stretched, raising her arms above her head, hair hanging down in black waves, flowing over her shoulders. "So much cleaner, the air up here. Fresh and full of—energy. Much healthier than in Bristol, Bath—or London."

"Our manor in Bristol has air near as clean, if you would but agree to make the move there."

Sinclair frowned. "We've discussed this before—and agreed, as I recall, that I will stay here until our child arrives, then maintain a shared occupancy between my estate in Bath and our manor in Bristol. I've already interviewed several candidates of proper background and disposition to assist Millie in the running of the homes for deserving women. And she's promised to stop threatening to hug them all to death, once they're placed in over-watch of each facility's finances, allowing for provisioning, investment in training, and support for the start-up of small businesses and the like."

Harold reached out and touched one of her long, ebony tresses, rubbing it between his thumb and finger. "Then we'll be off to my—to our manor first, upon leaving here?"

"Yes. As has already been made clear to you, upon your earlier request and our agreement made, my dear." Sinclair cut him a sideways glance, her eyes narrowed beneath the light washing across her cheeks and forehead. "Are you doubting my word?"

"Not at all." Harold sat up, circling her ample waist with his arm. He leaned in, adding the warmth of his skin to hers. "Just in a hurry to bring you both to a single locale—one with a greater measure of security." He felt her stiffen under his arm.

"Why choose that word, husband?"

"Only out of concern for the health of the child, preferring he be kept in one place, without need of excessive travelling made."

Sinclair's tone cooled. "It's good I left him in Bath then—before travelling here."

"I mean to say it is out of concern for the health of you and our son, when he-"

"Or she." Sinclair hadn't told him of Eira's prediction, having promised to keep it a secret between them.

"Or she." Harold looked into her eyes, the color of the moon, her skin as white and smooth as if formed of polished marble. "I am only a worried father in wait, wanting both wife and child placed in a single nest, where I can have them near to hand."

Sinclair studied his face. "You carry a vision in your heart?"

Harold hesitated. "I—have no wish to carry it there but must. An oath sworn nigh on two years ago to my Gran Da, shortly before he passed, promising to keep his vision buried, lest it flare up and burn my loved ones. Wife, children and all."

"Was it a sacred oath you made him? Greater than one sworn me—when we were wed in front of family—and God?" The room had grown cold, the small slate stove having burnt down to ash.

"More so—having made it to the man who made the woman—who made me. A three generational vow. One I must not—cannot break, without risk of dire consequence." Harold paused, his eyes set in a firm stare. "Which I will not allow to occur."

Sinclair drew in a deep breath, letting it out slowly, her chest rising and falling with the effort. "Does this vow involve risk to our child—or children?"

Harold shook his head, his eyes open to hers. "Not as long as it remains unsaid—with the vow, unbroken."

Sinclair sat quietly for a moment, then nodded. "Alright."

"Alright?" Harold mouth hung open in surprise.

"Yes." Sinclair nodded, then reached down, taking his hand, clasping it to her breast. "I trust you to do what's best for our family."

Harold smiled, then started to rub her skin, his fingers touching the edge of her nipple. Sinclair pushed his hand away. "There will be no more of that." He pulled back, then leaned forward for a kiss, her hand against his chest, finger in firm poke. "Nor any of that." Sinclair gave him a cold glare. "It was your Grad Ma made gift of this wee croft to your Ma. Passed on to me—as daughter and heir. Therefore, it is a—generational gift." Sinclair waited for a nod from Harold then made a dismissive sniff. "You may remain here for the night. It's cold—and I may require your warmth."

She slipped beneath the coverlet, her back turned to him, waiting for him to circle her waist with his arm, pulling her in against him. As she lay there, eyes closed until his breathing slowed and the wind sighed to a stop, a chill ran down her spine as she considered the unknown vision Harold's grandfather had shared with him, long before he'd become husband to her. Before having become a father to the child in the womb. She moved her hand, finding his, placing it on her belly where their wee one was at rest, covering it with her own.

∰

"The honorable Colonel Harold Knutt is recognized. Let there be order, gentlemen." A gavel knocked, sounding once; the mix of men in three political blocs falling silent; most with eyes of admiration aimed at the well respected and oft scarred warrior making his way to the raised section of floor, at the personal invitation of William Pitt himself. A few in the back rows exchanged knowing glances, eager to see their owned man take center stage, to begin building political leverage to effect political events to come. Ones their candidate had not been made aware of, yet.

Harold was beyond nervous, his hand trembling as he glanced at his notes, prepared for him by Charles, gone over again and again until they were a monotone blur in his mind. He took his appointed position, William Pitt having ushering him to the speaker's dais, then drew in a full breath, releasing it slowly before beginning his speech, looking at the faces staring back, seeing them as a single blurred image, as if a line of faceless soldiers approaching from one hundred paces away, their muskets shouldered, bayonets attached, glistening in the sun.

A familiar wash of heat flowed through him, causing a brief moment of panic in fear his bladder had loosened, not that it had ever occurred in the past with Robert's steady voice always at his side. He could hear it now as the faces of his fellow representatives slowly came into sharp focus, their mood receptive, attentive to his first oratory address.

"As Sergeant Major Scott—my good and trusted second used to say at times such as these, with the outcome in some measure of doubt —gentlemen, be at ease and mark your targets well, knowing they are as unsettled as yourselves. And remember that right—might—and our faith in God, King and Country are on our side. To the red, white, and blue—huzza!"

The assembled group of men with disparate agendas rose to their feet in thunderous applause. From that moment on, Harold knew he must bear again the title of Red Fox, wearing it proudly, knowing it would be necessary to wield in order to lead his force to the victory, sought.

❦❦❦

Richard and Thomas, granted privileged access to the upper gallery at William Pitt's invitation, exchanged knowing glances. Harold's speech had ended with loud cheers and shouts of acclaim made by men standing throughout the house chamber. Thomas nodded, a half-smile on his face.

"Our Harry is a—gifted orator."

Richard raised his eyebrows, lips pursed. "Not all were admiring his effort. A row of men in shadows along the side wall seemed less than pleased with his words."

Thomas nodded. "I noticed that too, although it seemed to me their issue was with the frenzied reaction of the assemblage to the speaker, and not the substance of the speech. As if his aplomb and stately manner of oratory was—unexpected."

Both men remained seated, their faces brightening as Harold climbed the stairs to greet them, a trail of well-wishers following close behind. Harold turned and faced them with upraised hands. "My friends, I'm to meet with my father and uncle—no doubt to receive their criticism of my wobbly presentation. If you will, sirs—allow my chastening be done in private." A flurry of claps landed on his shoulders, the boisterous group turning around and descending the stairs, shouting invitations to meet up later at the nearest public house to continue the celebration of his first speech.

Harold turned toward his father and uncle, his face sagging as he let go of his false guise of confidence, his feet heavy on the floorboards as he closed the distance. The two men rose, Thomas taking Harold by his upper arm, helping him to sit. Harold leaned back, eyes closed, voice tinged with exhaustion. "I'm as spent as when I was in a race to escape a fire—close behind the singed ass of an angry bear." Harold looked up at them. "Was I anywhere near as good as the mood of the mob seemed to be, in receiving my words? Or was I as terrible as the sound of them—in my ears?

Thomas smiled. "It was a fine performance, Harry. Opening with your mentor's words, helping to place them firmly in the palm of your hand—a brilliant maneuver."

Harold shrugged. "Was not by design, Uncle. Only a memory of a good friends words in my ear, where they will ever be." Richard looked down at his son, noting his speech-wearied eyes, watching as Harold drew in a deep breath, letting it out from between tight-pressed lips. Then he turned and watched the crowd milling about below as they worked their way through the doorways. The chamber was emptying out, with a flurry of men racing to find a place to bolster their patriotic fervor with tankards of ale and ribald songs. He sat back down, the three of them remaining in the gallery perch, waiting for the crowd to thin out, allowing Harold time to recover.

⸎ ⸎ ⸎

Six men sat in a close huddle around a table in a shadowed corner of a small coffee house. The establishment had been closed to the general public, the owner leaving a spare key behind for lock-up and eventual return. One of the men sighed, rubbing a hand over his face before looking up at the others. "He is—rather more gifted in vocal elocution, than was predicted."

A voice rose in support of his observation. "By far, especially for someone of his station in life. Do we know his place of matriculation?"

Another replied. "A third rank pile of bricks, stacked somewhere in the hinterlands of Scotland. Marischal, I believe. Fit only for those of —limited means."

The first man to speak waved a finger, bringing them to silent heel. "Evidently in host of advanced studies in public oratory. Let us hope they were more limited in provision of advanced courses in debate."

The rest of the group leaned back, arms crossed on their chests, eyeing the center of the table where a copy of the speech had been placed, having been transcribed by several young men taking turns capturing individual phrases. Each tasked with a sentence or two, every word written down, with full sentences compiled after the fact. The serious faced men at the table were already reconsidering the opportunities presented by the rousing success of Harold's speech, trying to determine who among them stood to gain, or to lose. All of them being powerful men of great influence. Not one willing to brook any deviation from their carefully defined plans for the future of both colonies and Crown.

When they finally moved to disband for the evening, one of their party turned left when the others turned right. He was soon picked up by a closed coach, the door opened from within. Once he stepped aboard and settled himself on the forward seat, he directed a stare at an obese man dressed in an immaculate white wig and white clothing.

Alfred nodded, slightly, then pointed a pudgy finger at a leather purse on the seat beside him. "You will make provision for another sortie, made in search of—personal details in regard to our young politician's expanded circle of family and friends. Additional leverage for our side, as it were, there being a measure of risk should public opinion be swayed by—the likes of him. The peerage has become— unsettled by news of the acclaim given his speech. Assurances of continued constraint and control must be made." The man sniffed. "And soon."

Nathan accepted the purse, adding its weight to the growing burden of his guilt. Too many years and risky opportunities endured in trying to reach the blood-sworn path, to risk leaning to a moral slant now. His own life in play and guarantee of financial ruin should he come up short in the measure of the cabal's expectations of him. Aware, should he be proven unreliable, it would insure a visit from one of the unnamed men. "Assurances they will have, with no—untoward measures needed, knowing this man and his instinctive awareness of the lay of the land—and any forces hidden there, ready to be mounted against him."

The obese man lifted one hand, inspecting the polished nail of his forefinger, angling it to catch the light from a small lantern. "This is not the western wilds. Nor are any of us soldiers—in play at war. Or savage allies—in search of scalps. Our members, heavily invested in our current enterprise, will not allow anyone—anyone—to cause the slightest deviation from the plan."

Nathan nodded in agreement, a wave of the other man's hand signaling his dismissal. Nathan gave a hard rap of his knuckles to the roof of the carriage, bringing it to a halt. He closed the door behind him as he exited, then took a moment to look around. The area was unfamiliar to his eye, the streets dark. Nathan sighed, hands shoved deep into his coat pockets, head down as he stared at the ground, slowly making his way back downhill to the lights of the city below, where his own carriage lay somewhere in wait.

Richard felt a familiar itch crawling along his spine. One not felt in over three decades and more of daily toil. Last sensed as a restless stir of the hair on his arms and neck while serving on the island of Gibraltar, just as the Spanish began their assault. One of a dozen men caught outside the fortress walls on patrol, forced to endure a handful of shattered hours trying to return, filled with bloody skirmishes. Only himself and three others surviving, the rest of his party falling victim to a hail of musket balls and honed edge of swords.

The same feeling pried at the edges of his awareness now, causing his head to slowly turn in a casual scan of the surrounding fields as he guided his steed along the outer perimeter of his son's manor. Nothing appeared out of place, the moment fading away as he watched Sinclair riding up to join him. His heart skipped a beat, seeing her radiant smile.

She reined in beside him. "Your brother is here. Along with his family. Eira sent me to find you."

Richard eased his horse into a slow trot back toward the stables, Sinclair at his side, her body in perfect balance, hands light on the reins, using a light press of her knees to guide her mare: a three-year-old gray with black mane and tail. A wedding gift from him to her, creating a smile as bright as the one she wore now when she'd first seen it, clapping her hands in glee when told it was hers. Richard was tempted to nudge his stallion into a gallop but refrained. Sinclair had only recently delivered a handsome, well-formed grandson, a few weeks ago. A boy with strong lungs, his occasional complaints heard throughout the manor when deprived of one thing or another, bringing a smile to Richard's lips, knowing he was doubly blessed by having Sinclair as both his adopted daughter and as mother to his son's heir.

"You are hale, Daughter?"

"I am, Father. In body and mind. Though I have been sitting a bit —uneasy, of late. A niggling—" She paused, looking around behind her.

"Itch?" Richard heard the word in his large ears, his face turning red. "I mean, in an awareness of something not quite right—and not in reference to—" He shook his head, hands tight on the reins, the stallion tossing its head. "Please say you know my meaning." The larger horse made a slight swerve, Sinclair able to match it, her body moving fluidly in the saddle.

"I do, Father—and read it the same as you." She paused, keeping a smile from her lips on seeing his discomfort from the untoward remark. "Do you mark its cause?"

Richard brought the steed under control. "Would have thought it nothing more than an old man's nerves, if not for your similar regard. I will mention it to Harold and see if he has any thoughts on the matter. His instincts are well honed—far superior to mine, age taking its toll as the years have slipped by."

Sinclair tapped her heels against the mare's side, encouraging a gallop. "Come along, dear Father—and see if you can keep pace with me. A short race to the stable gate, with the loser having to make the next change of under-garments for the wee heir to the manor, born."

Harold nodded, listening as his father related his concern. "I will contact my neighbor and ask if his gamesman can reconnoiter the area. He's eager to repay a favor granted and should be happy to oblige." Harold shrugged, gently rocking on his feet as he held his son, due to be christened with the name Aaron Robert, once the women of the house were ready to head to the local church, the horse and carriage waiting. "I will ask him after the ceremony."

Richard shrugged. "It's most likely someone passing through—in search of a meal and any work to be had. A soldier, perhaps—recently released from service and looking for coin enough to return home."

Harold smiled. "Then I shall oblige his, or their needs, if more than one is found lurking about. There's a well that needs deepening, and fence lines to be extended around a new plot, recently cleared for pasture." He stopped talking, young Aaron starting to stir as if he able to scent his mother's approach. Sinclair, dressed in a dark green gown, came into the room, her breasts swelling the fabric, ready to meet the lad's endless thirst for nursing. Harold started to hand her the babe, letting her know another change of undergarments was needed, surprised when his father stepped forward, volunteering to perform the re-swaddling, raising everyone's eyes in surprise, except Sinclair's.

Nathan made his way through a throng of dignitaries, family and friends gathered outside a church to celebrate the christening of Harold and Sinclair's son. He moved with a slow pace, an envelope clutched between his thick fingers, a gift to the child, now fully blessed, proud to have been named as God-uncle to the boy, the request coming from Sinclair and Harold both. He paused, waiting as several Lords, in escort of their Ladies, completed their own congratulations to the couple, having made their journey to Bristol from their London estates, eager to grace the christening with their presence.

While he waited for his chance to visit with the couple, Nathan considered how well Harold had taken to the execution of his duties, without a single misstep. His performance thus far had encouraged the ranking members of the secretive cabal to loosen the reins tethered to his own shoulders, allowing him a degree of independent action when it came to handling the reluctant politician.

Nathan stepped back, rehearsing the speech he'd be giving Harold later on that day, when the two of them had a moment alone. He wondered how his charge would react to suggestion of a more lenient attitude when it came to dunning the colonies for repayment of monies spent funding the military campaign against the French. As to Harold's suggestion of an independent and self-managed native territory, Nathan knew it had not received a single moment of serious consideration: the lands west of the colonies to be brought under firm control of the Crown, with minimal allowances made for a select handful of native groups having proven their loyalty, allowed to remain in limited control of a small portion of their ancestral lands.

A reed-thin, nasally voice from behind startled Nathan. Familiar to his ear, causing his hands to clench, wrinkling the envelope he was holding. "Our friend, the Red Fox—has proven himself to be a rather valuable commodity. Though, with the treaty regarding control of the New World nearing the final phase of negotiations, due to be signed next year with the French—his reputation and usefulness will soon fade."

Nathan turned around and stared at the unnamed man, the man he'd met with before, now dressed in elegant garb with a layer of white make-up covering his scars, no doubt in attendance as a guest of one of the other notables, and not as a direct invitee. He forced a smile onto his lips, knowing the man, despite his self-assured tone of voice, was only a minion, used to run errands for those wielding the real power behind the throne.

He stiffened his voice, taking a firm stance, having been encouraged by the secretive group to remain a close friend and confidant to the man in question. "I would humbly disagree, in believing Representative Knutt's value will only grow all the more important to our cause, based on his use of heartfelt words and well considered approach. He has a clear understanding of each side's needs, inclusive of the houses of both Commons and Lords. His proposals, as written and submitted —always careful to detail how to match them up with one another, ensuring the promise of increased returns on our initial investment of materials and men. A bright future, indeed—where the nascent growth of a restless movement away from Mother England—need not arise, left to wither on the vine, if you will."

"Yet it still may do so. Arise. That very word being circulating among—certain members of the aristocracy, including a few who are positioned within our particular group, holding the reins securely fastened about the neck of our boy king, in suggest of a deviation in course."

"This would certainly be news to me—if true."

The unnamed man frowned. "I would not wish to be—named a liar."

Nathan felt a cold pain slip through his abdomen at the look in the man's eyes. "Nor would I, my friend. My comment is aimed directly at the source of what you have reflected as a truth—one I assume is not based on your direct observation of it."

"My opinion is that someone standing close to me should be damn careful where he treads. As well as in his choice of friends—or family." The man sniffed, then smiled as he gave Nathan a hard look from hooded eyes.

Nathan stiffened his resolve. "I would not brook any actions being taken that would cause a negative effect to—"

"You are in no position to have a position in regard to this—or any number of like permutations in your little club's plan. Which, as you know, will ever be in motion, requiring constant need for adjustment. Which is where people like me come into play, paid to deal with events made to occur behind the scenery. Perhaps better for you to refocus your ears and eyes on events across the sea, too long left ignored, having spent so much time on this side of the briny divide."

Nathan eased his stance. "A message then—from our mutual friends?"

"A missive—from someone of note in attendance here. And in answer to your earlier surmise, left unvoiced—I am not an uninvited guest. Merely an observer, paid to gather information." The man placed a hand on Nathan's shoulder, his fingers in a stiff grip as he turned him around and gave him a slight nudge, moving him toward the well-coiffed mob surrounding the newly christened child's parents.

CHAPTER EIGHT

SCOTTISH HIGHLAND CROFT
SPRING, 1764

Eira watched as her three-year-old grandson raced about the croft, his legs in a steady churn beneath the needle-altered kilt she'd adapted to fit his ever-growing frame. His two sisters, Meghan and Marion, fraternal twins just over one year of age, were planted in the middle of a thick wool blanket, their chubby hands filled with flower petals and small stuffed animals. The sun gleamed on their heads, reflecting from Meghan's red and gold colored curly hair, while being absorbed by Marion's ebony-black wavy locks, both of them with eyes of blue, like her own.

Sinclair was sitting beside them, in watchful attendance as Harold trod the family sod with a measured step, back from having gone to pay respects to his Gran Da at the far end of the pasture. Eira watched him, tears in her eyes as she saw her father reflected in his movements as he passed by the wee croft home, built ages ago, with lichen-faced stone walls and a thick layer of moss covering its slate tile roof.

The day was half over, the weather brisk but clear, with a hint of warmth in build. Everyone's cheeks wore a tint of red, the sound of their laughter competing with a sighing breeze. Several long-haired Scottish cows and a handful of young sheep had been gathered up and driven to the small holding, the animals borrowed from the family manor, a two hours hard walk below. Harold insistent his son should know the use of a shovel for the mucking out of a stall, along with a pitchfork sized to his youthful hands, ready for the spreading of straw, same as he'd learned it himself, many years ago. Life lessons in abound to be discovered in the rolling hills and up thrust ridges, dotted with scattered collections of rocks, moss, trees, and ledges.

"Leave off the chase, Aaron! The sheep need time left alone to feed —same as you. To your Da, son. To your Da—or they'll be hell to pay."

"Language, son." Eira spoke the words through cupped hands, grinning as a blur of red and green kilted child closed the distance, leaping into his father's arms, his face split in a wide grin, releasing a shriek of laughter as his father spun him around. She felt a wave of warmth flood through her body, helping push back the chill inside her, still missing Harold's father, her husband lost in roadway accident, two months earlier. She closed her eyes, sensing Richard was near in spirit, despite having been cursed from the land by her own Da, shortly after they'd wed. She smiled, seeing him in a proud stance, now, his light-blue eyes watching over their son and wife, three healthy heirs, and a grieving wife of nearly thirty years.

"Come and sit with us, Mother. The girls need attention paid to their braids, and I've not the fingers or the patience as you." Sinclair patted the blanket beside her, a smile on her face, eyes a match for the sheen of sun from the gray-spun wool fibers beneath her hand. Once Eira had joined her, Sinclair clasped her arm around her adopted mother's firm shoulders, pulling her into a warm and loving embrace. "I miss my dear father so—especially at times like these, the children ever a joy to him. Wearing a smile wide enough to all but crack his head in two—as he always said." Tears fell from Sinclair's eyes as she remembered the father she'd claimed as her own, able to find him in the faces of her children and husband, all.

Eira reached up and covered her daughter's hand with her own. "He was never allowed to visit here, in life—but I feel his presence now. My own Da, unable to release the knife of hatred felt toward everything English, no matter how little of it was deserved in my choice of whom to fall in love with."

"His loss then. Your gain—ever since." Sinclair smiled, sniffing, her nose red from the thin, cold air. "The fool missing out on hours of harangue and exchange of heated opinions. Which, if half of what your son has told me is true—the two of them would no doubt have enjoyed."

"Ye have the ken of it, lass. The stubbornness of a highlander's soul making us hate them a wee bit less than the love we feel—most times."

"Something I never noted in Richard during our time together—or in my husband."

"Was the steed well broken you were knowing of. I spent years turning back the tide of his too-proper, stiff-lipped English pride and poise." Eira watched Harold carrying Aaron across the trampled pasturage, moving with careless ease between a handful of red-haired cattle with wide-swept horns. "Never had to worry about Harry or Jack, both of them open in full to the tart juice and sweet joy of their lives." She lifted her hand, wiping away a sudden rush of tears, a full smile on her lips. "True lights in our lives, the two of them in a fine balance of what each other needed and was able to share. Harold, left adrift through a heavy fog for several years after—once our sweet Jackie left. Away at school for months at a time, as I'm certain he's told you about."

Sinclair leaned back slightly, gazing at Eira, watching as the breeze teased the curls of her light colored hair, the red and gold having faded of late. "He has—although his brother remains a bit of a shadow to me, still. The edges clear enough in detail based on mention made of his physical features—found in common in our children, as both you and Harry have pointed out. But there has been only a brief exchange, here and there—of a more personal description of the loss he suffered. Due, perhaps, to the grief he still suffers from at the loss of my blood father."

She paused, sucking in her lower lip, biting her lip as she saw her son perched on the back of a small bull, his father at his side, though not holding on to him. "Though I confess I do not suffer from it at all, considering myself as daughter to the wonderful man who adopted me years ago, providing everything I could ever need—along with all his love. And then finding it again—with Richard, who I adopted as my very own—with him looking at me with such love and adoration."

Sinclair hesitated, then reached for Eira's arm, touching it lightly. "I miss him, so—beyond words capable to express it, though he is easy to find in your son and our wee Aaron—despite their kilted attire." Sinclair paused, lowering her voice. "Bloody Scots—and all that."

Eira smiled, covering Sinclair's hand with her own, enjoying the warmth of the young woman's skin. "Richard was blessed indeed with you agreeing to become part of our family. Yourself the daughter he and I had been missing all our lives, though our nieces have always been as close to us as could be. But it has never been the same—never the same for Richard—or me."

Aaron came on the run, tossing himself into their laps in a bony knot made up of pointed elbows and knees, laughing as they pulled him in, showering his red, sweaty face with dozens of kisses and chest squeezing hugs. Harold came on at a slower pace, stopping, hands on hips, face in a stern pose. "And where, pray tell—are my kisses and hugs?"

Sinclair disentangled herself from Aaron and stood up, then pulled back, her face wrinkling in disgust. "You reek—of cattle and manure. No kisses for—" Harold collected her into his sweaty arms, pressing his lips to hers as he swept her from the ground in a hug that stole her breath away. Then he folded her in his arms and moved toward the wee house, his voice in trail. "Mind the young ones, Ma. I've a bath to take and wife to bed—although the order of which comes first is a toss of coin in the air."

Aaron sat up straight, watching as his father carried his mother away, a serious look on his full lips. "What is it, child?" Eira leaned forward, her cheek against her eldest grandchild's. Aaron pulled away, then turned and looked at her. "Da wants to give huggies to Ma."

Eira nodded, casting a watchful eye toward the twins, huddled together, asleep beneath a thick goose-down comforter. "True, Aaron— and a fine ambition for you, some day, with a lass who loves you as dearly." She sighed, feeling another wash of heat sweep through from belly to eyes, missing Richard, wishing him there to share in the lives he'd been responsible of bringing into the world, with her.

His death was still a shock, his health good, other than the chronic pain from old wounds suffered from his six year term of service. He'd died while returning from a visit to his brother's estate, late at night, his coach going off the roadway when the team of horses had bolted, happening without warning as had been determined by those who knew of such things. The medical examiner's report had been achingly thorough, claiming death was caused by massive bleeding into his lungs, punctured by broken ribs, the result of an impact with a huge tree. The scene was as clear in her mind's eye today as when it had occurred, staring at the shambles of the carnage as dawn turned into day, with Richard's body carried to the side of the roadway, left stretched out under a dark cloak. Her son kneeling beside him, straightening his clothes, under the widespread limbs of a large oak.

Richard was eager to return home, in an excited mood based on news from one of his commercial partners in the American colonies. A letter sent several months earlier had invited feedback as to the temperature of the season and outlook for inclement weather, prompting a response indicating a continued stretch of a calm and moderate climate. Thomas had cautioned against his brother's outreach, sensing there was an underlying element lurking in the background, who might look unfavorably on such efforts made by members of Harold's circle of family or friends.

Richard had shrugged away his brother's concerns, reassuring him his subtle use of coded words would prevent any such issues to arise. He sighed, satisfied with the results of the meeting, his belly full after a fine meal, along with a half-bottle of a rich, full bodied wine imbibed, shared with his brother. He yawned, his eyes heavy with fatigue, starting to fall sleep, being gently rocked by the carriage as the driver eased a matched set of twin horses along at a moderate pace.

Richard was jolted awake as the wooden shell of the carriage rocked to one side, the impact causing his head to slam against the wood-paneled wall, dazing him. His vision clouded as a man dressed in black entered from the opposite side door. Richard blinked his eyes, trying to regain his senses as a small lantern swung from its handle, painting the interior with a gyrating strobe of flickering light and shadows. He forced himself upright, opening his mouth to ask the reason for the stranger's sudden trespass. The man grinned, finger pressed to thin lips, wedging his body on the floorboards between the forward and rear seats, bowing his head, secured against the next lurch and devastating impact, sending Richard chest first into the forward wall of the out of control conveyance.

$$\maltese\,\maltese\,\maltese$$

The lantern had been recovered and re-lit, rehung at an angle, the damaged carriage tilted to one side. The screaming of horses in pain radiated through Richard's head, along with the sound of moaning. His own, he realized, the outer banks of fog beginning to clear, his eyesight clearing. He drew in a deep breath, prepared to confront the man sitting by his feet, stopping when a searing pain tore through his chest and neck, connected to each other by a steady throb, timed to the beating of his heart. Richard felt himself staring to fade away, a slap to the side of his face bringing him around, the stranger's face swimming into focus, his eyes a penetrating blue-gray gazing at him as if a lover, concern etched in the corners of his chiseled visage. "Can you breathe? Your ribs took quite a punishment—from the effect of the sudden stop."

Richard tried to open his mouth, a spasm of pain clamping his teeth together as the shattered ends of broken ribs produced a coarse milling of agony in his chest. Darkness descended, leaving him adrift in a cushion of shock, preventing him from responding, from asking any of a dozen questions wedged in his throat. The silence when he returned was of concern, his heart fluttering, causing him to gasp. He tried again to inhale, struggling to breath, his crushed body belaying the order, forced to choose a shallow, rapid intake of air as waves of pain rose from within.

The stranger in black leaned closer. "You're bleeding inside. Your lungs no doubt punctured. Your face is as white as a bride's under-things, if still a maid." The face wore the same look of quiet appraisal as before. "A matter of minutes—half the turning of the hour, perhaps. No more than that, I'm afraid." He paused, his head angled to one side, listening to the anguished notes of the animals outside. "The poor things—in desperate need of being attended to. Broken legs, I'd guess —on each. As well as a crushed lung for one, by the sound." He gave Richard a warm smile. "Like you."

Richard managed to rasp the start of a sentence, his lips moving, trying to ask about the condition of his driver. The stranger leaned in, listening, his eyes on Richard's lips, nodding as he came to an understanding of the request. "He died—instantly. Head smashed in by a thick piece of wood. Held in my hand." Another breathless plea followed. "My name is not important, though my mission is. Only fair you should know the details of it, now you are about to be removed from the game." There was another slight pause while a considering look painted the corners of the man's light-colored eyes. "A rook, I believe. Yes—that's your piece. Or rather—was your piece. Your brother a bishop as yet, still in the game, with a longer reach then yours, preferring use of a more angular approach in his own search for information. Smarter than you. Luckier too—thus far."

Richard managed to condense enough air to express one word, making it clear and unambiguous. "Bas—tard." Blood trickled from the corner of his mouth, his eyes boring holes in the other man's, who grinned.

"I am actually—as much a bastard as anyone could ever hope to be. Bastard by birth, and bastard by deed." He slid to the floor, kneeling before the severely injured man. "And a rather rich bastard, at that. Made more so due to this lucrative caper, which must be concluded as I need to retire for the evening. No—for the early morning. There is a mail stage due before long, heading to London. One I shall beg a ride from, travelling to the nearest rural community where I shall disembark, raising a rescue party and bidding them return in force to untangle the means of your demise, and that of your driver." He shook his head. "And the poor beasties, too—the most innocent of all."

Richard made one last effort to speak, trying to show a small measure of pride-filled defiance. He failed, unable to resist as the man leaned forward, clasping his fingers around Richard's nose and mouth, sealing them, his voice tinged with a hint of regret. "I need to be up at the side of the road when the mail coach arrives—so your journey is over. Then the scar-faced man paused. "How did your son put it—in a speech a month or so ago—"

Richard raised his left hand, trying to move the man's hand from his face, failing, his fingers grasping the stranger's wrist as his eyes slowly lost their light. "Ah, yes. We all have stories to tell. From something or other to some other thing—the rest of his mesmerizing speech having faded from my memory. But your story is over—while mine has more chapters left to go."

He kept his hand in place, counting to sixty seconds, seven times over. Four hundred and twenty seconds, he said to himself, his audience of one in a lifeless pose. The measure of time needed to fold up a man's life and slip it away. How long one needs wait to see it properly done. Then he sighed, standing up and slipping through the missing door, wishing to be able to close the older man's eyes, and go attend to the injured horses with a sharp blade. It pained him, knowing the first men arriving to the scene of ruin and death would question why the dead man's eyes were not open to the world, and who might have slit the throats of the injured team.

He moved uphill, satisfied there would be no questions asked in regard to this terrible accident, result of a good nights work, paid for by the secretive cabal.

CHAPTER NINE

LONDON, HOUSE OF COMMONS

SUMMER 1764

Harold gave a short nod to Thomas who was sitting in a section of the hall reserved for guest and persons of note, surrounded by dozens of men with concerned looks on their faces. Harold took a moment to focus his attention on the members of the assembly, packed in together on the lower level, every seat filled. All representatives in attendance to see what his position would be regarding a proposed levying of new restrictions on the colonies right of free trade. A heavy levy to be placed around their necks by the remote hand of parliament.

Harold knew the bill, as written, would create a great burden, restricting trade of a commodity in great demand, soon to be heavily taxed under the bitter-sweet moniker bandied about in broadsheets as the 'Sugar Act', next of what promised to become a host of new levies issued by the Crown to recoup the cost of the war. One certain to increase strife between those still loyal to the Crown and their compatriots with sour voices, grumbling of a need for rebellion. All of them made pawns in the greater game being played between two destitute nations. France, and the British Empire. He raised his arms, waiting until the crowd fell silent, then began to speak.

"We are poised, today, on edge of a great precipice. One with a long fall to a hard bottom. Blood—soon to be spilt, with vast sums of monies lost, due to unwise words pressed on parchment that will create a gust of cold air. One that will sweep 'cross the wide expanse of Atlantic Ocean, when warmer words would be a far better choice." Harold lowered his head, waiting as a small but vociferous contingent of onlookers expressed their firmly-held opinions with a smattering of cat-calls and derisive retorts. The chamber guards looked to their commander for direction, with immediate expulsion the normal order given for such a breach of protocol. The heavily whiskered man in charge shook his head, allowing the men to remain in place.

Harold raised his voice to field-officer level, speaking over the fading sound of the angry outburst. He knew those shouting in opposition were hired men, earning their coin by interrupting with a flurry of rehearsed words, hoping to come to blows with the house guards, causing a scene that would be published in a flurry of broadsheets landing on both sides of public opinion. With lurid details of the event magnified in scope, used to build pressure both for and against the push to remedy shortages of governmental funding via an arm pressed firmly 'round the colonist's broad shoulders. For now.

"I have served my country and Crown—along with my fellow soldiers and the intrepid colonist militias, supported by native allies—who could be made our allies, one day, if we'll only allow it. All of us who stood shoulder to shoulder helping to achieve a great victory, then. And the promise of an even more rewarding victory—now, if given the time and will to see it through."

Several older men raised their voices in support, most with well-aged refrains of battlefield huzzas offered, dozens shouting his worn out moniker, an echo from past glory. The refrain reborn now to try and deter an impress of taxes on commerce issuing from colonial ports, heading to English and foreign trade partners. Harold raised one hand, bidding the voices to fade away, knowing the title Red Fox was no longer as well recognized or respected by many of those in attendance.

"Gentlemen, it is just that—time—which is needed now. Enough to allow financial recovery for our fellow citizens who manned the line then. When faltering would have meant a great loss for all! The French left in position for a steady gain, leaving us to abandon our dream of new territories sought out for trade. Our colonies weakened, if not for the support of our great navy." Harold waited as a different chorus of voices erupted, then slowly subsided. "These are the same citizen soldiers who stand ready to help us realize a greater dream now. Still struggling each day, in constant need of having to guard what they hold against continual raid and uprising made against settlements lying on the edge of Western borders. By equally aggrieved parties, looking for a measure of guarantee from us that will allow them to mark a line on the edge of their lands and say this far—and no further."

"Fook the sodding savages! No treaty they'll be made to adhere to!"

"No." Harold waited, knowing the man who'd shouted was speaking on behalf of many of those who otherwise were of a like mind when it came to forbearance of new taxes. "They are an ancient people, oppressed by incursion and a bloody trail papered with broken promises. Of treaties signed, then quickly ignored by a few opportunists—looking to stir emotional responses on both sides of lines, fairly drawn. Misleading our citizens with false tales made real by printer's ink—leading to fatal consequences for all."

"Indian lover! You had your prod in one of 'em—the tale told true!"

The headman nodded, three guards given permission to eject the drunk fool from the viewing area. His curses filled the hall with harsh invective as they carried him out. Harold used the time to step back and consider his response. Once order had been restored, he approached the speaking platform again.

"What he said is true—and something I've never kept from public disclosure. I was involved, for a time—with a woman of native origin, her people living on the lands of the Ohio for thousands of years, with valid claims to it based on blood and tears spilled holding onto it. The same color of blood as is our own. The same salt in the rivers of tears they've shed over loved ones lost. The same force of will as is in any one of us. Citizens of their own nation, sacrificing their lives helping us build an empire we can be proud of. And this woman, A'neewa—she saw us as we are, not only as we profess ourselves to be. Aware our knowledge was a far greater threat to her people than all our armies combined, or the power of our great navy. A'neewa knew this, and still encouraged her people to fight beside us. Beside me—aiding our conquest of the French. Long after settlers urged on by false statements leading to broken treaties, making permanent incursions into hunting lands that had long been their own. A woman who helped heal our sons and fathers, lying sorely wounded—myself included. All this and more, done by her and her people on behalf of our colonies—our empire."

Harold stepped back; the host of voices in opposition having subsided, their eyes starting to open, as well their minds. When he came back to the dais, he kept his voice low. "Of all the things A'neewa taught me—of all the times she looked into the future and shed tears at her people's inescapable plight—the lesson that has stayed with me to this day—unto this very moment—is that when words are spread from mouth to ear, the lie told is seen in the eyes and face of liars. Heard in the tone of their voice, revealing them as false. That the lies die with the one telling them." Harold paused once more, his throat tight, A'neewa's face before his eyes, her voice in his ears. He swallowed his pain, rising to his full height, hands clenching the sides of the lectern. "In our advanced and well considered culture, in our great libraries filled with books, along with broadsheets in abundance. With words inscribed in marble, stone—and clay. Words placed on parchment and paper. That our lies, once formed, live on forever—until and unless men grown wise enough sift them out from a vast sea of truth. The lie, once revealed—is tossed aside."

Harold hesitated, aware he was about to toss away his position of influence, four years in office and feeling the tide turning against prevention of another war. One of rebellion against the crown. A war he would give everything to avoid happening, knowing his father had been made to pay for attempt to aid his efforts. With the man or men behind his untimely demise; still undiscovered.

"And lies are being told—today. The motivation behind their being expression by proxies acting on behalf of men high above us based on birthright given, and not in positions earned. By purchase of false ranks, along with unmerited commendations—standing on the backs of good men, sacrificed to feed their lust for money, land, and the power given them by the hearts and minds of other good and common men, misled by half-truths, artfully worded. Half-lies strongly voiced. In public oratory— from where I am standing this day. Whether words in print, or words warming the air—and I ask that my own be judged no differently from those of any other man. Each citizen free to make their own measure of the truth. To judge the truth as seen in my eyes, on my face. Heard—in the sound of my voice in their ears."

Half the men rose to their feet in a mixed clamoring of cheers and robust applause. The rest remained seated, waiting for the other shoe to drop. Harold did not hesitate to deliver it. "This new tax on sugar is but the latest of many such blows to be landed in a grab for half-pence now, when countless pounds sterling are in ready reach. The lands west of the Ohio ripe for trade. For a fair exchange of goods and knowledge gained if—if the natives are allowed to retain lands that are already their own, to rule as they see fit. Providing safe passage through and beyond their borders—with access to the rest of an unexplored land lying beyond. One with limitless potential for untold wealth, with new allies made. Balanced against the pitiful sum of monies we seek to wring from the necks of our own people, themselves just now able to stand fully erect once more. To begin anew to prosper and grow, increasing our opportunities alongside their own. The natives able to provide tens of thousands of skilled warriors, eager to join our efforts in foreign lands, helping secure a bright future for those we seek to free from ignorant and brutal tyrannical leaders. Warriors born to seek name and reputation, no different than are our own good sons, fighting alongside them as allies. If—if we can only see the colonies as the cradle from which our willful children will soon be able to climb out of, helping our island nation lead the world into a new age of discovery. Of equality for all—here and abroad." Harold paused, raising one hand, the injured one, letting his words settle for a moment. "It is within our grasp—today. If we would choose patience— over greed."

Harold listened to the applause from most of the men, tears in his eyes, knowing he'd failed, despite the fervent reactions from the faces of those shouting his name. That A'neewa and her people were doomed to live out their lives haunting the thin edge of survival, or worse.

Faced with the slow extinction of their ways, their culture, their honor, their stories. He picked up his speech and folded it, placed it in his suitcoat pocket as he turned and walked away, leaving through a back-door exit without looking back.

William Pitt poured a tankard near to over-flowing with ale from a large pitcher. He lifted it with care, bringing it to his mouth, taking a long swallow, sighing loudly, then taking another, wiping his thick lips as he lowered it, giving Harold a friendly nod. "You know your enemies will be coming for your head. Literally—using angry words in the street and written in broadsheets, calling you out as a traitor, coward, Indian-lover—and much worse." The elder political leader paused, waiting while Harold sighed, his fingers on the sides of his head, rubbing away at the temples, in a despondent mood.

"And what, pray tell—what could be worse than those?"

"Hero. Savior. Savant." Pitt smiled. "Or prophet. Making your life a dangerous place to live in. The powers that be will not look kindly on you for having pried open the eyes of the blind. Opening the ears of. and expanding the minds of those tied with financial threads to every commercial enterprise. Here, there, and everywhere—all about the globe."

"I only told the truth as I know it to be. The future, as I hope it to be. The past, as it has always been—left littered with the bones of those who had the best of intentions."

"A bit wordy—for your epitaph." Pitt smiled again, raising his tankard.

Harold mirrored the movement, taking a long pull, wiping his lips with the back of one hand as he stared at Pitt, a firm expression on his weary face. "I mean to quit the Commons."

Pitt nodded. "That's why I am here—to talk you out of such a—rash decision." The older man leaned forward. "I mark your weariness, Harold. I do. But what you just so eloquently stated—is still very much in reach."

Harold frowned. "You would have me believe it to be, due to you having further need of me. You and your small army of silent backers, allowed to row against the current, keeping up an appearance of independent decisions being made on behalf of the common man's good."

Pitt narrowed his eyes. "We all are in service to one group, or another. Based on our own needs—as well the wishes of our masters."

Harold scoffed. "They are determined to bring both sides to their knees—those backing the crown, and their opposite number in support of the colonies. Good men on both sides, to be bled for their invisible master's greed."

Pitt cocked an eyebrow, his expression lined with regret. It caused Harold to flinch, a sudden concern passing through him of having brought threat to his family, his Grand Da's vision driving a knife blade of ice deep into his heart. When Pitt finally broke the silence, the tone of his voice reflected a hard truth, unaltered by emotion or concern for the common good. "The world we will awake to tomorrow —will remain as it has always been. In constant spin—the tides made to rise, then fall under influence of the moon. People in the thousands will die, and a thousand babes and more will be born. With nothing of any real consequence to have changed."

Harold tightened his voce. "The opportunity to hand does not have to be let go of—allowed to simply fade away. We can change the world, as you describe it. Have an effect on what is happening—if enough of us bind ourselves to the task—our hands placed to quill— speaking in one voice, raised to a level high enough to shatter the cold-stone hearts of those barring a new path forward."

Pitt shrugged. "I cannot promise you change—my impassioned friend, but I can relate that what you have just said in the House today has left a number of those standing on the other side of the issue considering if a—compromise might be made. If given enough time and the resources needed to gather support from a former colleague of yours in battle, helping to sway others to a like course. Perhaps then the beast might be led back into its restless lair."

"I cannot find your meaning, William." Harold pushed his tankard away, barely touched. "Speak clearly, as the hour is late and I am to be away on the morrow, back to a northern clime, free of the stench of foul city air—and politics."

"You would be better served in planning a return to the scene of your past successes. To reacquaint with those who may be persuaded to help you avoid the very thing you've warned us of." Pitt hardened his tone. "I charge you to bear away from your current course of relinquishing your representative duty. You will make a crossing before winter weather sets in, then return here, serving this year into next. Waiting until then for me to decide how long you are to remain in the House."

Harold leaned back in his seat, letting the silence stretch for a moment before raising his tankard and draining it, setting it down with a thud. He wiped his mouth then stuck out his hand. Pitt took it, both men staring into each other's eyes, knowing a pact had been made. Both left to question how it would end up working out. Both committed to seeing it all the way through, no matter the cost to reputation or self.

⸎⸎⸎

Thomas was unsettled, listening as his nephew explained his thoughts as to the reason for his father's death. The idea of foul play involved ignited an anger within the thin-framed man, causing him to leap up, cursing under his breath. His wife and three daughters were busy in the parlor outside the study door preparing a meal for Harold before he left for his family's manor in the southern Scottish Highlands where Sinclair and the children had been spending most of their time, well away from Bristol, Bath, or London, while the House was in session.

Harold studied his uncle's face. "I'm still searching for those responsible, my efforts failing to date without any firm evidence in hand—at the moment, though I know I'm on the correct path."

Thomas forced himself to refocus on the issue at hand. "I had warned him—your father—warned him of the danger he faced in attempting to subvert what he called the 'coalition of forces' underlying the government and the crown—our boy King's ability to rule sensibly in wane, of late."

Harold clamped his lips shut, unwilling to share with Thomas what Nathan had related to him in a grudging acknowledgement of the same thought. It had been a halting story told over two bottles of wine, with mention made of dangerous men lurking in shadows, manipulating the tenor and tone of recent events. The new King, painfully inept, making numerous mistakes, leading those who stood to lose or gain the most in fear of instability when it came to affairs of State. Stability, a key to profit. Profits, the progeny of plans put into motion generations before. A growing awareness by all sides lining up to tug at the reins of power, just how large an opportunity existed on the North American continent and beyond. With the French very much in play in the South. The Spanish with secure hold of lands north of Mexico, stretched along the western edge of what was estimated to be an incredibly vast and valuable unexplored region. Limitless wealth near to hand if the colonist's emotions could be held in check. The latest levy seen as an onerous insult by stiff-necked, prideful former soldiers, along with dozens of gifted orators and writers, all wanting their fair share of notoriety and the power going along with it.

Harold looked up, his uncle staring at him, lips pursed. "You know more than you're willing or able to share."

Harold shrugged. "I know more than can be shared safely. The consequence of a single misstep—unacceptable should I end up making a target of myself. Not worried on my own behalf, but—" He gave a nod toward the doorway.

Thomas's eyes widened. "They would not dare!"

"Depends on the ones in question. Most might not pose a threat to innocents—but I have been in the company of some who would consider it, with ties to men with the means and lack of morality to see it through."

Thomas shook his head, looking at Harold, his eyes filled with equal measures of questions, pain, along with disgust. "How you able to remain so—so damnably calm, in knowing—"

"Thinking, Uncle Thomas." Harold sighed. "Only thinking on things in play—for now."

"Still—my blood boils at the thought of it. I can't imagine how hot yours must be!"

Harold looked direct into his uncle's eyes. "My blood seethes for revenge of my father's murder. Lusting to drive cold steel through the hearts of those responsible. The urge to do so, constant, from the moment I found this in his pocket." Harold held up a wrinkled piece of parchment, letters pressed on its surface from what must have been a stub of a graphite stylus. The words were ill formed, shakily drawn. "I believe it to be a brief description—of his unnamed assailant." He handed it to his uncle, who held onto it as if a poisonous snake, with bared fangs.

Thomas studied it for a moment, his thin brows narrowed in concentration. "I can—make out the letters, recognizing them from when we were boys, in pass of hastily scribbled notes." He paused, wiping his eyes with the back of one hand. "I take it you've managed to make sense of it."

"Some of it, yes." Harold rubbed his forehead, closing his eyes. "The words are smudged—difficult to decipher."

Thomas studied the note. "Thin, gray—it's eyes, I think. Scars, cheek, neck, right side, mid age. Low birt—birth, I suppose." He handed it back, watching as Harold folded it, slipping it away in a pocket of his waistcoat, with a cold look on his face, his voice tight with anger when he spoke.

"Amazing, his having the presence of mind to do that, no doubt under direct observation of the guilty party." Harold paused, the sound of feminine laughter coming through the door. "Gray eyes—not common."

"Same color—as are your wife's."

"Another reason for us to tread softly, until this man and the ones who sent him are identified. Leaving me to find then back the bastard into a corner and finish him."

Thomas shook his head, fear in his eyes for his wife and three children in the next room. "You believe it possible to do so—safely?"

"I found Sinclair—with the help of a friend and his friends, or rather—his comrades in ink, as it were. I can always-"

"I urge caution, Harry. I've heard rumors, born of dark origin, pertaining to an underlying coalition-"

"-of gazetteers and the like, Uncle, with mutual interests on both sides of the Atlantic divide between hither and yon." Harold noted the look of confirmation in his uncle's eyes. "One of them known to you—on a personal basis."

"Nathan Bauer—made part of your family. Whom you would trust—" Thomas lowered his gaze, his voice hardening. "With an inquiry as sensitive as this?"

"I've not yet decided." Harold stared at his waistcoat pocket. "Why I've held onto my father's final words since discovery—or rather, recovery—of the note from his pocket."

Thomas came over and placed his hand on Harold's shoulder, squeezing gently. "Over three months ago—and not daring reveal it until now. I cannot imagine the burden you've been made to carry. Alone. I've known but these past few moments and feel as if my feet are clad in Thames River mud. Wanting to move—mired by doubt as to direction or identity of a target to aim my ire at."

Harold touched Thomas's hand. "I've been at the dance long enough to avoid a false step now. Career and reputation, used as leverage in hand against those behind the ordered deed."

Thomas stepped back. "What do you require from me?"

"Patience, along with your seasoned advice. And a promise to care for my family should anything happen—to me."

Thomas broke in. "As if there were a need to ask it!"

Harold shrugged. "I have never presumed—with family. My father's influence, I'm afraid. Stiff backed, irascible, and—" He looked at his pocket again. "Capable of providing details under what must have been extreme duress."

"As too yourself, Harry. With all you've been through, seen—been made a participant of. My own service ending without chance for valor. An empty vase, as it were, left in want of being filled."

"Consider yourself blessed to have missed it, Uncle. My own visage in a mirror, a stranger's face at times, bearing scars deeper than those on my body. A price I would gladly have avoided the payment of—the memories with me, to this very day." Both men fell silent, each recalling how the same malaise of spirit had affected Richard upon his release from service, his body left torn, in constant pain. Harold held out his hand, shaking his uncle's. "I'm off to be with my family, after I dine with then make my goodbyes to my dear aunt and three beautiful cousins."

"Of course." Thomas nodded. "I thank you for taking the time to share—all that you have. I hope in doing so, you find some relief of the burden, carried. Please let me know what I can do to help unmask the culprit—and the ones who sent him."

Harold paused, giving his uncle a long look. "I would charge you with working out all possible connections as to who, how, and why the ones lurking in the throne's shadows are weaving strings designed to pull us into conflict with our loyal brethren in lands across the sea. Creating rebellion where none need exist. That is what your brother—what my father would be asking of you. That is what needs be done—and soon. I will return in two weeks' time. Have your ideas firmly in place by then."

Harold moved into the dining room, allowing himself to be diverted by the joyful attention of his cousins and wonderful meal provided by his aunt, then left to be with his own family. Once he was gone, Thomas went into his study and clasped the back of a chair, staring at his fingers, the knuckles white, blood pressed from them as equal parts of bottomless anger at his brother's murder, and deep fear for the safety of both families washed through him. He closed his eyes, an unbound rage beginning to build within his thin, shaking frame.

CHAPTER TEN

PORT OF PENNSYLVANIA

AUTUMN, 1764

The bow of the ship rose and fell in a gentle motion, as if trying to rock Harold to sleep. He stared at the gray, hump-backed swells, watching the near horizon where a strip of dull textured green ran above the rugged coastline. It was still a lightly tamed land, once known as the New World before intrepid colonists had ventured here, willing to try and wrest a living from the wilderness. He counted columns of thin smears of smoke rising in a haze-fogged air, stopping when the number reached more than one hundred, thinking about all the changes made since those early days. Including those made since the last time he'd been there, the smoke from chimneys having doubled in number.

He marked native sites of ancient origin, their huge mounds of bivalve shells, or middens as the locals named them, anchoring the edges of protected coves where wharves and dock yards were festooned with countless small boats. Small towns continued to spring up where tribal fires had once risen, smoke drifting from chimneys centering houses reaching to second and third floors, visible in the morning haze as the ship made its steady approach toward the port of Philadelphia.

The three-week journey from London was nearing its end, Sinclair in their quarters below deck, trying on every piece of clothing she'd packed, trying to find the perfect look, quivering in her eagerness to venture into the world from which he'd been released a lifetime ago, or so it seemed to him.

"We are soon to part ways, my friend." Pierre de Coulombe, a fellow seafarer on the ship Celeste, based out of London on through to Boston and ports further south, stood at Harold's elbow, having made his re-acquaintance at the dock in London, three weeks earlier.

"As if that could happen, seeing how you keep—turning up." Harold flashed a tired grin, his sleep uneven over the last few nights, forced into social politeness during the day, then wrestling with dark visions populating his dreams, despite the loving administrations of his wife, trying to soothe his nerves. "Our paths seem inter-twined, as if we are making our way along concentric circles, intersecting as time and our mutual destinies decree."

"I bow to the wisdom of your words, Philosopher Knutt." Pierre stepped forward, hands on the rail, eyes closed against the light, sea-salted breeze, tilting his head back and drinking it in with a long draw and sighing release. "Why men would choose to leave this—I cannot fathom."

"The—sea?"

"Yes, my friend. The air is so clear. The mainsail unbound, and such nautical expressions as that."

Harold crossed his arms, his legs absorbing the roll of the ship. "The sting of rain, driven 'fore the gale. The deck in shuddering heave. Hull pressed between foam maddened jaws of a green-bodied beast, in violent shake and twist. Men sent aloft, risking their lives to secure sails in a storm battered whip."

Pierre stared. "You have—been in such seas as those?"

Harold shook his head. "No—thank God. But I've heard tales of the like told direct, from one who lived through them—when others did not. No less a battle fought out there, on the briny deep—then were our own." Harold paused, head lowered, feeling Pierre's hand on his shoulder.

"We now have new stories to share, my former comrade in opposed arms. The days have been filled with delightful conversations with our two wonderful companions. Along with music—sweet to ear and soul."

Harold looked over and nodded his head, hearing the notes from a violin sighing through the air, the words being sung, too faint to make out, though he sensed their meaning, sharing them in thoughtful silence alongside his former adversary. The two of them having been reacquainted at their journey's beginning, four weeks earlier.

Sinclair, her hand clasped in Harold's, raised her voice in order to be heard over a loud murmur of voices from people scurrying about the busy London docks. "A glorious adventure, husband! So much bustling between dock and boats, with goods and people moving from here to there. So many boats—"

"Ships." Harold squeezed her hand. "Not boats." Sinclair cut him a glare that would have sheared the ear from the side of his head if he'd not deflected it with a smile. "What the sailors call them."

"Boats, ships, vessels—gravy-pots for all I care, as long as they float and will carry us clear of land. I'm eager to see the ocean spread before me—with nothing but water as far as the eye can see."

Harold circled her waist with his arm, knowing he would use the same grip while holding her as she leaned over the railing, emptying her stomach later that night, or the next day. "As too am I, my Lass."

A voice cut through the mill of people passing by, with throngs of serious-faced seamen, dock workers, and fishermen in a hurry to get from one point to another as quickly as possible. Harold turned, hearing a phrase shouted in French, one he was least in favor of.

"Reynard Rouge!" Pierre de Coulombe approached, one hand wrapped about the corset-pinched waist of a young woman, the other raised in a friendly wave with a warm smile firmly planted on his lips. "My friend! A pleasure, indeed." He came to a stop, his face flushed with excitement. His richly attired partner stayed half-hidden behind a large fan with sachet attached, helping offset the odor of manure from horse-drawn carts mixed with dozens of fish rotting alongside the docks, along with the unwashed bodies of laborers at their sweaty toil.

"Major Coulombe. A—genuine pleasure, as well." Harold removed his hat and bowed to the lady at Pierre's side, switching to Parisian

French. "Allow me to introduce myself. I'm Harold Knutt, and this is my wife, Lady Sinclair Knutt."

Pierre stepped forward, taking Sinclair's hand, kissing the back of it then bowing in turn. "And I am Comte Coulombe — Madame Sinclair Knutt. Your husband and I were involved for a time on opposite sides of a — national disagreement — a few years ago. Each of us performing some small assistance to the other — in time of need."

Sinclair nodded, aware the man had tried to kill her husband, then helped him bury the soldier who'd been her blood father. Pierre stepped back, hat in hand. "Allow me to introduce my travel companion. Miss Aimee Chevalier — of Paris."

Harold bowed again. "A pleasure, indeed — Miss Aimee Chevalier." He could feel Sinclair's cool gaze on the back of his neck as he leaned in, kissing the other woman on her powdered cheeks. Then he stepped back, reaching for Sinclair's hand, giving Pierre a hard gaze. "A stroke of luck, you finding us here — in London, on the same dock, one of a dozen or more lining the bank of the Thames."

"And on the same ship, as well — your name noted on the passenger list when my man came here and booked our passage last month. We are bound for the colonies, with call at ports from Boston on through to Williamsburg, where business opportunities await my arrival there."

Sinclair nodded to Pierre. "A fortunate event, which we must take full advantage of." She stepped forward, taking Aimee's hand in hers, leading her away to a nearby cart, loaded with flowering plants in ornate vases, waiting to be loaded aboard ship for placement in guests' quarters.

Pierre watched as the two women moved away, arm in arm. "She is an — incredible beauty."

Harold nodded. "Yes, my-friend. I still have my eyes. Your young companion is-"

"I am speaking of your lady, my friend. I've never met someone so — so naturally beautiful. So-" Pierre looked at Harold with an expression of awe on his handsome face. "I will understand if you wish to strike me — for my untoward appraisal — but I can assure you the blow would be a small price to pay for having revealed my true feelings. She is the most beautiful woman I have ever had the pleasure of meeting."

Harold shrugged. "I will not disagree."

Pierre stared back, hands at his side. "And as to the blow to my jaw, earned by my unconscionable behavior?"

"I am—pondering the matter."

Pierre laughed, then placed his hand on Harold's shoulder. "Then ponder away, my friend, as we once again engage in artful probe and parry." Pierre guided Harold toward the flower carts. "In the mean-time—let us join our lovely ladies as they make plans for what promises to be many wonderful days and nights of delightful entertain-ment to come!"

❦❦❦

A meal made up of simple, though delicately flavored fare, was laid out in a reserved cabin with a large window open to the sea air. Four settings, in a circular placement, were centered by a bottle of red wine left open to breathe. Glasses of the finest manufacture were matched in quality by vases placed about the room, filled with fresh cut flowers providing a delicate bouquet.

"It is an incredible array, Pierre." Sinclair brandished a warm smile, her eyes moist with appreciation of the gift being presented Harold and her on their final night aboard, scheduled to reach the riverfront city of Philadelphia in the morning. "I am so glad our dear Aimee has passed through her recurrent bouts of nausea—the sea in a more tranquil state of late."

Harold needed all his willpower to keep from rolling his eyes, recalling the frequent trips made above deck late into the night, escorting his wife as she suffered through bouts of seasickness once the ship had reached open seas. He watched as Pierre slid out a chair for Sinclair, then mirrored the elegantly dressed man, seating Aimee, who graced him with a warm smile.

The two men took their seats, Pierre ringing a small silver bell for service. They spent the remainder of the evening in light-hearted banter, ending with an arrangement of songs in English and French, performed by both ladies, along with Pierre, whose rich baritone voice perfectly complemented Aimee's contralto, and Sinclair's alto-soprano notes.

The scent of tobacco hung in the air, backlit by the odor of burning oil from lanterns hanging along the railing of the ship, along with a line of others strung alongside the dock they were tied to. Pierre had declined an offer of Harold's spare pipe, choosing instead to lean against the railing, staring into the river in steady flow, his mood quiet. Unusually so, Harold though as he considered his former foe, given his normal disposition. He leaned back against the railing. "You are in a sullen state. Is this the hour you will finally relate what's been gnawing on your soul of late?"

"Are you asking that I make a confession of my sins?" Pierre looked over, his eyes reflecting a hooded expression. "If so—no more worthy a person to unburden myself to than the man I tried with all my will to kill—during our final encounter in western reach."

"Would have been the same on my side of the coin in toss—the moment left to fate's dictate."

The slightly younger man nodded, crossing his arms on his chest. "It is a heavier burden of guilt I carry, no matter your casual dismissal of it. I have information to share of—mutual concern. Charged with its delivery by someone known to us both."

"I could hazard a guess as to his name—and likely hit the mark dead on."

Pierre narrowed his eyes, his carefully plucked brows furrowed. "If so—and correct in your aim—I would make claim against you of practicing witchcraft."

"Or only a logical interpretation of your odd choice of making your crossing from a London port, on a ship whose original manifest did not include the names of one Pierre de Coulombe and his—escort."

Pierre sighed, lowering his gaze, staring at the recently scoured deck. "A last minute decision, both the passage booked and—hired passenger in tow. She is an employee of a friend's establishment. A sweet enough blossom for this bee—though in considerable pale to your wild rose, the Lady Knutt an exquisite bloom." Pierre paused, considering his words. "I do not mean to speak so freely of my feelings, my friend—aware how prickly you English can be when it comes to affairs of the heart."

Harold shrugged. "You speak a truth we share in common." Then he paused, a wry grin on his lips. "Besides, my friend—seeing as I'm half-Scottish by blood—if I felt offended by your comments, I'd simply shoot you out of hand—without resorting to the naming of a second."

Pierre bowed his head. "You are a far better man than I, Colonel Knutt."

"I am as good—perhaps."

"I will allow you to re-consider after I've provided the information, previously mentioned."

Harold waited, silently appraising his former enemy made friend, aware Pierre would always be an adversary, despite the swing of the compass needle of their relationship. He also knew he could count on the other man's sense of honor.

Pierre stiffened his posture, looking Harold straight in the eye. "I am a member of a group that has ties to people of power in your country, as well as mine. A group made up of powerful men throughout the greater-European collective, and beyond. A minor member, as yet— perhaps not even that, but made privy to shadowy gossip—enough to form substance from it. Enough to-"

"The man you mentioned earlier—would his name be Nathan Bauer?"

Pierre hesitated for a single heartbeat, then nodded in reply, his shoulders lifting slightly as if a weight had been removed. "In point of fact—it is."

Harold shrugged. "I have had similar conversations with him. Enough to form my own conclusions as to his motives, and those of this same group you speak of. Motives I feel are very much still in play, much like the game we were involved in—a handful of years ago."

"Then you too feel the blade of concern—held against your back."

"It has already struck me through—my father made to pay for his —unwise, but well intentioned attempt to try and determine the cause of ill feelings being raised between crown and colonies, trying to protect me from a threat he could not see, or come to understand how great it was. Until he was murdered—at their order."

"I had heard—from my source—the news of your loss, though he did not reveal any untoward action having been taken. Only relating to me that an accident had occurred. For which I extend my full and most heartfelt sympathies to you."

Harold nodded, his voice low. "I thank you for them."

Pierre turned and spit into the water alongside the dock, clearing the bile from his throat, built up while waiting on an opportunity to clear his conscience, his soul still fouled by secrets that would need to remain untold. "I would release myself from their grasp, were the price not too great. I let myself—my foot—to be placed in—I'm not sure of the English phrase to use."

"Your toe—placed in their trap." Harold cocked his head, eying Pierre. "Drawing you further into the grind, each day."

"Exactly! Just so." Pierre flashed a thin grin, his eyes remaining dark. "Your analogy is a perfect description."

"It was my father's, told to me just before I left home to join the British army in repulse of—you."

"A man with clear foresight. Yourself, an image of him, are you not?"

"Better, perhaps, than him. Having started from a perch on his broad shoulders. As it should be from father to son. As I would hope it will be with my own."

"You are fortunate in your children, from all that Sinclair has related of them. Most fortunate in your son—as described."

"Yes. The laddie just having turned four years of age. The twins, a few months short of turning three."

Pierre sighed. "My own circumstances in regard to a family—are rather bare on that account. At least as far as I know of—the thought both a fear and hope at times that some lovely lady will come and knock at my door with an infant in swaddle, bearing my grin. A dream I awake from in sudden start, whether from potential loss of a small part of my personal freedom, or of dying alone—without an heir. I truly cannot say."

Harold shrugged, turning to look at the waters of the river, sighing past the end of the dock. "Enough, perhaps, that you contemplate the idea of it now. The future a bank of fog on the horizon these days. And, speaking of days—"

"Yes. The hour draws near for our final goodbyes, with a sense that —that it will be the last time we meet, though I would have it be otherwise. But I am left satisfied at having been given the opportunity to unburden myself of what has been related to me—and believe to be true. To provide as much to you as I can—safely offer." Pierre smiled, this time letting his eyes betray his emotions, gleaming in the light from the ship-rail lanterns. "Consider it a parting gift, my friend in return for that of my life—when first we met."

Harold listened as the man, who was and would always be an enemy to him, told him of the inner workings of the cabal and their ongoing efforts to put in place and one day ignite a handful of slow burning fuses that would lead to eventual conflict between the English Empire and its willful colonies. When Pierre finished, Harold nodded his thanks, wondering how much of what he'd heard was a back-door message from Nathan, the only person other than himself aware of the details of his passage back to the colonies, booked with an agent of one of dozens of ships making regular crossing from the docks in London.

George was still the same bear of a man, his girth enhanced by a belly starting to fall over his belt, his hair going over to gray around his temple, tied back in a ponytail, eschewing use of a powdered wig. His greeting to Harold was a loud growl, his strong arms spinning his friend in circle as if a child, leaving him breathless once back on his feet, his mind in swirl.

After regaining his senses, Harold smiled, watching the same reception given to Sinclair, who had the presence of mind to lift herself up, using the burly man's arms to hold herself above the ground, her smile a gleam of white as her dark hair flowed about her shoulders in a cloud of thick, ebony ringlets, laughing as she made a circular tour of the crowded dock in George's boisterous twirl.

George finally released her, coming over to stand by Harold, towering above him. "I could not allow myself believe it true—your letter arriving with the news over a month ago. I've near died from anticipation these last few days, word sent from Boston by coach, letting me know you had survived the crossing. A dawdling trip made down the coast, your Captain in no hurry to see you safely delivered here." He turned, staring at Sinclair, who was surrounded by his mother, and several relatives as a flurry of introductions were being made. "Which I can understand and all but forgive the man for—in wanting to hold onto the—both of you a bit longer before letting go."

"A fair assessment, my brother—and well said."

"Good to see you have retained some small measure of respect for one holding the higher rank within our two families, now joined."

Harold smiled. "You've been—promoted from Colonel? Have you rejoined the colonial militia?"

"No. I left with rank and commission earned, my status—still retired. Politics my choice of battlefield now—as I understand to be the same for you."

"Then it would seem we are equal in rank, with Ayden kind enough to promote me to full Colonel, upon my own separation. Which I'm certain you were aware of then, when we last saw him."

George shrugged, his smile losing some warmth. "Must have slipped my mind." Then his face brightened as Sinclair looked over and waved at them. "But come on, my friend—our carriages await. You, to ride with me—and your beautiful bride to accompany the others, their claim on her seeming to be secure. Possession considered the lion's share of claim to ownership—on this side of the waters, now crossed."

Harold followed his brother in arms over to where a matched pair of black horses with silver-gray manes and tails were harnessed to an ebony colored coach, the driver tipping his hat as they climbed into the open conveyance. Harold twisted in his seat, watching as Sinclair gave a wave of one hand, the other clasped by George's elderly mother who leaning in, saying something that brought a smile of delight to his wife's joy-filled face.

⚜ ⚜ ⚜

Sinclair exuded excitement. "They all were so—wonderful in display of their affection for one another. And for us, myself included—though they know so little about me."

Harold watched Sinclair, his wife dressed in a robe with the belt left unfastened, revealing her legs and lower thighs as she moved between bed and closet, her long hair let down, framing her face and shoulders. "One need not touch the rose—to know it's beauty, or breath in its delicate scent."

Sinclair missed his comment, her eyes filled with excitement as she spun around and smiled. "I'm feeling—as if a young girl again. Giddy from the quick tour made of your friend's holdings. The thousand acres of woodland and fields—and the stables. Immense, with brood stock as good as any I have ever seen—in all of England. Amazing, the scope of architecture and innovative design in abundance throughout the region.

"You have some sense of it—but not all is as it appears to be." Harold sighed, pulling his eyes away from Sinclair's partially exposed body, the robe hanging open. She came over and stood in front of him, her hands on his forearms, eyes looking directly into his. "You have been—somewhat out of sorts—ever since our last night aboard ship. No doubt having to do with your top-side conversation with Pierre."

Harold stared out a curtained window, the view filtered, the grounds outside a hazy green beneath the fabric softened bright blue sky. "I am not at liberty to broach any of the subjects discussed, that night. Suffice it to say, I am made more aware today, than yesterday, of what lies at stake in the greater game being played between short-sighted men with handful of flints, eager to light fuses that could—" Harold stopped, Sinclair's arm on his, turning him around into her naked embrace, her robe puddled on the floor at her feet.

She gazed into his eyes. "Enough, my husband—carrying the weight of the world on your shoulders, as if Atlas himself. We have an entire evening ahead of us, with dinner, drink, and dancing to get through before we will be free to make our way to the bed provided us by our gracious hosts."

Harold glanced at the four-posted frame of a large bed placed against the far end the large bedroom they'd been shown to, their baggage already there. Sinclair had been busying herself in removing their clothing, hanging everything in a set of spacious closets, then arranging her shoes, of various colors and shape, in a perfect line before a wall of polished walnut: the entire room a work of opulent design. "We could take a lie down—to recover our wits. An hour or so before the ride George has arranged for us, to get a closer look at his holdings."

Sinclair shook her head. "It is not an act of recovery I see in your beautiful blues eyes, you liar." She paused, seeing a slight wince flash across his face. "I'm only making a jest, Harry."

He forced a smile, then took her in his arms, burrowing his face into the coils of her curls, breathing deeply, drinking in her natural scent. "It is enough to hold you—for now." His lips found her earlobe, nibbling gently as his firm fingers pulled her in against him. Sinclair sighed, then pulled away slightly, looking at him with a heated expression in her eyes. "Not for me—it isn't. So, gather me up, husband mine —and carry me to the bed."

Music was in full balance, filling the large ballroom with a mix of background sounds from stringed instruments and woodwinds. The delicate notes hung in the air, gently stirred by a host of elegantly attired women and men moving about. They were an assemblage of local dignitaries, joined by others from further afield, having made their way from coastal cities to the expansive estate at George's invitation.

Harold paused as he entered the room, Sinclair on his arm, waiting as a thin man in powder dusted wig made their introduction, with everyone's eyes swinging in their direction. Harold glanced at Sinclair, wondering if they were at a celebration of a holiday, or anniversary of a significant event. He was shocked when George stepped into the center of the hall and announced, in a booming voice, that the evening was meant to welcome a war hero to the colonies, returned.

The large man waited until a load roar and sea of applause died down, then continued, one hand raised and pointing at Harold, who's face had gone a deep shade of crimson. "My brother in arms—who shed his blood, sweat, and more than a few tears shared between us in the effort against the French—has been a respected voice of support in Parliament on behalf of our pleas for redress of onerous taxes, risking his position of power and prestige on our behalf."

The crowd of people pressed closer, surrounding Harold and Sinclair as George led them into the center of the floor, the music increasing in volume as Geore beamed at the two of them, sharing in the acclaim as the others came forward and made their thanks known.

"I am still upset with you, brother—knowing I deserve no such credit for what you said last night!" Harold stared at George, the two of them on horseback, leaving the stables. George laughed, loudly, his hands grasping the reins of a large steed, the animal shying at the booming sound and sudden movement. The large man's gentle touch and reassuring tone soon returned the magnificently formed animal to a relaxed canter.

"You're as blind to your importance as ever. Never in a clear mind when it comes to your own ambitions—seeing only what's in the best interests of those around you. Selflessness can be a capital crime, my friend—when practiced in extreme."

"I spoke the same truth that you, or anyone else with experience from this side of things would do. Nothing more. It's not worthy of the thanks given me."

"You spoke it in the very face of the boy King—along with his rump-muddled consorts, with their heads so far up the royal orifice, they might never find their way out, if they were so inclined to try." George leaned back in his saddle, the horse coming to a stop, its head dropping to search the side of the narrow lane for twists of grass. "Hark, was that a glimmer of a grin on my taciturn brother's lips?"

Harold shook his head. "A fleeting memory of someone else of like energy and build similar to yours, offering a similar opinion told me long ago—myself a young officer in training, and thousands of leagues away."

"As wise a man—I take it."

"Yes—he was." Harold clucked to his mount, a long-legged mare with sweet build and sweeter disposition, who moved ahead without need of further encouragement, eager to get back to the barn and a stall filled with sweet hay. "I can accept your introduction of me as brave, or more accurately—brazen in my opinions concerning the proper treatment of the crown's subjects, over here. It helps strengthen your personal ambitions, in having a close tie to the political scene back in London—but I assure you, it is not from strength of will but my sense of fairness that bids me rise, interjecting myself into the fray. Something any man of like mind would and should do—in defense of logic and reasonable treatment given to all, by all."

George caught up, returning to a side-by-side position. "If you choose to frame it so, that your actions are being done on behalf of— likeminded men in England, then I shall call off the gathering of those wishing to make known their personal thanks to you. Telling them it is not needed and will not be well received. Though it will be you who will share the news with my lovely lady, whom, as we speak, is having alterations made to one of her favorite dresses so your wife will have something spectacular to wear while meeting with those who hold prominent positions in our political and intellectual world—on this side of a deep and widening sea, between."

🌿🌿🌿

There were two doors leading into a side-room, where a small circle of chairs had been placed, each holding a person of distinguished name and reputation. One of them supported a man who could not keep from gawking at the others, knowing them by name and words in publications circulating abroad. Harold continued to slew his attention from one such personage to another, as each took center stage, voice raised above the murmuring background noise of the others, making one insightful point after another. George remained silent, waiting until all had opportunity to say their piece, as was his right in having hosted the affair. Then he rose to his feet, a towering figure, his hand firmly pressed on Harold's shoulder.

"We have all had ample opportunity to fire our loads—wadding lying in burnt tatters upon the ground." Several men in the background crowd made ribald comments, among them a handful of men with parchment sheets in hand, quills poised, each tasked with the front or end of every sentence spoken, an overlapping effort designed to capture every sentence in its entirety. "And it now falls to the one we are here to honor with our attentive natures—as he gifts us with the benefit of his own understanding of the cause and effect of taxation without representation in parliament, and the like. I present our guest, and my brother in arms and in life—Colonel Harold Knutt, retired, a decorated veteran of our war against the French and Indian allies, and a respected representative to the House of Commons."

The assembled dignitaries stood up and clapped their hands. Harold, his face reddening before the applause, stood and nodded at his brother, then lifted a hand, waving at the crowd of well-wishers. He motioned for silence, the room falling away to a hush, then cleared his throat, starting his unprepared speech.

"I am but a soldier. Still. One sworn to protect those I hold dear. No more and no less than any man, in any home, in any city, township, or settlement. Whether in hovel or manor, or from a hole in ground—a man's place, or position in life means little when measured against his pride or desire to fight for what is an inalienable right—for all. The freedom to decide one's own fate, one's own destiny—from a highland croft to a log home at the edge of the wilderness. From castle to manor, born. Allowed to choose freely the path he will lead his family down. Willing to fight—if need be. To stand and avenge dark deeds, when retribution is called for in support of his neighbors, friends, and allies. Only that—a simple man with a simple view of the foundation on which his house is to be built. Ensuring that each man shall have equal share of the promise of this promised land that we are bound to by shed of our sweat, blood, and tears. To help raise it up, to defend it, detesting our sins, when wrong. Admiring our successes when right. Serving with full measure of will and might. No more or less than would any of us gathered here, tonight. To take our rest when the fire finally burns down, touching our loved ones gently, bidding them all goodnight. And then, when our lady love is safely off to bed—to leave through the backdoor and join our fellow soldiers and friends for a great carouse!

The room erupted in joyous laughter and shouts of hurrahs. George wrapped his huge arms around Harold's chest, lifting him into the air, where he waved one hand while trying to draw in breath to survive the embrace. Those whose buttocks had been glued to their seats during the earlier speeches, joined in. George released Harold, who collected himself, noting a few men of regard standing in the back of the room, somberly nodding their heads, as if considering how the moment could be used to their own advantage.

Harold was forced to look away, ducking his head as George and several other well-wishers picked him up, carrying him through twin doors into the stateroom beyond.

CHAPTER ELEVEN

WESTERN PENNSYLVANIA WILDERNESS

LATE AUTUMN, 1764

The woods were unchanged since the last time Harold had been through them. Thick canopies of deeply rooted trees in shadowed pose were posed above scattered lines of rocks; framed by weather-smoothed ledges bordering cascading streams. He closed his eyes, seeing the charts, maps and other identifying features noted in his journals. Left behind in Bristol at his parents' home, in a small chest stacked among other personal items stored from his days in service to the crown.

He did not miss them now, his recall crystal clear. The native guides hired, left to follow as he led the small contingent of men, and one intrepid woman, deep into the wilderness. A mostly untamed land, stretched from the edge of one now being carved into settlements by the metal blades of plow, axe, and saw.

"Another day?" Sinclair's voice was at his elbow, Harold reaching back to help her up a small step of limestone. He could tell from the rasp of her breathless words that she was near to being done for the day. The sun hung at a low angle, signaling a need to stop and set up shelter for the night, now in swift approach.

Harold nodded. "One more." Sinclair stood beside him, still

holding his hand, leaning her head against his shoulder. He drank in her scent, then sighed. "I'd hoped to reach there this day, my desire to do so greater than my recall of the time needed to cover the distance."

"Better, perhaps, to reach it during the day to come. Well rested—and fed."

Harold pulled her in, the heat from her body providing a pleasant warmth. "Agreed." He could feel the rumble of her hunger beneath the press of his hand on her side. "Is not the first time I've placed my desire ahead of common sense."

"And we have the twins to show for it. Our sweet brood having appeared earlier in our lives than I'd planned on, but here, none-the-less. Or rather, there." Sinclair's face dissolved in worry, every mother's burden to carry with children not ready to hand. The three children left cupped in Eira's capable hands, safely tucked away at the manor in the highlands of Scotland, along with a host of adoring relatives drawn there to share the manor, eager to have their turn with each one.

Harold eased his grasp, leaning back, looking into her light-colored eyes. "We will be hard-pressed to be pry them away, returning them to our firm hand on their reins. But to their lovely mother's sweet voice they will come on the run. Just wait and see—and soon enow, our journey near its half-way point and near the reason we are here, my beautiful lass."

Sinclair grinned, her tears unshed. "Your honeyed words reveal a hunger of another kind—but my body desires food and rest." She shoved him away. "Issue the order to make camp, sir. Before threat of a mutiny is made."

The air was cold, due to the higher elevation, with several fires kept going throughout the night to keep weary bodies warm. Sentries were posted in four-hour shifts, moving between firepits, feeding wood to the flames. The men's eyes were in constant watch, despite the lack of threat from the natives whose land they were moving through. Their passage, made through several tribal territories, had been prearranged, the native leaders in agreement as to the reason for and time needed to complete the brief incursion into their lands. All of them having made visits to the caravan, presenting gifts and speeches in a show of respect from former allies, and foes.

George sat beside Sinclair, his arm wrapped about her shoulders. Harold asleep beside them, his own turn to stand watch and tend fires still a few hours away. "Are you warm enough, sister-mine?"

"I am." Sinclair snuggled in, resting her head against the large man's chest, knowing she was as safe as anyone could ever be, placed between two men with courage and means to defend all against all, no matter the odds. "Speaking of sisters, I know so little about yours. About Meghan."

George considered a moment. "I suppose you would consider it to be a point of pain—asking me to share my memories of her—as it must be for your husband. She evoked strong feelings in all who came to know her. As too perhaps, for yourself—if wanting to be made subject to my telling you of them."

Sinclair pulled away, looking up. "You are—a much deeper person than you let on."

George grinned, then lifted a finger, placing it to his lips. "A secret —between you and me. People assuming the bigger you are, the thicker your head—and skin." He pulled Sinclair back in, unable to speak while under her gaze, waiting for her to relax into his embrace. "I was witness—blessed to see it in full express—of a one-sided love between two people I dearly cared for, and still do—to this very day. Not to mention a growing affection for a new member of my extended family, recently met."

Sinclair smiled, enjoying the sound of his words resonating in his chest. She listened as he began to tell the tale, in emotional detail, her arm squeezing him whenever he faltered, his voice halting until he was able to continue. When he finished, Sinclair used a fold of his shirt to wipe her eyes, her tears in full stream as his hand caressed her shoulder. Emotionally exhausted, having heard the tale told firsthand, along with what A'neewa had shared with him of Meghan's final moments.

Sinclair sighed, looking into the flames of the fire, watching as sparks spun in small twists of heated air, rising into the night sky. "So —painfully—beautiful. Her love—their love—and yours." She faltered, her voice fading away.

"My sister, for her husband and son—yes, though unable to provide it in full to—"

Sinclair pulled away, her eyes gleaming from the light of the flames. "No. Not Meghan's—but A'neewa's. Her love—for your sister. The reason she—helped her find a release. To be with her family again. Done out of a shared love—a shared pain—in common. Both of them victims of a world with little regard for right or wrong. With good, overwhelmed by bad."

George returned an understanding gaze, feeling the truth of what had eluded him for so long, thinking the deed A'neewa had done was meant to protect Harold from further injury, his sister's pain having driven her to strike out without awareness. "You are—worthy of his love for you. All of it. Every drop of his—in return. Along with something I saw in his eyes, from the very first time we were introduced. Always there—before and after every fight, each battle, performing a soulful recount of the people lost on either side. A gentleness of spirit, wrapped within a will and vision beyond my ability to fully measure up against." George hesitated. "A man I hold great respect for."

"The same as Harold feels for you."

George nodded, pulling Sinclair close, giving her a long, heartfelt embrace. "You have the right of it, dear one. Now lie down alongside your husband and I'll spread a cloak to keep you warm."

After George had tucked her in, he stood up and moved away, finding a rock to shield himself against. Wrapping a blanket around his shoulders, well outside the circle of fire and hidden from view, he leaned forward, clasping his large hands around his knees, allowing a wave of painful memories of his sister to wash through him, his shoulders heaving as his heart was torn in two, again. Crying soundlessly until he had no strength left, falling off into a deep and dreamless sleep.

♼ ♼ ♼

The weather broke with a bright sun rising into a clear sky, warming air in close follow. The blaze of light and clear air painted Sinclair's cheeks rose-red as she made her way uphill, arriving at the top of a steep ridge, her light-gray eyes gazing down at a vibrant panorama of thick-quilted forest, threaded through with small waterways in silvery gleam. She stood still, trying to catch her breath, drinking in the beauty of the western highlands displayed in full splendor below. It was a rich tableau of colors in dab and daub, of texture and tone, as if a painting placed on a vast round wall, revealing a scene that could only exist within an artist's vivid imagination.

"You—are good?" One of the native guides touched her on her shoulder. He was speaking in his own language, knowing she had some understanding of it, having been in constant practice the past two weeks. She turned and gave him a smile, placing her hand on his, squeezing slightly, letting him know she was in fine spirits. He returned a knowing gaze, aware of the purpose of her journey, then shifted to French. "Reynard Rouge—he loved your father. More than himself, as it is between men who fight as one. He placed him here, where all this—" He swept a wiry, muscled arm in a full circle. "His to watch over."

Sinclair closed her eyes and nodded, using a linen cloth to wipe her nose. When she opened her eyes, she was alone and for a brief moment thought it had been an illusion: the native an apparition sent by the man she'd come all this way to find. Sinclair turned her head, watching as Harold made his way over to where she was standing, hat in hand, hair in a ponytail, eyes soft with slight concern showing in their corners.

"We're only a few hundred paces away."

Sinclair was tempted to ask if he'd seen the native. "I'm fine. How many are coming with us—to where he—to where my father lies?"

"Only you—my own goodbye made years ago."

"My father could not have asked for a more perfect resting place." She paused, wiping her nose again. "Or a better friend."

Harold came up and leaned against her, his arm surrounding her waist, feeling her toned body beneath the press of his fingers, having become even more beautiful in his eyes over the past two months and more since they'd left London. Three months having passed since leaving the children with the Scott clan. Five years on from when he'd met her in the doorway of the boarding house in Bath. Over six years, since seeing her likeness in a carved cameo, resting in Robert's hand, his thumb in constant rub. He leaned down, burying his nose in her ebony hair, inhaling the scent of oil, sweat, and woodsmoke. "Yr wyt yn fwy mewn harddwch nag erioed o'r blaen. Mae'n gosod y tir o'i gwmpas."

Sinclair angled her head, her eyes filled with motes of silver from the mid-morning sun. "What does it mean?"

"Thou art more in beauty—than ever before. It pales the land, in surround."

Her eyes swam as tears flowed down her crimson cheeks, a match to his own, in watery sea of blue. Their lips met in a salty embrace as they allowed their unfettered emotions to be fully released.

⅏ ⅏ ⅏

Sinclair pressed her hand on a large, weather-stained rock, her fingers lying flat on the cold stone. It seemed to be absorbing the warmth of her flesh, as if a wick in reverse, pulling it deep inside, as if hungry for the blush of life, returned. Sinclair was alone, having asked Harold to stand away. Near to her call, if needed. Determined to have a private moment with the man who'd troubled her thoughts for so long.

She'd been prepared for any emotions that might arise, including anger at his abandonment of familial duties, of the loss of the love that Harold had assured her was sent each morn and night, for as long as she'd been alive, over the distances stretched between them, through their lives spent apart. She felt a stirring of childhood hatred, fueled by lies told by the woman who'd birthed, then used her as emotional leverage, offering men of means, without families of their own, the love of an innocent child. Presented to them as a priceless gift should matrimony be proposed, leaving them once financial security had been secured, in a trail of destitute, emotionally destroyed victims. Then a search for another victim begun, continuing a steady climb up societies ladder.

Sinclair lifted her hand, aware her anger was poisoning the moment, unwilling to share it with a man who'd been as innocent as all the others. A half-smile painted her lips, remembering how the last victim selected had turned the tables, leaving her mother a tortured, syphilitic husk, repaid by fate for a hate filled life. And herself a daughter to a man with a loving and compassionate soul.

She leaned forward, her voice a whisper. "I wish to have known you direct, left trying to touch you through the veneer of memories shared with me by one who knew you best, trying to paint the brightest picture of you told true. But I would have you fully revealed, warts and all—with cursing in frustration at my failings, then the clumsy caress of your scarred, rough-skinned hands. With a scowl on your face, when angry. A quiet reflection of pain in your eyes as you recalled battles won—and lost. To hear your voice in my ears as you bade me goodnight—" Tears fell onto the surface of the stone as Sinclair reached out and leaned down, her face poised above the hard, unyielding surface of the stone. "To have heard your whispers of love for your little girl, made in the night. To have felt your love—given you mine in return. Left without having ever known you, trying to touch you through this cold, unfeeling—"

Grief began to well up from deep within, her body trembling as she was overcome by waves of long buried pain. She sobbed, her vision starting to fade, feeling Harold's hands on her shoulders as he pulled her into his lap and cradled her, his warm hands cupping her head and face. Her own, grown cold, wrapped around his in a talon's grasp as she gasped in half-breaths, then looked down at the stone, feeling her heart dissolve, then slowly reform as a wash of love rose within her. She looked up at Harold, his eyes revealing his willingness to help her embrace her pain, causing her heart to swell beneath her breast until it was large enough to hold all she was feeling, adding her father's love to the familial stew.

⸙⸙⸙

A green swath of scythe-cropped grass was topped with a light dusting of frost. The headstone bearing Meghan's name held a slight stain of light-gray lichen and black-mold growth. The ones to either side were in the same condition, each with inscribed letters and numbers, telling stories of their own. Sinclair reached out, tracing the carved shapes one by one, sounding out the names inscribed, ending with Meghan Elizabeth Patterson. She turned and found Harold's eyes. "There are not enough—here—to hold the meaning of her in your life. How much she loved you, as dearly as she could. How she saved you from death, holding you close when the pain in your life was beyond your capability to bear—alone."

"She did all that—and more. As did another who was equally as capable, gifted with a clear view of the world—one far exceeding that of my own."

"A'neewa."

"Yes." Harold nodded, then looked away.

Sinclair leaned back. "Who the native guides said was in good health and active on behalf of her people's needs." She paused, waiting for Harold to look over. "And but a few more days of travel away—to the south and slightly west."

Harold gave her a considered look. "You—were quick to learn their language."

She fixed him with a patient look. "Why?"

Harold hesitated, then took a deep breath and let it slip away. Sinclair reached out, touching his hand, encouraging him to take hers. The air was still damp, moisture soaking through a small square of rough-woven cloth provided by George's mother, knowing they were off to visit the family plot. Harold shrugged. "I couldn't have faced her, knowing I've failed to deliver what I promised. Security of and guarantee of self-governance for her people—for all those living along the Ohio, from the lakes to the north on through to lands in the south, still in French hands."

"And you know this failure to have happened?"

"It will." Harold released her hand. "As surely as the sun rises from out of the east."

"This imagined dawn you speak of, as if it has just now risen—may be many months, if not years away. There is still time enough to see what can be done to produce a fair and equitable arrangement."

"And what of those lying beyond the Ohio? Those in dominion in western lands, yet unexplored? Are we to exclude one group from our insatiable need to rule over them all, cursing others with the spread of our—disease? Which can no longer be ignored as coming from our own encroach and not, as some would claim—God's will, made real. Striking down over half and more of those who follow 'pagan' ways, along with the loss of their lands and ancestral lore."

Sinclair leaned back, her eyes widening as she heard her husband's words echoing through her mind. "You—speak blasphemy, my tortured husband. Our Lord and Savior is not-"

"Forgive my words made in frustration due to my own failings. They are rash and rough-edged, requiring a rub of your sweet love to make them smooth once more." Harold took her hands and brought them to his lips. "It is only my shame of the promise made—and left unfulfilled."

"As yet. An impossible burden for you to try and carry alone." Sinclar angled her head, her eyelashes in a soft flutter, looking to Harold like the wings of a resting butterfly. "Let me help you with your righteous—and God supported cause."

Harold looked away, his jaw clenched. "As too were the Great Crusades, ending with thousands of innocents slaughtered, from the first on through to the last one made."

Sinclair frowned. "You are in an impossible mood to be dealt with gently this day." She rose to her feet, attired in riding-clothes. "Come, husband. Let us take to our horses in a fast gallop to jar you out of it. George has promised a tour of the local lands, with a race between you included in his plans—if I have not missed his intent."

Harold knew he was more than equally matched by his wife's ability at strategic insight and critical reasoning, thanking Robert once again for having brought him to his daughter's door. "I am, as ever, in your capable hands, my lovely bride. Lead on—and I shall follow, as closely as I am able."

🌱🌱🌱

George slowed his large steeds pace, allowing Harold to catch up, the horse angling its head to check on the loping approach of the gray mare. George kept a firm hand on the reins, knowing the male was edgy, reacting to the beginning of estrus, sensed in the mare. George muttered under his breath, aiming a soft curse at his hard-headed friend who'd insisted on riding the mare, ignoring the matched stallion selected for him to help make a close race of it.

Harold reined in, his face beaming. "Your horsemanship is impeccable, my brother. My own uncle, gifted as he is, would have been left in your dust, despite his having earned a reputation as one of the Empire's best cavalrymen."

George bowed his head in recognition at the compliment, his pout let to slip away. "I am but a humble rider—the animal owed all the credit. I offer him to you as a belated wedding gift. One long overdue."

"I could not properly manage him, his being a better match to you —in size and strength of will." Harold paused, raising one hand and cupping his chin. "As to consideration of a wedding gift—I would gladly accept the mare." Harold noted a flash of an emotion close to fear showing in George's eyes. "I jest, of course, recognizing her value and knowing she is central to your breeding plans. Which are extremely well thought out, as have been most of the decisions you've made since our first meeting, years ago."

George let out a sigh of relief, his heart fluttering in his chest at the thought of having been held to a gift of the mare. "I have another mare —of similar disposition and build."

Harold reaching down and rubbed the neck of the horse, who whinnied in response. "I would miss this beauty all the more, when mounted on an animal of—less potential. Your hospitality and provisioning of our journey to the western reaches, fully funded and safely made was more of a gift than was deserved. Far more, my brother."

The two men closed the conversation, each silently recalling the look on Sinclair's face as she'd regained the company of the group after her visit to her father's grave. The natives had looked on with admiration at the young woman's poise: her perfect face streaked with tears, freshly shed. Head held high and firm of step, with a strong voice as she'd announced she was ready to head home.

George had been envious of his war-bonded brother, wishing to have found such an incredible woman of his own to wed, knowing he would need to alter his approach to find another like her. Though his search to date had not been in vain, resulting in a series of satisfying, though temporary relationships.

"Your speech—at the celebration I arranged on your arrival." George paused, reaching down to stroke the neck of the stallion, calming it as its nostrils quivered, nose angled back, eyeing the mare. "It was well received—and I've been asked to request you to make another. With some of the same men in attendance—at an out-of-the-way locale, halfway 'tween here and the city of Boston."

Harold angled his head, studying George's face. "When?"

"Are you agreeable to the suggestion?"

"Need you ask?" He nodded. "My faith in you is, as it always has been—complete."

"Yes, Harold—I do need ask it of you, considering the possibility of harsh accusations being tossed your way, exposing you to feelings of righteous anger—from powerful men."

"Harsher than to be found in the House of Commons, where angry curses are the usual greeting offered once I'm through the door? Our guards are armed with spears for a reason—are yours?"

George smiled, then frowned as the stallion edged sideways in a sudden turn, looking to mount the mare despite the presence of the riders aboard. "Damn you! Get quit of the idea and now—or feel my whip on your randy ass!" Harold backed his mount away, the mare fully compliant, eager to avoid the stallion's intent. George glared at Harold. "I'm as angry at you, brother, in choosing to ignore my offer of a more—suitable mount."

Harold grinned. "I had hoped the advantage of this pretty lady's condition might divert and distract your own. Giving me a fair chance of winning the race."

George jabbed his heels against the side of the snorting beast, bringing it back into a semblance of control. Then he leaned forward, stroking its thick neck with his hand, using a soothing tone of voice until it settled down. He turned and looked at Harold, matching his grin. "And how did that stratagem work out for you—Red Fox?"

Harold leaned forward. "Not well—my arse covered in soot and eyebrows singed." He drew in a deep breath, then released it, sitting up straight. "My ego also bruised, but no other significant wound suffered. And as to your invitation to speak to your friends—count me in. I will do my best to deliver them as much and more invective than received, in turn."

CHAPTER TWELVE

MILL HILL, CONNECTICUT
EARLY WINTER, 1764

The meeting place was a square-framed building, large enough to hold twenty men or more, though only fourteen were in attendance, including George and Harold. The others were a mix of politicos and men of industry, their fortunes built on the back of waterpower from an abundance of rivers and streams, running from inland mountain ranges to the sea.

Harold understood that a dependable source of power was one of the main reasons behind England's interest in continued expansion of the empire's reach into native lands. Water, when under the influence of gravity, produced power needed to drive the wheels of commerce. Along with thousands of towering white-pines throughout the northern colonies, needed to mast the vast ships of line in constant prowl along sea lanes, protecting countless threads binding the Empire together, around the globe. An interest Harold knew was shared by the men staring back, waiting for him to speak.

He'd been introduced to each of them in turn, three of whom he remembered having met before at George's manor, their reacquaintance made with firm clasp of hands and tight-cornered smiles. Harold could sense the tension running within the walls of the open interior of the building: a law office owned by one Thomas Fitch, the fourth,

Governor of the Connecticut colony. A man of sixty-five years of age, nearing the end of his story, his eyes a faded shade of blue with poor vision and trembling hands, though still sharp as a razor in mind and stiff worded opinions offered.

Harold took a moment to measure the collective mood. It was a ripe mix of energies, balanced against the potential of an interruption to the flow of monies though each one's holdings, and in firm opposition to levy of new taxes, seen as an encumbrance to their ability to expand. A balancing act to be performed, with Harold hoping to keep the political needle pointed near the center of the financial scale.

"Friends—and fellow citizens—I am honored to be invited as guest into your common house, at large." He pointed, both arms outspread, as if a minister at Sunday sermon. "Here at your invitation. Not to preach, though many have claimed it is my inclination to do so—but only to inform of the collective mood and intentions of those on the opposite side of the watery divide. To provide insight as to how, when, and why a levy is to be—has already been inscribed on parchment and signed—waiting for imminent delivery. Each of you, holding positions high enough in accord to hear of it direct. Others made aware, once word begins to spread—of the weight of further burden, added about your collective necks."

Harold kept a weather eye on George, marking his slouched demeanor as he stood in one corner of the room. His reaction neutral, mirroring that of the audience, with the shell of his speech, barely cracked. "I did not support, nor ever will—the signing of any document that places restrictions upon your work-weary, worn, and knowledgeable hands. You and you alone understanding how best to manage your own affairs as independent representatives of our great British empire." Harold paused, seeing a few of the men beginning to nod, their jaws clenched, the others remaining unmoved. "And I make this additional claim—as a loyal and sworn representative to people ruled over by good King George, the third—and as a former soldier wounded in actions accomplished here—that what I've seen firsthand in the colonies and know to be true—must be put before all of England, including the King in royal pose, along with those standing in his shadow, offering advice. Men of commerce—much like yourselves

—with reach into seats of political influence on both sides of the Atlantic, proposing financial actions against men who spilled red while fighting the French. Stalwart men, such as my comrade in war and adopted brother, Colonel George O'Malley—along with many others providing honorable service. Many of them giving their all—in order to secure this land. Men with the will and strength to hold onto it—claiming it as your own, on behalf of England."

Harold waited as the assemblage rose in robust cheers and frenzied applause, knowing he would need to disappoint them once they'd regained their seats, taking note of a handful standing apart, their faces set in stony stares as they leaned against the outer walls. "I have learned, these past few years—that a few men with good intentions often end up causing piss-poor consequences for the rest." The coarse expression drew a chuckle from several of the men. "Imagine, if you will—especially those who shouldered a musket alongside my brother and I—imagine my surprise at learning that one's prior service to crown and country holds little value to those clutching the purse strings of the government. People eager to see them loosened in oder to procure munitions, and other materials to support forces to be sent here, against potential challenge from those who are already here—tonight—your voices raised in lawful protest, with no say as to what might be a reasonable share of the costs of the recent war, assigned. Forced to provide compensation now that it's been fought and won! An unfair demand made of the prodigal son by a stern-faced father, his hand held out, asking the return of monies spent in raising them. As if the child owes the parent for food, clothing, and crib—with the parent bearing no fiduciary responsibility at all—desiring all the gravy, and most of the meat in the meal, as well." Harold paused once more, noting George nodding his head. "And gentlemen—I for one love my gravy—as well the meat it covers!"

The assembled men rose again, louder in their vocal agreements, fixated on the tenor of the speech, overlooking the hard truth Harold had exposed. They remained on their feet, assuming it was over, until Harold waved them back into their seats, his face fixed in a cold stare.

"There are dark days ahead, my friends. I am not by nature a messenger of doom, believe me—but I wish to bring insight into the shadows of governance in England." He stopped, looking at each of the men present, making eye contact. "I know that, within this very room, there are some with prior knowledge of what I am about to reveal. Themselves tied in with likeminded men of my acquaint, both in the colonies and abroad, who would see a reasoned approach be made by those on both sides of this impending conflict. With words written in broadsheets, uttered in meetinghouses, reflecting opinions for and against any increase of levies, despite their own regard as to what is right or wrong. Charged with maintaining order, willing to confront those who would encourage rebellion with threat of jail—or death. The gallows for those engaging in insurrection, knowing they will be made martyrs, rousing more who will rise, willing to march."

Harold shook his head. "A steep and slippery slope, formed by those who stand to profit from strife on both sides of the same coin tossed downhill, gathering speed, promising to lead to the spilling of blood that will fatten their purses. Ports closed, cities made to suffer— up and down the coastline with ships seized, commerce dwindling before the threat of ships of the line, with transports full of soldiers close behind. All this and more, in store—lest we come to an understanding of the motivations of those involved, eager to see it made true."

He gazed out at the group of powerful men of influence and wealth. "A *shadowy* group of men with allegiance to their own cause, without patriotic ties to any country, to any King seated on an ivory throne, or to citizens of both sides who represent the needs of the common man. A dark group with darker hearts, their fingers in greedy rub as they count their gold, earned for each keg of powder or cask of shot placed in holds of ships, returning filled with the blood of our best and brightest, gone to war—with no idea of who it is they were in service of."

The mood dampened, as if the roof had split, a torrential downpour let in. Harold lowered his voice, his words subdued. "I am a soldier. Always will be. The scars on my body are a constant reminder of the folly visited upon it due to my ignorance of the ways of the real world. One with rules I had never learned about, having been raised by a man with honorable service done on the crown's behalf—taught to support the rights of all, each man equal to the next. So—heed my words, or not. They are not meant to beseech, only to inform—as previously stated."

Harold paused, taking a deep breath then releasing it slowly. "I thank you for your time and ask only that no ill will be reflected on my brother, who had no idea of the speech I would be giving here today. I yield the floor to any who would gainsay my thoughts, promising to listen with an open mind. With promise to make them known to the honorable and well-respected William Pitt, who charged me to make my journey here in order to read the temperature of those with their fingers on the pulse of our colonies mood, making a full report to the House of Commons."

Harold paused, a sly smile on his lips. "And—before any might question my omission of mentioning the House of Lords—I say to *hell* with those *poxy* bastards!"

The steady clop of horse hooves on the trampled roadway were a match to the thud of Harold's heartbeats, felt in his chest. George was quiet, his posture in the saddle one of sober reflection, as it had been since the two of them had left the small meetinghouse. An owl on a nearby limb called out, questioning their identity as they passed by, the hour late. Harold resisted the urge to return its mournful inquiry with one of his own: 'a fool, that's who', tweaking himself for having lifted up men's spirits, before dashing them onto a floor made up of hard truths.

George finally broke the silence. "You have—a way of getting to the heart of the matter. To the hearts of those who cannot see the cost of battle 'fore it has begun. Your approach more refined, now—than when I first met you. Though I feel, despite their claps on your shoulder while agreeing with your portrait of a storm in approach, each of them has left for home with their minds on potential threat to their own hides, not wanting them pinned to either side's wall."

Harold lowered his head. "I had though it to be a complete and utter failure—"

"On the contrary, my brother—you reached deep into their pockets, plucking out their fears, holding them up for all to see. Myself, as well—which is the cause for my sullen mood and dispirited tone."

Harold looked over. "I brought a flask."

George grinned. "I have never loved you more—than now. Hand it over and be quick!"

⸙⸙⸙

Sinclair was sitting alongside Harold in a carriage, stopped alongside the manor grounds. She was in a full pout, her full lips turned down at the corners. Harold shrugged, knowing she would recover her sunny disposition soon enough once George had her alongside for a final ride throughout the local region. Strangers, made fast friends, were waiting to be called on for a final round of tearful farewells, Sinclair having been accepted as a member of their tight-knit community due to her candor and open-minded approach to those she'd been introduced to.

"I'm anxious to return home, but know our wee ones are in good and caring hands. Still, the tug of their tether to womb is difficult to ignore. Especially now, as the moment of departure draws nigh."

Harold came over, placing his hands on her hips. "I could, perhaps try again to—loosen the knot."

She gave him a look suggesting he would fail, her body sore from his vigorous return to vitality, his mood having lightened of late. "You have not yet bragged of beating George in a race, his mood grown sour since you returned from your meeting."

"We did not race, my love. His mood is due to the words I used, painting a dim picture of the future, once thought bright."

"Was that—wise?" Sinclair moved away, looking through their bedroom window, the light on her face revealing a frown.

Harold joined her there, reaching for her hand. "I sense a reprimand—or an alternate suggestion in loom."

"I only mean to point out that a different angle of approach might better have suited your intentions—as the bee is drawn to blossoms by promise of pollen, not the scent of manure."

Harold released her hand, his arms crossing on his chest, staring straight ahead. "I did what I thought best—based on my read of the room and men in it."

"But again, husband—might you not have chosen another path to better convey—"

Harold turned, facing Sinclair with a quiet look, one she'd seen many times before, able to predict his words before he spoke. "The horse is lying on the ground, dear wife. Its death observed, and thus assured. So why, pray tell—persist in the clubbing of its broken body?"

Sinclair stuck out her tongue, Harold reaching to pinch it, quickly retracted, flashing him a mischievous grin, daring his kiss. Harold leaned in, in full compliance to her need.

"You're *late*, my brother. Hand the lass to *me*—we've no time for such as that. A boisterous ride is near to hand through glen and glade." George rode up, gray mare in tow, saddle already adjusted for Sinclair's shorter legs. She smiled as she leapt down from the small carriage borrowed from the stables, the two of them having spent the morning collecting flowers for Meghan's grave, as well for those of her husband and son.

Harold watched as they rode off together, then clucked to the horse harnessed to the carriage, guiding it in a wide circle, heading to where his other loved one lay at rest.

⸎⸎⸎

He arranged the flowers along the bottom of each of three headstones. Bluebells for the son. White roses for the father. Yellow ones for Meghan. Then Harold knelt, pressing his hands on the sun-warmed earth, the day heating quickly from the pulse of a south-westerly breeze. He closed his eyes, reaching out to Meghan, picturing her face, her sky-colored eyes. Hearing the sound of her voice, with a light Irish lilt. And the scent of her hair, the warmth of her embrace. Tears slipped down his cheeks, falling to the grass.

"You still love her—my dear sister. As do I."

Harold opened his eyes and looked up, seeing A'neewa standing several paces away, backlit by bright sunlight, her features in shadow. "You're—here." He wiped his eyes. "To find me?"

A'neewa stepped forward, coming over and kneeling beside Harold who could see that her face had thickened slightly, her raven dark hair now tinged with gray about the edges, the corners of her doe-brown eyes framed with fine lines. Still as beautiful, her looks enhanced by the quiet energy radiating from her body. He reached out for her hand, surprised when she pulled away and looked at him, speaking in French. "I came to visit my sister. You—were already here."

He shook his head. "The guides—one of them spoke your tongue. A man I'd known before. He must have found you and told you I had made a visit to tribal lands." Harold paused, then smiled. "A'neewa's words are those of a serpent."

She smiled, despite herself. "I have a hatchet if you need it—to find the truth."

Harold pulled her in, waiting until she relaxed and folded into his embrace, her head against his shoulder as they gazed at the center stone. He whispered, his throat constricted by his emotions. "I know your love for her—was as great as mine. Greater, perhaps—having shared a common pain."

"It was why I gave her the gift she yearned for—at the end. Allowing her to reach the place you people believe lies at the end of your path. So that she—she could be with them." A'neewa pointed with her chin at the other two stones. "A gift she could not give herself. Or ask of you."

"That was explained to me—when visiting Robert's grave. A gift of insight. One I could not fully understand—until then."

A'neewa leaned back, her head angled, the light finding her eyes. "He is well—our brother George?"

"As large as a bear, still. With more girth about the middle. Say's it helps keep him anchored to the saddle, which he is in—most hours of the day."

"And how is your wife?" A'neewa straightened up, looking to one side, her hand reaching out to rearrange several of the flowers lining Meghan's headstone.

"She is in good health. As are our three children—left behind in their grandmother's care, along with a small army of relatives."

"Only three?" A'neewa pulled back, regaining her prideful posture, Harold letting her go, knowing the bridge between them had been washed away by the currents of distance and time. "Would have thought you would have a dozen or more, based on your—enthusiasm for such things." She sniffed. "Your woman must have grown tired of you, with your nose always in your books. Or in the wind, in scent of another challenge, leading you from one hard lesson to the next."

"You see it clearly—as always. Wise A'neewa."

She shrugged, remaining silent for a moment. When she spoke, her voice was tinged with sorrow. "So, tell me, Reynard Rouge—have you retained your innocence? Or rather—your wish to succeed, without causing pain to either side?"

Harold hardened his gaze. "No. I have learned to let it go, as a child tosses a toy into the corner of its room." He fastened her with a stare, his eyes a bed of coals in glow. "They killed my father. The ones I am in search of. And they will be made to pay—with their lives!"

She smiled, her eyes gleaming, a smile on her face, as happy as he'd ever seen her. "Good! As I said before—I have a hatchet you can use. And a knife—for when you find them."

Harold nodded, his eyes softening as he searched her face, capturing every detail, breathing in the exotic scent of her hair and skin, all the flavors of her thoughts and expressions. Knowing, from where such truths reside, that he would never see her again.

A'neewa nodded. "You are finished, here?" When Harold nodded, she touched him on his cheek. "You will leave me—now. I have words to speak to my sister. Alone."

Harold stood up, tears on his cheeks, revealing all the pain they'd shared between them, and how much she would be missed. "Farewell —Silent Doe."

A'neewa turned away, kneeling before Meghan's stone, her back to Harold, waving a hand in dismissal. Once he'd gone, she bowed her head, overwhelmed by sadness. She clenched her hands, heart aching, know the vision seen a half-moon ago, a day before coming to find him, would come to pass. That Harold would have his revenge. That he would be unable to save her and her people. Unable to prevent the storm in rise between the English father and his children. That their world would soon shatter, leaving her own in tatters, too.

She reached out, tracing the carved lines of the chiseled letters with the tip of her finger, reading each word aloud, as she'd learned to do. Losing herself to memories of sweeter days. Sweeter moments. Of a love shared between them all. Harold and Meghan. Meghan and her. Knowing, as she leaned forward, pressing her head against the stone, that she would never feel such warmth again.

CHAPTER THIRTEEN

PORT OF PHILADELPHIA
SUMMER, 1769

The riverside docks were larger than Harold remembered from his last visit made, four years earlier. The city had expanded from horizon north on through to the south, a thick haze of smoke drifting into the surrounding countryside from multi-storied buildings and houses rising over cobble-stone streets. Every field, once there, had been relocated to environs further out due to the appetite for buildable land, needed to meet the rapid expansion of manufacturing. Holdings made far more valuable by far to those whose names were on the paper, assigned. Dozens of families enriched with each plot they'd acquired, then sold.

There had been a large group of such entrepreneurs aboard the ship Harold had boarded in London. Men eager to invest or to re-invest in port cities up and down the bountiful coastline, countless opportunities springing up along the mouths of rivers in constant flow. Water power, as always, the heart-blood of any country with a claim to it. Power in evidence everywhere Harold looked, pumped by gravity throughout the inner workings of the original grist mills, turning the wheels in scores of new factories, driving the flow of commerce. Commerce driving the policies of politicians, ensuring their firm hold on the reins of public support and monies gained. It was enough, at times, to cause an ache in his heart, yearning to take his family in his arms and release them into the wilds, in search of a humanity he'd once shared with the natives living there. One unbound by restrictive laws, rules, regulations, and deceit.

"There is our hero of battles, yore!" A corpulent man in a slow waddle came on, a tankard of ale in his hand, his feet splayed as he moved along the ship's upper deck. A beam of light seemed to be emanating from between fat-creased eyelids, his eyes dark beads, gleaming from within. "No doubt with his political lantern held high, seeking fair treatment for all. As if Diogenes—in a hopeless search for honest men."

"One would do for now, friend Albert." Harold reached out, pressing his fingers atop the much shorter man's fleshy shoulders. He'd enjoyed the company of the like-minded man during their crossing. A person of influence in both England and the Colonies. The two of them in parallel agreement as to the travesty of the recent occupation of Boston by British troops, due to unrest over additional, heavy-handed levying of onerous taxes. Fuses being laid, leading to kegs of powder, waiting to be lit. "May I count on you, sir?"

"As long as ale continues to run in amber flow—sobriety a curse upon my genial mood. The world as it not a pleasant view, of late."

Harold nodded, his eyes narrowed in concern. There had been talk of the colonials wanting to relocate their seat of political power from New York to Philadelphia. One that would raise the eyebrows of those with their fingers firmly pressed to the pulse of people, on both sides of the watery divide. "There is a definite effort being made—by some—to avoid facts clearly stated in words written in their thousands, both for and against any weakening of ties. Better perhaps, to take leave my leave of it all—and hie to the hills, shutters barred against the storm that is certain to rise."

Albert, having identified himself as an investor in several publication houses sown throughout the colonies, shrugged. "The words you claim to have been avoided—place half-pennies in my purse. With myself remaining a verbose and skilled orator of the truth—as I know it to be. In ready disagreement with your lofty vision of a world made sane, as sanguine men would have it be. Yours is an overly optimistic viewpoint, my friend, when balanced against each man's inner turmoil. Most left wanting more. Unable to settle for less. While a few are born with an unquenchable thirst for all."

"There is always Scotland—where I might propose an opposite view of the world to apply."

"Yes—or rather, aye!" The florid faced man raised his half-empty tankard. "To the vainglorious Scots, ever and always to a man in steadfast adhere to their delicious hatred for those wishing change—or daring offer challenge to ancient, ancestral vows, made in solemn swear." Alfred drained the last of his ale in a series of long swallows. He wiped his mouth, then searched for a place to leave the metal container, settling for a precarious perch on the side-railing of the ship. With a searching look along the dock to one side, he belched, loudly, then yawned. "You are—to meet a friend—as I recall you making mention of during our last night aboard."

Harold nodded. "Your mind, numbed as it ever is by ale, or wine—is truly a vault." He paused, measuring the other man carefully. "I am to meet a man who is a true friend, and brother, as measured by our service together—supportive in word and deed to my cause."

"That would be Mister O'Malley. Or Colonel O'Malley, soon to be elected to a position of political prominence, if what I have heard from my people over here is true. Those who have blue-black stains upon their hands—and morals. As well their very souls—according to you."

"Another matter of fact. Their words formed into bricks of metal, inked with greed, pressed to parchment—thrown by your ilk through the open windows of people's minds. Their own view of the truth, once shattered, becoming a small reflection of your own, depending on the slant of what's written."

Alfred shook his head, then smiled. "We are a necessary evil, Harold. You see that. I'm certain of it, knowing your reputation for strategic insight, which I have determined for myself during these past few weeks, is in no way an exaggeration. Your keen-eyed vision of what is to come—dripping from every word you speak, when the podium is in your grasp. Or perhaps pulpit would be a better word, more suited to your somewhat—sacrilegious viewpoints when it comes to the 'beliefs' of your native friends."

A voice from the other side of the railing drew both men around, Nathan standing there, arms crossed, in a stout pose of confidence. "Now that's a splendid suggestion, my friend. You as a minister — opining to a flock of thousands. There would be no church in the colonies, or England itself, large enough to hold your faithful flock, once gathered. A mountaintop would be the better choice. A voice from on high, as it were, the populace swayed, eager to march to capitols in every country, demanding what is felt owed them."

Harold shook his head. "You are too late to share a bottle, Nathan. George no doubt waiting on me at piers end with a glare in his eye and curse on his lips." He leaned down, retrieving his bags, giving both men a nod as he left the ship.

Nathan gave a slow wave to Harold as he reached the end of the pier and turned around, receiving one in return. Then he nodded to Alfred. "I have made arrangements at an out of the way ale house to make our re-acquaint." Albert shrugged, then stared at his bags, waiting for Nathan to pick them up, a smirk on hid plump lips as he followed him to his carriage.

⚹⚹⚹

A middle-aged barmaid delivered another tankard of ale, served in a pewter stein. She slipped the coins on the table into her apron pocket, leaving with a nod of thanks to the men, heading to the kitchen to check on their meals.

"A comely Lass. Of stout hips, with the air of a practiced lover." Alfred lifted a hand, in study of his nails, neatly trimmed. "Do you miss it. Nathan? The dark mark of your earlier toil at the press, always there, the stain embedded into your flesh, reminding you of the power wielded."

Nathan gave Alfred a cold stare, no longer in awe of the man's power, having earned his seat at the table. "I am having trouble, my friend in hearing you, for all the gold in your mouth — and the thirty pieces of silver in my ears."

Albert nodded, lifting his stein without offer of a toast. His eyes were in a constant sweep, watching the entrance into the shadowed room where they were seated, providing a modicum of privacy. "Our local group is up to date on the latest news sent and received? Your innovative plan working to perfection with packets of information delivered each day to ships sailing from port to port along every sea lane, hither and yon."

"A continuous flow, with daily adjust made of recent happenings, along with options offered for alteration of actions to be taken. Extremely useful in our efforts to shape, then reshape opinions—private and public."

Alfred sniffed, glancing at the door, his stomach rumbling with hunger. "Yes, your idea has proven to be an excellent solution in a world of constant evolution. Allowing for rapid response to events while they are still in motion." He paused, seeing a young girl passing by, carrying a tray for one of the other tables in the inn. "Our revenues had increased significantly, of late. As have your own."

Nathan nodded, accepting the credit richly deserved. Formulating an idea that had elevated his position within the club. Trade decisions made, then changed based on the latest news, with items pulled or put into holds of dozens of cargo ships each day, creating a growth in the fortunes of the politically motivated members, both here in the colonies, and abroad. He sighed, the sound drawing a stare from Alfred, who leaned back, his voice lowered. "You are weighted, my friend. No doubt due to some measure of worry as to our other friend's future status."

Natha nodded. "I find it difficult, separating myself from a genuine affection for the man and his family, having known of him since he was but a young strategist of note, playing at the game of war. Until the beast picked him up and shook him to his core. Torturing his mind and morals—yet still willing to face it again, and again. Undaunted. As if—"

"Not a novelette, needed. Find a narrower point of aim, if you will. The meal is soon to be presented, and I for one, plan to enjoy each bite."

"Rest assured I will do what needs doing. My oath signed in red, same as your own. My feelings will not be a deterrence when the time arrives for any alteration to the plan—if needed."

"Then we are in accord." Alfred reached down and stroked his round belly. "I too am rather fond of the man. He exudes a light that is rare in this dark world we are made part of. But—the beast, as you so eloquently put it—needs to eat. As do we." He turned his head, his nose detecting the food as it came through the door. "Huzzah. We are served by a lovely young lady, who moves as if a dancer on the stage, tray in pose—all my appetites, about to be met."

Alfred smiled, receiving an inviting one in return, a young girl barely of age placing their plates on the table, leaning in as she did so, allowing Alfred a view of her budding breasts.

⸙⸙⸙

George ran his hand along the neck of one of the matched set of gelded horses, each a perfect specimen in glossy coats of ebony black. "Their sire? He is available for stud?"

Nathan smiled, standing back watching as the influential politician fell under the spell of a new bloodline being brought into his stables, enhancing his reputation as the prominent breeder of quality horse-flesh in the colonies. "I've kept him from all others making the same request. Saving him for you."

George spun around, eyes gleaming. "Name your price. I'll pay it."

"Your forgiveness, for having delayed your brother from meeting you upon your arrival at the docks this day."

"It is given, though I bid you to accept some small service in return. A mare is about to deliver a foal who will reset the bar, again. Within hours, if I know my girl, and I do. You will stay the night and be one of the first to witness it. I insist!"

Nathan nodded, making a small bow. "This night only—with an early leave on the morrow. A meeting in the city, you see. One I dare not miss."

Harold remained silent as he watched the two men continue their discussion of all things equine related as the three of them slowly strolled toward the stables, a handler leading the tethered team, carriage in tow.

"They are as much our enemy as were the French. More so, acting as agent provocateurs against the crown. With no limits placed on what might be done—is being done to undermine the common good." Harold was pacing, a glass of wine in one hand, going over and looking through a large window, overlooking an expansive garden being tended by a host of dark-skinned men in simple garb. He sighed, the sight reminding him again of the disparate viewpoints on both sides of the issue of enforced labor. He realized George was lenient in work-load expectations, and generous in support of his workers, providing attention to their health needs and a nod toward limited education. Though the degree of freedom lost in the exchange was difficult to balance in the right versus the wrong of it.

"You are upset, my brother. This new world is far removed from how we found it, then fought to hold onto. And are prepared to fight to keep it, now—with troops in occupation of Boston. Their presence there a constant spark in a room filled with fuses leading to kegs of powder. Men, with investments at risk, in a constant dance to snuff out the flames, keeping everything from exploding in everyone's faces."

"Your investments, as well, I take it."

George refused to answer, knowing Harold deserved some leeway in regard to his political slant. Aware he too was allowed respect in return. "You are to meet with men of my acquaintance in Boston, I hear. A—dangerous mission."

"A friendly excursion, designed to defuse—the very situation as you just described."

"If such a thing is even possible, given the current temperature. Hot, and growing more so with each day in passing. The red-coat heels pressed upon our neck."

Harold turned around, looking at George. "You do not appear to me as overly burdened—or aggrieved."

"Freedom is not found in our being burdened unfairly by our would be overseers. Their physical presence is insult enough. The idea of having the smallest slice of self-determination lost to us, left without any direct representation in Commons, is more weight than those of us

with pride can be expected to take. Reduced to fighting for full reten-
tion of the freedoms we've earned. Ones we are willing to fight to hold
onto—keeping what we've built with our own hands."

It required all the force of Harold's will to maintain his focus on
George. The image of men toiling a few feet away, coming into painful
conflict with the clean, uncalloused hands of the man he loved as much
as any, knowing George's moral blindness was tied to his fear of the
loss of all that he owned, should rebellion arise. Any desire on his part
to push the extension of personal freedom to all men, having to be left
aside. For now.

"I concede the point you make. The need of you making it, as well.
It is why I have been charged by Pitt, once again, to place finger on the
pulse of the beast in its lair, taking another careful measure of its
mood."

George frowned, his lips tight with concern. "Again—a dangerous
task."

"One I am willing to take on, if there is anything that might be
done to prevent blood in run—on both sides of the street."

"Perhaps that should be the first line of any speech given. My
fellow compatriots made to see, clearly, what we saw firsthand in the
western wilderness—a lifetime and more ago."

The small meeting room at the inn was full, the doors secured, a guard
posted outside, the men within sitting in rows of close-set. They had
adjourned from an earlier meeting just down the street, in a building
with a large interior used to assemble wagons for the movement of
materials on roads stretching from lands in the far south on through to
northern holdings.

The men had been invited there to listen to Harold's plea for a
measured approach, with assurances made that William Pitt was on
their side, hopeful of being able to form a coalition wide and deep
enough to force a change in regard to levies ordered. Time, the
weapon needed to alter the Royal decree. Short term financial pain
incurred against certainty of financial ruin should trade be shuttered

by soldiers in city postings, their ports closed by warships on the horizon.

The men who'd gathered at the inn watched as Alfred slowly mounted the platform, his hands resting on either side of the lectern. He raised his voice, issuing a stirring call for unity, promising that powerful men in England would do all they could to wrest control of government greed away from the few, in transfer to the slightly less few. The movers of opinion and shakers of financial markets to be brought further into the fold, providing a wide base to absorb any temporary, financial pain, balanced against a far greater gain should the flames of open warfare be avoided.

They stood in polite response when Alfred finished his speech. More than half in mild applause, his words having stirred little emotion. The rest nodding, their fingers remaining in firm clasp of their fat purses, knowing there was wealth to be made in careful manipulation of the markets, on both sides of the political divide between. Time now, per their speakers words, for rational examination of where each of the collective group might be, in support or opposition. All those in attendance bound together with ties to printing houses in each town and city of note, including those found throughout Europe.

Nathan called the vote, the issues having been laid out in clear writing, with no embellishment or vitriol added to spice the stew. A simple choice, the vote secret. The tally made in full and open view of all. The numbers close but leaning to an avoidance of conflict, for the time being. Promises made to solicit passionate words from those who had one eye fixed on feelings of patriotic zeal, and the other carefully measuring the likelihood of personal gain and historical perch. Hamilton. Jefferson. Adams and Washington, though the latter two were apt to offer their thoughts in a more subdued script. Hired men, with scars on their bodies, paid to wave banners inciting action be taken, as had just happened with bales of tea tossed in Boston Harbor. Other men, not yet sworn to membership in the club, but passionate in their feelings, used to provide goods, munitions and monies needed to lubricate the fears of decision makers in England, leading to slipways filled with transports and ships of war being build, poised for imminent launch.

Alfred stepped forward. "We are agreed, then, of our course for the immediate future. Poke a small stick in the King's eye, while handing him a palm branch. So—good men of a New World Order, we are to seek wealth from the promotion of war and peace. Go all ye forth and stir well your respective pots."

No one smiled, each aware of what lay in store. Each looking to their neighbors, wondering how many would survive the flames, if too carelessly fanned. Each confident they would win through. One of them, larger in stature than any of the rest, standing in the back of the room, eyes steady, hands in clasp between his knees. Knowing his brother had failed, despite his impressive effort made earlier in the evening. Knowing he'd just voted to tear the world, as known, in two. A new one to be raised in its place.

Harold was where George knew he would be, with his knees pressed into the soil before his sister's stone. His hat in hand, his fingers tracing the letters of her name. The very portrait of fidelity to a love that had never been fully offered in return. A love George knew he could never be in possession of, aware of his limits when it came to feeling such emotions. Except for the rare horse or two, he added, his mind wandering to the upcoming meeting arranged between his prize mare and the stud responsible for Nathan's matched pair of geldings.

"Have you heard anything?" Harold was on his feet.

"Shortly, I imagine. When next at Nathan's estate, or rather—his stables. Small in size, but with a fine brood stock in hand."

"Your read—my speech made at the meeting?"

"Dour. Sour. Storm of lead raining down—and something about pain." He smiled. "Every soldier's refrain, each time we were preparing to man the line."

"Amen, brother. Amen." Harold glanced down at Meghan's stone. "Do you need a moment alone with your sister?"

"No. Not much of a need for that."

"Pragmatic to the core—as ever. Except in the presence of prime horse-flesh."

George shrugged. "Men have all sorts of weaknesses. Mine is mine.

Thine is—well, without identity as yet. But you must have one buried within you—somewhere. I'm certain of it."

"A reluctance to let go of my effort to expose the truth. Placing myself and loved ones in potential danger. Only that."

George considered for a moment, then shook his head. "Would not consider that to be a weakness."

"A weakness on either side of the coin. Whether to be true to one's natural destiny—or bury it away beneath a desire for wealth, increase of one's reputation and position in society, until left prone—" Harold glanced at the wide circle of granite markers. "Beneath headstones, such as these."

"Would an offer of a gallop in woods and fields improve your mood?"

Harold came over and clapped his brother on his back, trying to rattle his teeth, failing to do so. "Wisest thing you've said since my arrival." He smiled. "If given my choice of steed."

George nodded, knowing he would still win the race. That he would always come in ahead when in a contest with Harold, who did not hold the same measure of heated desire for power and prestige as himself. One overwhelming everything else.

CHAPTER FOURTEEN

SCOTTISH HIGHLANDS MANOR

MID-WINTER, 1765

Harold' and Sinclair's world had come full way around once more. Their ship to a Scottish port. Overland by coach to the family manor. To children asleep in their large bed, their mother's arms wrapped around them all. Harold left standing outside the door, looking in with loving eyes, work to be done before he could join them there.

Thomas waited in the kitchen of the highland manor, eager to fill Harold in on the work he'd put into crafting a plan to guide the family to and through a host of hidden threats, as if wolf-packs lurking in a fog-shrouded wood, along with a host of other, equally deadly, two-legged beasts, employed by men with cold and calculating souls.

"I have sourced articles in past printings, bound up in collections revealing several companies with an outward appearance of being in opposition to the government, though backed by men in support of it. Their motives tucked safely away from the eyes and ears of the common man. They own a host of smaller companies, manned by former military personages of note, controlled through proxy vote with bank notes held by numerous personages of little note — some of them long dead, their estates transferred to distant relatives, deeds held by international firms."

Harold thumbed through several stacks of paper, eyes narrowed in thought. "I do not need ask, as to attention paid to need of security in-"

Thomas drew himself upright, his hands on his hips. "Then do not, Harry. I have the highest respect for those we are in the process of carefully nosing out." Thomas stared over, his age showing on his face with sagging jowls and squint of his eyes. "I have never faced direct conflict before, with expectation of suffering deadly consequences—as have you. And do not wish it to happen now, with an army of grand-children to arrive." He softened his expression. "A parent's just reward, 'tis true—with two wee ones already in hand. A blessing from God. And another soon to be delivered, helping to expand Clan Knutt—if you will. Though the increased worry for them does drag at me, leaving me feeling every day of my advanced age."

"You're not so old as that, dear Uncle. I've seen men in the colonies near twice your age, as hale as ever they were."

"Due, no doubt, to better food and air." Thomas sighed, reaching to rub his lower back. "We are a cretinous breed, Harry, living in cities bound hand to foot in a wallow of filth and black air—most days. A diet of hard work and feast on food grown in one's backyard soil would be a tonic for my soul." Thomas looked at his nephew, who seemed the picture of health. "Perhaps you should adapt your plans, and consider uprooting your family and—"

"We'll not chase that squirrel up the tree, again, Thomas. The lands here-about are as hale and fertile as any to be found over there. Safer too, with eyes on every hillock, eager to call the clan together at a moment's notice. Whether for a feast—or in stiff-necked defense against the least of slights to clan honor." Harold came over and clapped his uncle's shoulder. "As my Grand Da used to say—damn all lowlanders, wherever they may be. Little better than the bloody Irish."

"Careful, lad. I've clients, friends—and relatives too, tucked amongst the wide-spread roots of that lot. As do yourself."

Harold returned a grin, rubbing his eyes, trying not to yawn. Thomas pointed at the door. "Get thee to bed with your family. We'll leave off all this 'til next time we meet. It'll wait a fortnight until seeing you in London again, with more details to share."

"Heels down, Aaron, lad. Hands—loose on the reins. Your back straight. Let the animal find its own pace." Harold kept a close eye on his son, another on his wife, who was pretending not to be the least bit nervous as Aaron cantered around the manor paddock on a small horse, too tall by any measure of comfort to his mother's eye. "She is a gentle lady you're aboard, son—not some temperamental young filly, liable to make a misstep or shy away."

Harold knew Sinclair trusted his instinct's when it came to their son, allowing both her men a long tether. He knew as well that each time another boundary was bridged between a safe life and one with some risk, however slight, his wife's womb delivered another tug to the firm-lined frown of fear, pulling down the corners of her full lips.

The sound of a rider approaching coaxed Harold away from the paddock rail. He turned around, watching as a man, tall in the saddle, his red hair tied back, rode up on a large steed: a magnificent sorrel-gray, with snow-white mane and tail. It was his mother's cousin, known to Harold since his youth as Uncle Shaun. A tall man of narrow build, with an iron-frame beneath light-colored skin, he was the nominal head of Clan Scott, in constant movement along the highlands as if a guardian saint, watching over all things clan related. The older man pulled up, allowing his mount to come on at a slow walk, seeing the youth in the paddock, not wanting to startle the small mare he was riding.

Harold spun back around. "Ease back on the bit, son. Bring her to a stop. She'll know you're looking to dismount and will abide it."

"Can I nae take her oot and aboot?" The boy's eyes widened as he lifted his arm and pointed at the paddock gate.

Harold shook his head. "Nae, Aaron. Your Ma is watching as if a hawk on wing. We need be wary of vexing her." He paused, waiting to see if the frown on his son's face would stick, or be let to slip away. "Another time, son. Get down and hie to give your Gran Uncle Shaun a hug to crack his ribs."

Aaron looked over his shoulder, noting his great uncle standing beside his father, the lead to his large horse in one hand. He swung his leg over the saddle of the mare, slipping down, coming on in a flash of red and black clothing, scrambling up and over the rails of paddock fence, then making a dash into the waiting arms of his favorite male relative. Shaun placed him on back of the stallion then climbed up behind him, giving him the reins and an earful of encouragement as they loped away.

Sinclair came over in a more sedate pace, stopping beside Harold, her long hair unbound, hanging in soft waves, the air dry of late, easing its natural curl. She searched for Harold's hand, securing it with a firm grip, leaning in against his body. He returned the pressure, taking in a slow, deep breath, savoring the light floral scent of heather, blended with the natural oils in her hair.

"He'll be the worry of me, unto death—no matter his age. Seeing in him the man he's to become, a mirror image to yourself." Sinclair paused. "It is a rising tide—one I cannot hope to stem."

Harold watched as his son tugged on the reins, encouraging the large animal to turn toward a nearby ridgeline, Shaun's voice over-riding the command, bidding caution. Harold grinned, feeling Sinclair's hand squeeze his, knowing she would scald Shaun's hide, if given the least opportunity. "He will become the man he is meant to be, and neither a mother's concern nor father's spur will alter the course of the life he's to lead." Harold looked down, struggling to keep from falling into the mesmerizing depths of his wife's eyes, still fascinated by her natural beauty, unadorned by the latest in fashion or glittering jewels. His love for her as deep and pure as from the first moment he'd met her: a cameo brought to life.

Sinclair shook her head. "I know that look. Lose the idea before it forms. I've chores in need of attending to—involving the lad." She raised her voice, the horse coming along at a moderate pace, stopping a few steps away. "Aaron, give your dear Gran Uncle Shaun a squeeze, then hie to me." She waited, as he looked at his father, seeking a reprieve. "Now!" Her firm tone cut through his protest, bringing him on the run. Then she gave Harold as firm a look. "See to your uncle's need for you—and return before dark. Sober, if possible. Alive—with no more than a few broken bones or missing teeth between you—if not."

She gathered her son beneath her arm, heading to where Thomas was engaged in a game of hide and seek, chasing after his two grandnieces, his arms widespread as he lurched about the garden paths. Sinclair was grateful for his presence, and improved mood. His demeanor had been weighed down of late, his face creased with deep lines, the vigor gone from his body leaving him unable to ride. Grown old before his time with a shadow behind his smiles. A worry to her as well, though she knew Harold would share it with her, in time.

⁂

The croft mill was in disrepair, the door of its small building hanging from a broken top hinge. The floor was stained with mold from water seeping through the back wall, thought the wood was still solid when Harold pried at it with the tip of a knife blade. Shaun reached down, brushing a finger against the grain-polished face of the millstone, tracing the inscribed lines on its smooth surface, rough-worn from small pebbles gathered up along with bushels of wheat and corn kernels, ground into meal.

"The wheel will need refacing." He looked over at Harold, who shrugged, a dismayed expression on his face as he considered the work required to bring the mill back into operation.

"Are you proposing to harvest corn, hauling it up from the fields below? Same as when I was here in my youth, bonny and braw? Gran Da, back bent by years of hard work, in a fine cackle at the thought of concocting another batch of the water of life?"

Shaun shook his head. "Nae, lad. Those days are gone. Ghosts in the shadows, though I still have claim to his last bottle, sealed under his mark, reminder of where we once stood. Proud, tall, with the future of Ireland 'neath our kilts." He grinned. "For a certain your kilt seems loose enow to produce an heir and two fine lassies. Your Aaron, a son any father would be proud to have, in carry of his name."

Harold nodded, coming over and touching the stone. He touched his uncle on the arm, knowing he had always protected the interests of the clan, convincing the English to spare them and their lands during the Highland Clearances, in large part due to his own father and uncle's political influence back in London. "Not only a father—proud of the lad." He gave Shaun a considered look. "My son looks up at you —and cannae find your top. Like the mountain he begs to be let free to go and climb, each day. Wanting to go up in your footsteps, like I did when near to his age. Years before Gran Da would allow me to go on my own, with young Jack in tow."

"Your Ma was fit to be tied, that first time I took ya. The two of us coming down the next day, being snow-bound at the top. Half-frozen, wind-whipped—and near dead."

"Was yourself, only, in any danger of that. Me on your back, wrapped inside your cloak and mine, fit as an Irish fiddle, as I recall. The only reason your sister let you live."

Shaun leaned back, his arms crossed on his lean, still well-muscled chest, age no deterrent to whatever action might be required of him as head of Clan Scott. Eyes, as blue as Harold's, with firm jut of chin and a thin scar on his cheek, marking him as a man who wouldn't back down in face of threat to kith or kin. "You'd be sore pressed to make the climb, this time home. The weight carried on your shoulders enough to buckle a strong mule's knees." Shaun reached into a pocket of his greatcoat, removing a metal flask that drew Harold's eye. He held it out. "Are you in want of a dram—or perhaps, in need of it all?" Shaun watched as his nephew shook his head, a shadow on his lined face, near a half-mirror image to his own.

"I'll stand a swallow in toast to Clan Scott." Harold took the flask and removed the stopper, holding it up. "To the men who stand shoulder to shoulder, back-to-back, with any and all of us—good to their sworn word to deliver for, and defend the Clan no matter the day, the cause, or the numbers for or against. To all our brothers of Clan mothers, bonded by the blood we share—and shed." He took a long pull, then handed it to Shaun who did the same, then tipped it to one side, splashing a healthy amount onto the ancient wheel. "O'r cae i'r cnewyllyn, cnewyllyn i stwnsh, a stwnsh i anadl angel mewn potel, wedi'i arllwys—efallai na fydd ein bywydau byth yn brin o fenywod cain, wedi'u cusanu—ac fel chwisgi cain, wedi'u chwipio."

Harold repeated the words beneath his breath, in English, a nod to his father's memory. "From field to kernel, kernel to mash, and mash to angel's breath in bottle, poured—may our lives never be short of fine women, kissed—and as fine a whiskey, sipped."

The two former soldiers, on opposite sides of the highland hills when it came to oaths of loyalty sworn, hung their heads and made a silent count of those they'd served with, and lost. A soft whicker from Harold's mare outside drew them to the door. Aaron, mounted in front of a large man with bushy black beard, was in full beam, kitted out in tartan kilt and garb, his hands loose on the horse's reins, easing it to a stop.

The man nodded in greeting. "Found this lad on the trail, punching holes in the ground with angry heels at having been left behind. He would not name his Da—tight-lipped, as any good Scotsman should be." The man was named Duncan, a close friend of Shaun's, following behind wherever he went in order to protect his laird from harm, or haul him home after over-indulging at any number of boisterous meeting houses scattered throughout valleys down below.

Harold stepped forward. "I'll lay claim to the lad, though his Ma will have a piece of his hide for his having run off. And blister my ears for the deed, as well." Harold reached up, gathering in his son and setting him down, then grasping Duncan's hand, half again as large as his own. "How far along was he?"

"More than halfway here from the manor, in a lather of ripe curses as I rode up. Words I hesitate to use myself—most times, along with a few new ones sprinkled in." He gave both men and the boy a nod in turn, then tugged his horse away, heading back down the narrow trail.

Harold looked down at Aaron. "You've gone and stirred the hornet's nest, son. Hope you're up to the punishment coming from having poked a stick in your Ma's eye."

"Ya should'ha brung me. I have the right."

"And what right is that?" Shaun knelt, placing his hand on the young boy's shoulder. Aaron looked up at him, his eyes the same color as his mother's. "As heir. What I'm to be. This will be my—my—" Aaron swiveled his head, taking in the mill. "What is this place?"

"A millhouse. Used to make the flour from which bread is made."

Aaron scoffed. "Gran Ma makes it in ovens." The young boy looked around. "No ovens here." He pointed. "No chimney."

Harold reached down, pulling his son into his arms, taking him inside and showing him around the interior, thick shutters having been opened to let in the light. "The path to your Gran Ma's oven starts down there." He pointed to the sloped shoulder of the mountain, where a zig-zag trail wandered up a steep slope to the top of a ridge, then over and down to the valley floor, far below. "From a place where grain —the same as your own horse eats—is grown for our food. Standing in the sun 'til ripe, then scythed and threshed. Which is what your Ma will be doing to us both—once we're home to the manor again. Then it was gathered up and brought here—a long time ago—and poured onto this—" He placed Aaron's hand on the millstone, making sure his small fingers felt the chiseled lines. "The mill stone made to turn by water flowing from the spring pond above, grinding the kernels of wheat, rye, or corn—placed here." Harold touched a wooden sluice, placed just above and at an angle to the face of the stone.

Aaron's eyes followed the flow of his father's words, taking in each step described. He wriggled until Harold set him down, then went over and knelt down, looking at the underside of the stone, his kilt revealing wiry legs as he leaned forward, touching the wooden geartrain in the shadowed enclosure. "Make it go."

Shaun glanced at Harold, eyebrows raised at how quickly the lad had picked up on the sequence, understanding the means to move the large mass of stone. He knelt beside his nephew. "It will nae work as it once did, Aaron. Would require a handful of workers to clear the sediment from the spring outside, as well make repairs to the spillway and other-"

"Cannae ye and my Da nae fathom it oot?"

"Aye, laddie—with time. But your Da and me—we have more than enow on our minds to discuss as it is. There is nae need for t'other things done wi' no use for it—once restored."

Harold took Aaron's arm, helping him to his feet, noting a grimace on Shaun's face as the older man got to his feet. "Come along, son. We need to be getting you back 'fore your mother comes through the doorway, knife in hand, murder in her moon-kissed eyes."

"Then close the door and bolt it. Keeping her oot."

Harold shook his head, gathering up his oldest bairn. "Your Gran

Uncle Shaun has not room enough to keep us wi' him in his own manor, were we to do that. Best we go and do our best to make amends." When Aaron started to protest, Harold gave him a measured stare: the boy in quick retreat lest the lesson become one of a physical nature. He lowered his head against his father's chest once aboard the mare, his gray eyes struggling to stay open as they slowly rode away.

Aaron was sound asleep in his own bed, having been found sound in body by Sinclair, little enough worse for wear of having his nap delayed. The two men had beat a hasty retreat to the salon room, a fire in glow and bottle of family branded whiskey to hand. The wind had risen, its mournful voice against the eaves penetrating through thick panes of glass in two large windows that overlooked a road winding its way down to the valley floor, a full day's travel away.

"The shutters will need replacing. The hinges too—all but gone." Shaun sipped the clear bodied liquor, enjoying the warmth as it drew a line from his throat to stomach. "They'll be needed to protect the glass against winter storms—or men with bad intentions."

"Little worry of that, Uncle—all the way up here."

"Nae, Harry. There's always a worry of it when money and politics are involved—which is the case with yourself and your uncle as well, based on whispers I've heard in the wind. The reason he was just here. While you were over there with your wife—in lands beyond the western line of the horizon these three months and more in pass."

Harold took a sip of his Gran Da's whiskey, holding it in his mouth for a moment, savoring the unique notes of its mingled flavors. Then he tilted his head, allowing it to slip down the back of his throat, knowing he would never develop a need for it, as his father had. But he did enjoy the energy bound up within it, created by the hands of those who'd brought it from field to bottle, bottle to glass. He sighed. "I'll have someone come and make repairs. Tend to whatever else needs the doing of."

"Someone already has done so, Harry. Workers are due here in two days to mend the shutters, as well as replacing the door in back. The storage room door—having replaced the kitchen one, a year ago."

Harold raised his glass, looking at his uncle over the rim. "Is not your responsibility, Uncle—but I thank you, truly, for all you've done. All you do to keep my family and the Scott clan—safe from harm."

"It is my nature to so." Shaun nodded. "But your thanks are welcome, none-the-less. No different than yourself would do, in return—were you not in labor in trying to hold back the winds of change."

"You've heard news of what is coming?" Harold looked at Shaun, who shrugged.

"Your recent speech in Commons has ignited a storm of broad-sheets, in support of and against your request of the boy King to ease his grip on colonist necks, overseas."

"Along with my suggest of a self-administered nation of native tribes, serving as our allies in defense of current and future needs. Whether against French or Spanish incursions in lands to the South and west of the colonies. Intent on maintaining the current boundaries of our colonies, while encouraging eventual and mutual expansion, alongside our allies. A coalition of native tribes." Harold paused. "A native nation, if you will."

Shaun looked back at his nephew, a confused expression on his face. "Native—nation?"

"Yes. A central theme in every speech, made. One third—one leg, if you will, of a triumvirate—fashioned into an unbreakable coalition. Of great benefit to all sides."

"Only two sides mentioned—in news I've seen provided from publishing houses below the southern border."

Harold stood up and went over to the fireplace, resting his hand on the mantle, the amber liquid reflecting the light from the flames. His voice was soft edged when he finally spoke, his words tight with emotion. "It was said—and written—in my own words, made clear. The bastards denying their spread." He looked over at Shaun. "I was shown copies that correctly stated my intent. For distribution to all corners of England, on through to Ireland and Scotland. To the colonies, themselves."

"I cannae speak on anyone's behalf but my own—and my words on the subject are as offered."

Harold's voice hardened. "Damn him. Damn *him* and his slippery ways. He swore to make my thoughts clear to those who would rise in support of them. To prevent what is bound to result from my daring to challenge—to stand against those who are manipulating the King. And influential members of Parliament. Cold-hearted men—gathering together in clandestine meetings."

"All the more reason to prepare here—against what they might sent us from there, if you are made out to be an obstacle to their plans. Which, it seems—you are in danger of becoming."

⸙⸙⸙

Thomas disentangled himself from the grasping arms of two young ladies in laughing assault, his face florid, covered in a sheen of sweat, despite repeated calls from Sinclair to not allow the twins to over-tax him. He finally made good his escape, assisted by the children's Gran Ma's call to hie to her, a basket of fresh bread recently pulled from the oven.

Harold raised his eyebrows as the older man closed the distance, wiping his face with a cloth pulled from his pocket, shaking his head, albeit with a satisfied smile. Thomas joined Harold on a wide slab of rock, made into a bench in the center of the gardens surrounding the manor house.

"They are much as I remember my own sweet girls to have been, indeed. Though stronger in body then ever were my own sweet cherubs. Due to a rigorous routine of daily chores, no doubt, fostering a healthy and—robust stamina."

Harold nodded. "I am often accused of neglect—by two woman who profess to love me dearly—in spending so little of my time entertaining the lassies. Though, when left to myself as the responsible parent—they ply me with endless requests for time spent on horseback, or hikes into mountains, yonder. Same as their brother does, leaving me betwixt and between."

"Would have made good names for them, each—though Meghan

and Marion are well suited to their natures. One a beautiful pearl, strong and resolute. The other—with a cunning mind and mood as changeable as the sea." Thomas tilted his head. "Was it Sinclair who named them?"

"Eira. The honor going to her. Prepared for it with names in hand, well before I was born. Herself always hopeful for a daughter."

Thomas blushed, mindful of his place in the family line. He cleared his throat. "The alliteration, as well as their meaning, perfectly matches them both. A fine pair of brawny—or is it braw I'm reaching for? Yes. The two of them make a 'braw' pair. You're blessed by the women who love and adore you—as is your right—earned from your loving attention to their every need."

Harold considered a moment, then nodded. "I will not disagree. And it will be a matter of great interest to us all—the lads showing up daring to take them on as partners in life."

Thomas flinched, raising his hand. "Too soon, nephew. Too soon. It will be but a blink of your eye before you'll have opportunity to regret such cavalier words, so carelessly uttered." He paused, a finger lifted, pointing into the air. "Beware request of time to fly. A single moment or more in store—when night draws nigh—time more precious to you then, beyond the gleam of gold or jewels in cling of hands, to chest."

Harold narrowed his eyes. "The Bard?"

Thomas shook his head. "One Thomas Knutt."

"I bow, sir—to your philosophic soul."

Neither man spoke, their thoughts their own as they watched dark clouds gather on the far horizon's edge.

Harold's thoughts spun in circles, though he was standing still, his mind processing the words in his ear. His uncle's lips moving, relating a dark tale of an approach made and warning delivered, his voice shaking in fear, eyes shifting, unable to land in a steady gaze. Thomas had made his leave from the manor house a week earlier, then returned at a rapid pace by carriage, his face sagging with fatigue as he clenched his hands at his sides.

"It was as clear as if a message launched from the shore of a deserted isle, placed in a sealed bottle by the castaway in Defoe's tale. A note—left inside an actual bottle—placed sometime during the night, a few days ago. Warning me to cease and desist, or be made deceased, if choosing to continue my—our present course."

Harold reached out and clasped his uncle's shoulder, feeling the bones beneath the skin, the older man's weight having fallen off of late. "You must stop, then. Immediately. Take your notes to the front yard and burn them in the middle of the day, where an observation can be made."

His uncle hung his head. "Already done, Harry. As if I were a dog to master's call, tail curled between my legs." He looked up, his face having aged ten years since the thin slice of time when he'd last come north. "I have failed my brother, your father. I've failed you both."

Harold took Thomas by his shoulders, straightening his bent frame. "It is not you who has failed, but me. In laying my trust at another's door. A hard lesson learned with time running out, unable to avoid what will happen, must happen now—against all measure of common sense to the contrary."

"Common—sense. As if enough of that could ever be found and made go round the world."

Harold released his uncle and moved over to the window of the manor that over-looked the gardens. He watched Sinclair and the three children as they knelt, pulling weeds from the soil. Aaron began tossing tufts of grass into the air, the blades settling on the curled hair of his sisters. Squeals of protest followed, along with handfuls of weeds tossed back. Sinclair came over, scolding Aaron, bent over at the waist, hands on her hips, a rain of green grass falling from the sky, covering her head. She lifted her skirts and chased the children in small circles, the four of them tumbling to the ground, the thick glass of the window-panes all but preventing the sounds of their playful laughter to pass through.

Harold pressed his palms against the cold glass, tears in his eyes, knowing he must leave them, making a final attempt to right a ship in danger of sinking. To try and gain some measure of value back for all the precious blood he and his men had shed, so many years ago.

CHAPTER FIFTEEN

KENT

SPRING, 1774

A member of William Pitt's household staff left an open bottle of wine on a dining room table located at his estate in Kent. Harold had made the half-day ride out from London, invited to meet the respected politician there. He'd arrived early in the afternoon, lured into spending several hours in hard toil, helping the elderly man with a project in his beautiful but expansive gardens.

Harold had enjoyed the work, his clothes changed out for those of a laborer of similar build. Pitt, limited by pain from gout, a lifetime affliction he'd managed to put to one side in service to the Crown, had given orders while Harold finished his efforts then changed back into proper clothes after a wash up. The two men shared a meal, hearty in portions for one, and a carefully administered plate for the other. The wine was shared between them, with the lion's share left for Harold to finish.

"Your report of—the strong emotions of those with influence in the colonies, was thorough. The notes with observation as to a potential move of political base to Philadelphia, insightful. I assume your sources were to be trusted?"

Harold had finished his meal, the dishes cleared when the wine had been brought. He tipped a small helping into his mouth, letting the flavors settle for a moment before swallowing. "They were—and are. Though they suffer from the same issue as do those on our side of events."

"You will now make your usual charge of this—this unnamed, underground society again. One in control of all things related to State, commerce such. A pot of weak tea, my boy. Rumors, and nothing more, I can assure you." The stout man with mane of white hair waved one hand, indicating another half-glass of wine be poured. Harold quickly complied, refilling his own before returning the unlabeled bottle to the center of the table. Then he made a final attempt to bend William around.

"I fail to understand how you can so easily dismiss the information I've presented you. In strict confidence, without any attempt made to corroborate it independently, with the safety of the lives of my family at—"

"Tosh and posh, Harry. It's true I have not followed up on these rumors. But is not because I'm ignoring your claim of risk to you or your family. The charges you prefer have been ignored in order to avoid having a net thrown over my shoulders, followed by a forced move to Bethlem Sanatorium. The gardens there are decent enough, I will admit. Still, not in compare to my being left alone, remaining here in tend of my own."

Harold shrugged, knowing the aged politician and former war hero would never admit to an incursion by a secretive group, one established in every corner of the civilized world, with intent and the capability to control the power of governments around the globe. He could forgive the older man's omission, knowing him to be the genial face of protest permitted by the group in question, allowed to rail against the crown's unfair treatment of colonists abroad. Ever in the press, speaking out for the common man, insisting in protections of a free, if sometimes vociferous press. Unaware, due to his myopic view of it, that those in financial backing of the press were themselves being tugged by strings leading back to the hands of men placed in their position without any public vote. Without thorough investigation of their moral code, or hidden motives. A German bloodline ran through most of their veins, with inter-familial marriages arranged to maintain momentum from past generations of like-minded ancestors.

"Your gardens are a treasure to behold, William. A pleasure indeed, my being invited to assist in some small way—truly. Takes me back to days spent in highland pastures, from dawn to dusk, in sweaty labor."

Willian cocked his head. "I'd thought you English, by birth. Your father a man of—some military distinction. A spot of hard service in Gibraltar, as I recall." Pitt closed his eyes, shaking his head. "So many mistakes made there, and elsewhere. So much good English blood spilled." He looked over, waving his hand. "Not on your father's orders, mind you. No slight intended."

"None taken, sir. We all have tales to tell, along with the burdens we carry."

"I forget, at times, your own good service. You appear much too young to have been there with Ayden. Many of those fine fellows gone —the country poorer for their loss." William shrugged. "Your former leader is still hale enough. Riding every day, his horses his passion —still."

The room grew silent, a low fire in bank against the cool air as the evening made an approach. Harold finally broke it. "I would have the papers I delivered you, safely back in hand. A matter of a nervous relative, with three married daughters and a handful of grandchildren under his wing."

"Yes, of course. They are here in store, somewhere or other. My man will bundle them up and you can take them with you in the morning. Are you certain I cannot convince you to stay another day? I have fresh cuttings due in—with numerous holes needing to be dug."

Harold shook his head, the last of his wine emptied with a careless swallow. "I must beg off the pleasure, my back aching from my small dose of honest toil, this afternoon."

Sinclair was in a sour mood, reflected in the look on her face as she watched her son handle the bow that his Gran Uncle Shaun had provided him in celebration of his thirteenth birthday. The gift, a three-quarter sized longbow, was ideal for hunting rabbits and grouse in the lower fields. A quiver of iron-tipped arrows was part of the bundle, along with thick mats of bound rushes, leaning against a triangle of sticks.

Aaron had been quick to take instruction from his favorite person in the entire clan, proving to have an excellent eye for the placement of arrows in tight patterns, his draw and release made with one smooth motion, the bow flexing in arms already thick with well-toned muscles. Harold took note of his wife's sullen scowl, remembering the same look on his father's face, decades earlier, watching as his two young sons poured through thick tomes on battles fought during military campaigns.

"He will use if for hunting, wife. Not in battle. Those days are long gone, with recreational use or the taking of small game the only use fit for such a weapon, this day."

"Weapon. The word itself indication of its potential for damage."

"Even so, it would not be to him, as might be the result with pistol or musket, which was bandied about last night, until I quashed the thought."

Sinclair turned and looked up at him, her eyes going wide. "He is not to be made part of any such activities as those! Not the least of encouragement made, or so help me I will use the bow to place a shaft in Shaun's arse, where it will not be easily withdrawn, having to be pulled out along with his thick Scot's head!"

Harold tried not to smile, managing to keep it to a weak upturn of his lips as he nodded. "I have made such clear to all." He noted her stare. "I will make it clear again." He paused, his eyes narrowing in a hurt expression. "Do you nae ken how much in oppose I am to any of that? Nae, Lass—I've no more thirst for my son on a battlefield than my own Da did."

"And look how that worked out for your poor Mother."

"The boy's spent more time here than in England—since birth. As difficult to remove him from these highlands as a thistle from horse's mane. He does not see himself as a son of England, his nose drawn to the scent of Scottish sod, as tight knit to it as the kilts he's constantly growing out of. Each season in pass seeing him stretched taller, and broader in the shoulder."

Sinclair took in a long breath, pursing her lips, letting it out slowly. Then she nodded, her mind made up to accept this step in advance of martial arts, knowing from the look in her son's eyes that he would never be made to let go of the bow in hand.

"It will be you who'll teach him to hunt. Not your fool of an uncle, with his endless tales of raids and uprisings told with a glass of whiskey in his hand."

The hare was sitting upright, paws posed upon its thick chest, ears upright, amber eyes making a careful study of the surrounding sea of grass. A snip of it was sticking out from one side of its mouth, its jaw working away, pulling it in. When nothing moved, it dropped to the ground and made a small hop ahead, dipping its head and nipping another long blade of green growth from the edge of a narrow field pinched between two small ridges.

Harold watched from half a hundred paces away, trying to make out where his son was hiding, having been watching for the better part of an hour, a chill wind painting his exposed skin red. There was no sign of Aaron, only stalks of bright green field grass, stroked by the restless stir of air.

A faint sigh announced a shaft in flight, the head pinioning the large hare, left kicking its feet in a vain attempt to flee as its life slipped from it, lying on its side in leg-stretched pose upon the grass. A grin centered his son's dirt stained face as he rose to his feet a dozen paces from the kill. A blanket of cloth strips, mimicking the color and texture of the grass, lay upon his shoulders, Harold staring in amazement, recognizing it as a ghillie suit, used by poachers to steal game from their laird's lands.

Aaron walked over and snatched up the hare, snapping its neck, taking care to avoid the hind feet with sharp nails, capable of causing a serious gash and possibility of infection. He drew the shaft from the loose-limbed body, checking the arrowhead for sign of damage, nodding in satisfaction as he dragged it through the grass, cleaning it, putting it back inside the sheath at his feet.

Harold stood up, his legs stiff from the long wait. "I saw no sign of you, your choice of garb a clever touch." He paused. "Your Gran Uncle's doing?"

"Nae." Aaron grinned. "Read about it in a book. Made it from old gunnysacks, needling them myself. The strips, torn rags — dyed from a dip in a pot of boiled grass."

Harold felt an ache in his chest, his son's face calm, certain in his skill, no longer the boy, now fully a man in carry and forethought. Too much like himself, he thought, when at the same age. Concern washed over him, borne of thoughts of what might come, despite his and the lad's mother's firm conviction he was never to be exposed to any untoward risk. "You've become a skilled archer. Deadly."

Aaron looked at the hare. "To such as these." Then he looked at Harold, his face widening into a crooked smile, his eyes lighting up. "But if allowed to take a stag! Now that would prove a worthy quarry." Aaron's eyes and words were an obvious plea for a full-sized bow, the first sign revealed thus far of his actual age. "Will you nae allow me one? And guide me yourself — with a musket, in case the animal is wounded, and not struck true?"

Harold lowered his eyes. "Your mother would nae approve of it." He watched as his son's face fell into a frustrated look, waiting to see if he would recover his balance. As soon as Aaron nodded in docile acceptance, he pounced. "So, we must not let her know I've left one for you back in the wee croft house, tucked away in the corner, with a bundle of arrows fit for the job. To practice with over the next few months until your arm is up to the full draw of it. A tale shared between the two of us." Harold saw his son's smile spread from ear to ear. "At least — until we're back to the manor house later this summer — with meat and rack strapped to your sturdy mountain horse."

Aaron came on the run, tossing one arm around his father's waist, the other holding the hare and longbow out to the side, careful to avoid letting them touch the ground.

⅏ ⅏ ⅏

"I would have forbidden it, if such a command could ever alter your course, once heading downwind." Sinclair tossed a pillow onto the bed, another picked up and soundly plumped. "You've taken him to the edge of a line that cannae be uncrossed. A hare or grouse on one side. Stag, boar—then men, on the other."

"Too far wife." Harold frowned, giving Sinclair a firm look. She'd managed to wring the secret from him, having noted the increased size of her sons arms and thick calluses on the fingers of his right hand over the summer. "A stag is not the same as the killing of a man." His voice was as taut as a bowstring at full draw. Sinclair came over and put her hand on his shoulder.

"I withdraw the words—said without thinking it through." She touched his cheek, softening the line of his lips with a kiss. "I know you would never lead Aaron to the thing you abhor most of all—the taking of someone's life. Is but a hunt, made on steep rise with his Da in attend, your chest swelling with pride at the killing blow—well struck." She rose on her toes, looking him straight in his beautiful eyes, her voice soft, her mood shifting to thoughts of creating another child. "Bring me a great stag—" Her hands slipped to his waist. "One with a grand rack." She touched him, feeling him start to respond. "To mount —on the wall—with our son's name engraved on a metal plaque beneath."

Harold softened his stance, reaching to undo the laces of Sinclair's nightdress.

Shaun raised his glass, toasting the wind-scored face of his nephew, made to stand upon a chair in the great room of the manor. Aaron held a cup of ale, his eyes bright with pride at the gathering of Clan elders, there to celebrate his first kill of significance. Harold stood to one side, accepting the clap of hands on his shoulder, acknowledging his braw son, become a man of the Clan.

Shaun cleared his throat, bringing the others to a sudden silence. "I have long held the distinction of being the name hanging below the greater rack on yon wall. Now made to bow my head to a hunter who has surpassed my claim to lead huntsman of Clan Scott. To Aaron—first born son to my nephew—a young man using a bow, mind you—and single arrow, downing a stag of twelve points. Twelve. A magnificent beast, who now hangs drying in yon meat house. The choicest parts laid before you, provider of said hunter of note. To him, Aaron Richard Knutt, raise your glasses in a three note cheer, gentlemen, if you will."

Harold joined in as the group of serious-faced men toasted his son, watching the boy as he turned into a man before his eyes, nodding his head and smiling, accepting their acclaim. A whisper of concern ran through his ear, gone before it could form into an image. One he let slip as he drained his third cup of ale, basking in the reflected glory of his son's improbable first kill.

Shaun came to stand beside him. "He is a fine young man, nephew. Both halves of him, Scot and Brit." Shaun touched his glass of whiskey against Harold's cup. "And the sound you hear from the wee croft on high—is the boys Great Gran Da spinning in his grave 'neath the pile of rocks, hearing that said."

"Thank you, Uncle. It was a fine effort made, with himself the guide and in no need of me to be there, backing his effort." Harold paused, his eyes far away, recalling the approach made. Standing to one side of a narrow pinch in the rugged mountain terrain. Aaron moving as if born to the chase, the kill made clean. His mood—serene, at the moment of arrow's release, bringing an end to a two day stalk. They'd followed the large animal, moving in a steady graze far above its normal range, keeping to the higher points. Each shift of wind requiring a slow retreat and new approach having to be made. Aaron had never once made any complaint, the two of them going without hot food, making cold camp during the night. The final stalk made beneath two suits of gray cloth, the stag unaware of its impending death, the wide-blade of the arrowhead cutting through both lungs and heart, left standing in a cold mist until collapsing on the ground.

Shaun pointed with his glass, aiming at Aaron, surrounded by members of the clan asking for details of the hunt. "He will needing a musket, pistol—and sword, as well, no matter what his sweet Ma has to say about it. A bow is fine for taking of the occasional stag—but a man of the clan must be armed and properly trained. Are ye nae in agree, nephew?"

"We will speak on it and other things on the morrow. For tonight, we celebrate the lad and stuff ourselves with his first kill, of note." Harold touched his cup to Shaun's glass, fixing him with a firm smile. "Are you nae in agree with me, uncle?"

Shaun nodded, accepting the mild rebuke. He raised his glass, the amber liquid slipping down his throat, eyes fastened on his Gran Nephew, knowing the lad's destiny would be to protect any he felt threatened, no matter the wishes of his mother and father.

CHAPTER SIXTEEN

LONDON

MID-SUMMER, 1774

Nathan sniffed, his nose poised above the back of his hand, pulling a pinch of snuff into his nostril. He blinked several times, then straightened up, Harold watching him with an inquiring glance. Nathan offered him the box, but Harold raised a hand in polite refusal.

"Enlighten me, my friend. Your family—they are in good health?"

"Yes. As is yours, I hope. Meaning your wife—there being no children in evidence as yet."

"You have the right of it—though how you came by the information is—news to me." Nathan frowned, then released it on the back of a thin smile.

Harold knew he'd made a mark on the other man's confident demeanor. "I asked a friend, who asked a friend. My interest one of concern as to your health. Children—a blessing. Though they can be a worry, at times, depending on the cause for one's concern over their wellbeing. As I'm certain you're in agreement with."

Nathan stiffened his posture, feeling a shift of the ground beneath his feet, understanding a message was being sent. Uncertain as to the reason. "Of course, my friend. Quite right. One's family is and should always be of primary consideration to all. Which I can assure you, yours is with me. Including yourself."

Harold didn't hesitate, having set his course and not to be deterred. "I am aware of your influence on both sides of the arguments being made—for and against the impending conflagration."

"You exaggerate the significance of recent events, Harold. The— activities are but window dressing to underlying concerns. Trade, the issue always at hand, and how best to carve the beast. Nothing more. No one wants blood to run in streets soon to be paved with gold. Surely you can see your way clear of such a negative mood and brighten your outlook with my promise that all will soon be mended between colonies and crown."

Harold scoffed. "There is money to be made in sale of arms, as well other materials of war. Transports, settled deep in the water with iron and lead in their holds, returning with goods confiscated and sold to highest bidder, with a healthy percentage retained by the crown, the rest to men without direct exposure to risk."

"You read too deeply into spurious broadsheets." Nathan stepped closer to Harold, lowering his tone to try and ease the tension he felt between them. "The truth is those suppliers you make mention of are not in favor of disruption in commercial trade."

"The disrupt, as you call it, has been in place since soldiers decked out in red-coats seized Boston—with no chorus of voices in protest heard over here. Only whispers, without consequence to those pulling the strings leading to fat purses and fatter personages."

Nathan stepped back, his mind working on how much of what was being said was opinion, or only chum, cast upon the water. Aware the famed strategist was more of a threat than others in the club were willing, or capable of admitting, including Alfred. Harold's descriptive words bringing the obese man's image to mind. "I will go—once more—and make inquiries there. Again. Trying to ferret out the least rumor concerning your fears. If it is real, I will find it and join with you in exposing it for all to see. You have my promise, Harold. On my honor—I so swear it."

Harold nodded, then reached out, taking Nathan's hand in his, shaking it once then stepping back, turning toward the door, stopping when the other man called out to him.

"I would ask that you return to your family, where I will send you my answer, as soon as any such discovery is made. Rest easy, my friend. Your concerns, as well those of our dear and highly esteemed William Pitt, shall be answered with utmost resolve."

Harold pushed through the door without another word, knowing he would be aboard ship just after midnight, tucked safely away before dawn, his name withheld from the crew manifest, clad in sailors garb assigned to galley stores below. Hidden from view of those above deck until the shoreline of Pennsylvania colony was near enough to reach by small boat. His plan set in motion, with only an ocean crossing left between him finding his own answers.

⅏⅏⅏

Early morning off the coast of the North American continent was a gray blanket to those wandering the deck of the ship. A thick fog bank greeted Harold as he exited the shadowed hold, climbing into a small boat lowered at his directive with four men at the oars, pulling away without comment, knowing the tide was on the rise, reducing any chance of an accidental grounding.

Harold waited until he could smell the forest, the scent of pine trees hanging in the mist saturated air. "Close enough. I'll wade the rest of the way." Harold tossed a purse to the sailor manning the rudder. "My thanks. I'm sure the fishing will be good, this far from the city."

The squat man grinned, his teeth a medley of hit and miss notes. He lifted one hand in a slow wave, turning the small craft back out to sea. Harold waited for it to depart, then angled along the shoreline, moving a thousand paces northeast until reaching a small stream. He followed it inland, the land rising to fields bordered by a group of small homes. He sparked a flint, lighting a small lantern he'd been carrying, waving it from side to side, responded to in a count of a hundred heartbeats. Both lights were quickly extinguished, a group of three men making their way to where Harold stood, every man with a hand on the pistols they held, wary against a trap sprung by either side.

The oldest man spoke first. "Did you manage to catch any fish?"

Harold let out a short breath, nodding. "The bait—was not to their liking."

The man offered a hand, flanked by two younger men. "Pity. Had a taste in my mouth for some." He gave the other two a nod, sending them ahead. "Follow me—my nameless friend."

⁂

"From the farm on into town, we'll have a free run of it, nothing of account hereabouts to bother the sensibilities of the red-coats." The grizzled face man grinned, his eyes reflecting the oil lamp burning in a small barn. "Or none known to them to be a threat."

Harold trusted the man, a veteran of the wars in the west and steadfast colonist soldier who'd survived the massacre of the Big Burn. He and his sons had guided him through sections of dense woods and underbrush, skirting boggy mires, ending up at the end of the first phase of his mission, the second about to begin.

"The supplies I requisitioned?"

"In a broke-back barn across the way, behind a house burned down to the chimney. Land too poor for farming with no one left to make a claim, the original owners killed by British lead, their bodies tossed into the fire." The man turned his head to one side and spit. "The deaths deserved—for having remained deaf to our warnings to cease their efforts against the English forces."

Harold reached out, taking the man's hand. "I will be leaving before dawn. My thanks—for all you've done."

The veteran held on, his grip tight. "And more yet to do."

"Nae." Harold shook his head, then eyed the man's two sons. "I'll not put you or your family at further risk."

"My country, Brit. My risk to assign myself and mine as I see fit. Them supplies will be a bit heavy in the hauling away, and I'll not have the Red Fox left with a strained back on my account. What kind of a story would that be to leave my grandchildren's children to tell?"

Harold lowered his head, his chest tight with pride from having led such men in the past, willing to follow him into battle with no promise of winning through. "You have my thanks—and further appreciation if keeping my former 'title' between the two of us."

"Unlike the previous owners of the small farm left in ruin, I'm neither daft nor deaf." The man glanced at his sons, who smiled back. "Only old—as I'm often reminded of."

Harold nodded. "My own Da said that old age is the reward earned for having lived so long."

"Sounds like a sensible man. How many years has he earned?"

"Not as many as deserved." Harold tightened his expression, his eyes reflecting the shadowed light of morning in full approach. "Killed by the bastard I've hunted for ever since, done at the orders of those who will be made to pay the blood price."

"Then we will make our way home and have a drink, toasting your father and effort made on his behalf."

A jug of rum was produced from a cupboard, no glasses required, the container balanced on forearm, opening pressed to lip, a long pull made by each of the other three men. Harold, the last to drink, winced as the strong drink hit his throat. He lowered the jug and wiped his lips, his eyes finding those of the older man who grinned and clapped him on his back, taking the earthenware vessel, a final swallow made, then raising the jug. "To my brother in arms—well met."

Harold nodded, knowing there was promise in the air, supported by thousands of colonist veterans of like determination ready to assume the mantle of war, if called on. Willing to wrest control of their destinies away from the greedy grasp of those who would have it otherwise. Aware any strike against the shadowy mix of men, playing both sides of the impending conflict against the middle, would not alter the direction of the storm in rise. But it will be enough, he promised himself, to avenge the death of a father gone before his time, with chapters yet still to write.

Nathan was in an irritable mood, the other members of the local group gathered for their scheduled meeting having refused to heed his sullen words of warning. Those most deaf, men of power and social prominence, had dismissed his fears, leaving Nathan standing in a corner of the room, shaking his head. He was both hurt and disappointed that one of them, a great bear of a man who should have been a voice of support, had agreed with the others.

"You are a woman at bleed, in tither and tears, hands rubbing your apron as you worry and fret. Belay your whimpering, printer. Go back to your twist of truths in pretty prose. And take your mucking nags with you." George, well into his cups, had needed the back of a chair and the shoulder of the portly man sitting in it to provide balance, his feet spread, supporting his massive girth which had increased by half due to an excess of appetite and lack of exertion. His stable of horses made to do the work of conveying him throughout the colonies, seeking opportunities to increase his wealth.

Several others had laughed, more joining in as Nathan had walked away, leaving the room, his face red in shame at having failed, once more, to wake his fellow members from their false dream of being able to maintain control of people's emotions. He went to the outer doorway, staring out into the night, wishing to have someone to confide in, to help salve his wounded ego. Nathan spotted his target: a tall, thin, and dangerously quiet man hired to provide a measure of security, standing near the side of a road, watching the approaches to the assembly building. He walked up, making his approach known with a scuff of boot soles on the path. "A study in nonchalance—no doubt based on the full purse on your belt and little concern as to what's to come, either way."

The unnamed man shrugged, turning his scarred face and focusing on Nathan's, one arm held in a crooked angle behind his back, a pistol always near to reach. "Do not aim your hurt in my direct. I'm no one's mother—or whore. Although, if shown enough silver, I will stand quiet while you make your whine."

"As always—a true delight in speaking with you." Nathan stepped away, finding a seat on a bench alongside the outside wall of the large hall. No one was in evidence, the small town situated at a quiet crossroads, with several buildings of commerce holding down the corners of four red-dust lanes. A scattering of houses nosed the edges along both sides, crowded around two public houses, with a pub nestled between. The accommodations would provide enough rooms to hold those who would be gathering throughout the next day to attend the quarterly meeting, being held in an out of the way locale. The core of the colonies power base invited to assemble to discuss on how best to leverage recent events to their advantage, based on the latest financial review of market variables, both local and overseas.

Nathan sighed, wishing to discover the means for a timelier transfer of information, beyond that of the system he'd helped develop a few years ago, with messages in code sent aboard every ship departing or arriving at ports all over the world, carrying the latest buy and sell pricing suggestions for men of commerce, in wait. The information adjusted as the next ship arrived, subject to additional change as a new series of messages would be delivered, a day or so later. Commercial decisions to be juggled to leverage as much money as possible from a steady flow of shipments made over the churn of wind and waves along protected sea lanes, drawn in lines between hundreds of ports, domestic and foreign. Word carry by men on fast horses up and down the coastlines. Men, with fluid minds and firm fingers pressed to the pulse of Royal throat and colonists' wrists, sitting in the center of web their webs. One of them, far more intelligent than he was willing to let on, standing in the other room, inebriated, though his eyes remained watchful, as if gauging the moods of his men before the start of a battle. In the hopes that his magnificent estate in the countryside outside Philadelphia would be far enough away from the threat of conflict to avoid the worst of the conflagration, once it began.

A nudge of hand on Harold's shoulder was followed by a point of forefinger from the veteran, who leaned in against him, his eyes focused on a building with light streaming from its windows and doorway. The air was cool, evening's arrival helping to dissolve a blanket of heat left over from the summer solstice, left behind barely a month ago, daylight in slow retreat each day since.

"The core of the group you seek—gather there—two days before the rest will arrive. Always some who are late to the party." He shifted his finger slightly, his voice a mere whisper in Harold's ear. "The ale house is just there, with an inn to either side. That's where they'll retire to once the meet is done. Then host the main event tomorrow night before disbanding for three months—more or less. This time their reunion seems to have been—hastened a bit by what's happening to the north. Those damned Bostonians always itching for a fight. Trust me—when the shite finally hits the milk-cow's tail—the spark to the fuse will be lit from there."

Harold kept the smile from his face, the veteran a fount of earthy wisdom. "A small window of opportunity, then—for my prepare?"

"Two, with no promise of another. Travel won't be hampered much by storm or mud, according to my ache less knee." The man hesitated. "Tomorrow night's the best time to get it done." The he gave Harold a hard look. "Whatever it is you're of a mind to do."

"Then so it shall be."Harold nodded, refocusing his eyes on the face of the man on the bench, too far away to make out who it was. No doubt one of the group of men guiding the beast from its lair, led about on thin tethers formed of words in print on both sides of the big briny. Any change to their influence would prove difficult to achieve by a single man, performing speeches to close-minded men. A significant change requiring God himself to roll up the sleeves of his robe to help make happen, with a bolt of lightning from the sky or some other natural event. Harold looked around, measuring in his mind the distance to the sea and possibility of a great flood made to rise. Too far, he thought, as he leaned back into the shadows of evening's approach —even for God.

CHAPTER SEVENTEEN

HIGHLAND MANOR

LATE SUMMER, 1774

Several red grouse were moving along a narrow footpath, heads down, their beaks probing for bits of grit, unaware of three thin coils of twine lying in wait for them to step into. Two of the snares were tied to the trembling hands of two girls coming of age, lying on their stomachs, their older brother between them, his fingers on his own braided cord, ready to let them know when to yank back, hoping to secure a couple of fat hens for their supper.

Aaron nodded, the three snares tightened with three birds caught, their wings beating rapidly as they struggled to rise, landing in angled fall back to dew-soaked ground. The two girls joined their older brother in a rapid pull and gather in of the twine, keeping the large-bodied birds from freeing themselves.

"It worked! Just like you said." Meghan pounced on her victim and snapped its neck, the way Aaron had taught her a few days earlier, made to practice with a chicken destined for the pot. Marion looked over with a wide-eyed stare, mouth open in shock from seeing the feral look on her sister's face, framed by her light-colored reddish-gold hair and spray of freckles, just like her Gran Ma. Her own, a thick, fog-kissed black mane falling over her wide shoulders.

"You—you *killed* it! They were to be made our *pets*, not dinner!"

Marion clutched her captured bird to her chest, feeling its heartbeat quivering beneath the press of fingers on its back. It fluttered its wings, stronger than a chicken by far, freeing itself enough to drag a clawed foot along her arm, leaving a deep scratch. "Damn you!" Marion grabbed the bird by its neck, a hard twist ending its struggle. Meghan smiled, then looked over at her brother who was shaking his head, a grin on his lips.

Aaron freed his captive, releasing it into the air, watching as it beat a hasty retreat. Meghan came over, the heavy bird dangling from her hand. "Why?"

Her brother shrugged as he gathered in the twine and coiled it. "Two is all we need. More would be a waste—and no life should be used to pay for the greed of another's."

Meghan looked at Aaron, loving her older brother dearly, seeing their father in his face, his build, hearing the echo of his voice hanging in the air. Gone more than a month already, with no mention of where to or when he might be returning. "Another lesson. From our father —right?"

"Yes." Aaron frowned, turning to check the path. Then he gave Meghan a smile, reaching out to tuck a loose spray of curls from the edge of her face, her cheeks a wind-kissed rose. Then he checked on Marion, her fingers rubbing away at the small wound, the bird lying in the grass at her feet. "We'll need get back to put liniment on that, little sister. The birds are known to carry a wee bit of a curse, at times. Easy enough to counter with a dab of Gram's salve."

Marion stared at him, a stamp of her foot indicating her displeasure. "Then why did you not think to bring some with you?" A pout tugged down the corners of her mouth. Angry, Aaron knew, not at the lack of salve, but having to return from the croft meadow to the manor house below. She gave him a glare then flounced away, heading back along the trail, the bird's feet dragging along the path, its broken neck in her hand.

Meghan came over and stood beside him, leaning in against his body, enjoying the warmth. "*That* one's gonna be a tough match, for certain."

Aaron slipped his arm around his sister's shoulders, pulling her in.

"Nae. I think not. She's too open with her feelings, making her easy to manipulate." He gave Meghan a considered look, knowing that having turned thirteen years of age, the day was close to hand when her eyes would turn away from hunting rabbits with his small bow, or spending hours in snaring grouse. "You're the one who will prove to be a difficult chase for some young stag. With ya running him near to death in trying to keep up wi 'ya. Making him sweat blood for the holding of your hand. But knowing when he does—he'll be there for you at the end of the chase. Once you turn around, letting him catch you up."

"Because of you. And Da. In causing me to set my sights so high." She twisted her eyes away, tears beginning to spill down her cheeks. "I miss him, Aaron. Miss him so much. Ma, in constant worry, day and night. Her hands in a twist, though she hides it well enow." Meghan stared at Aaron, her voice breaking. "Please tell me, brother—swear it to me true. Do ya see him coming back to us?" She reached out and clenched his hand. "I ken ya ha' the sight. The fey."

Aaron took a deep breath, tasting the rain in the air to come. He closed his eyes, more for effect than need, his voice as soft as morning mist on heather. "Aye. He will. Men like him—they always come home again. One way or another. You'll see."

Meghan threw her arms around her brother, the bird left to fall to the ground as she squeezed him hard enough to force the air from his lungs. He didn't mind the loving assault, his own arms wrapped between hers, the words echoing in his ears, knowing he hadn't lied. That their Da would return. With a measured step, or in a wooden box.

⚜⚜⚜

Eira watched her adopted daughter as she paced about the manor. "A walk out of doors might do you good, my child. The floor—in imminent danger of being worn through."

Sinclair stopped, hanging her head, her arms at her sides. "I am unable to let go of a vision from last night. I heard Harold's voice—as if a whisper in the wind. The sound of it frightened me, as much a wailing, as words."

"The wind was in a braw blow, and often raises a howl around the north-west corner—at times."

Sinclair stiffened her resolve, keeping her fear from her lips, not wanting to burden her adopted mother with worry. The older woman was still strong in body, though her mind had softened some, along with the sound of her voice. Their once vibrant and vociferous conversations had become more of a one-sided effort, with Sinclair's tone taut with fear for her husband's well-being, causing Eira to shrink back in surrender. A thrust of a dagger to Sinclair's heart each time it happened. "My husband will return home. I know it. Feel it in my bones."

Eira waved a hand at an open window, the air outside warm, her eyes drawn to the hills where sunlight was painting a gleam of gold on wet grass, between drifting tendrils of fog. "Then it be told true, dear one. You have the ken of it, I can tell." She let a wistful sigh slip through her lips, shaking her head. "Had it myself once—as strong as my Da's. Then lost it when my sweet Jackie died—having missed signs of the fever in lurk."

"Was not a lack of vision, Mother. Those things happen, most often down below, in more crowded environs. Like harmful spirits, rising from sewers and clogged rivers. People living elbow to elbow, with little room to draw a clean breath." She went to the window, searching the path leading up to the croft, as if sensing her children's energy. "It's my own lack of vision, plaguing me of late." Sinclair turned around, arms crossed on her chest, looking directly into Eira's. "I was cross to your son—the night he left. Beyond angry with him telling me he had to leave. To let—to let go of me and our children. Of you. Off in search of some measure of—I cannot find a name for it, nor could he. I only know that what I saw there—could see in his eyes—was in direct conflict with what was in his heart. As if he was trying to find some way to slice himself in two. To leave the best part of himself—here. The rest, sent to find a balance to be struck against imminent threat of pain, and loss. As if he could prevent it—to find relief of it—through a righteous action, taken at great risk."

A youthful voice outside pulled Sinclair's view to the window, her youngest daughter by a handful of minutes came into full view, stamping her feet with down-turned lips, a large bird in her hand, swinging loosely from a broken neck. Sinclair turned away, facing Eira, who looked back in silence. "I did not stop him. I knew I could—if I'd begged him to stay. But I let him go, Eira. Released him to his destiny—with a stream of harsh invective, levied in full force. A curse placed upon him by myself, causing me endless nights of aching heart. And now I fear I may never be shed of them. What am I to do—should he not return home safely again?"

Sinclair stared at Harold. "You care naught for the children, or I—heading off on some vainglorious adventure with no good coming of it, in attempt to salve your conscience. Which should be clear—due to your endless efforts made to reverse the tide in rise."

"I—cannot disagree." Harold met Sinclair's ripe anger with a shake of his head, which inflamed her ire.

"Then why—husband?" She stared, her eyes pleading for him to help her understand. Harold unable to answer, shaking his head, eyes aimed at the floor. "God curse you! I will have an answer from you, if only to nail it on your forehead when you return, as reminder of what you risked losing—for no gain shown. No medal pinned to your chest, or promotion earned. With me left in the shadows, while you hide your reasons behind your eyes. As if trust no longer exists between us. Why? Can you not at least lie, so I have some useless thing to hold in my hand while waiting for the sound of your step outside our bedroom door?" She grasped the bedpost, unable to contain the hate she felt welling up from within her. Hating herself for hating him. "Can you not give me a simple lie—if nothing else?"

Sinclair gathered strength enough to move to where he stood, pushing him back through the doorway, into the hall, pushing him again as he turned and descended the stairway, heading toward the door. She stopped at the bottom of the stairs, waiting to see if he'd turn and face her. Her heart aching as he left without looking back. Without a single word left behind, the light gone out of her world.

She went to the window, watching as he headed toward the stable, her hand pressed against the glass reflected her face, a steam of tears falling from her eyes as if blood from a heart torn in two. Salted by the hurtful words used to send him off. Her voice fell to a whisper as she placed her cheek against the cold surface of the window. "Go—my love —and don't come back to me. And when you do return—I'll not return the love you deserve. And when I do return it to you—it will be a fortnight before my legs will open to you. And when we again lie as husband and wife and our strength is spent—I will not kiss you and tell you how much you've been missed. Will not weep onto your scarred shoulder, kissing it gently, refusing you the best part of me, that exists from your vow given me—my own given you. Go—and find your answers in the dark, my love. My light. My solemn-faced soldier to a final battle—in a righteous march."

The sound of a pained call twisted Sinclair from the window, Eira rising, the two of them walking to the kitchen to attend a child in need. Two mothers, sharing the same nudge to womb in wanting their children home safe, once more.

CHAPTER EIGHTEEN

OUTSKIRTS OF PHILADELPHIA

LATE SUMMER, 1774

The building where the secretive group were to meet had been successfully infiltrated, with supplies carried in that Harold had requested two months earlier, by a coded note sent from England to a go-between in Philadelphia, handed on to the veteran, along with a large purse for their acquisition. The items, secured in a closed off storage area that ran along the back of a large, open room, had been carefully lowered through a small trapdoor in its floor that opened to a cavernous rock-lined room below. The shelves in the upper section held cases of wine, silverware and serving dishes packed in cloth covered crates, along with other items needed to serve dozens of guests attending social functions.

Harold moved a heavy chair with wide arms into place, leaving it to one side of the access door cut into the floor. He used a hammer to drive several spikes through the legs, securing it in position. Then he drilled two small holes through the floorboards to the room below, providing ample room for the poke of a thin metal rod that had been included in the list of supplies. The three men who'd helped Harold roll in, then lower several large kegs and a dozens of sturdy canvas bags through the narrow opening, were released to make their way back to where they'd come from. Two small carts, used to haul the supplies from the ramshackle barn behind the burnt out farmhouse, had been moved to the edge of the small town. Followed by a careful sweep of brooms, removing evidence of wheel marks and boot prints in the dirt walkway leading up to the hallway door from the side of road.

The former soldier had hung back a moment as his two sons completed the tasks. "You are not coming with us." It was a quiet, solemn faced statement of fact. "I could see it in your eyes when we first met up. I will not ask you why. Your reasons—are your own."

Harold didn't try to speak, just reached out and touched the man on his shoulder, seeing in his sons the men his own son might one day grow to be, in time. He handed him a leather bag, heavy with the weight of gold coins. The man took them, judging the heft with narrowed eyes, looking at Harold.

"Are you daft? We've been paid, and more than was agreed. This is —a lifetime and more of wealth earned, for little enough effort."

"I would ask you to use some portion of it to purchase a small fishing vessel, capable of seeking out a hold-full of cod pulled from northern seas. You will find one suitable in any of several small ports just north of Boston. Make certain you hire on a captain with experience, and crew—with your choice made of the men. The ship to be renamed—the Neewa." Harold spelled out the name, waiting for the man to nod. "Make short voyages to sea and back, checking on its worthiness for a longer voyage, made under threat of rough weather. It will be worth the monies spent, as you'll have the ownership of it. A seed, if you will, leading to a handful of such ships, with money earned on the Grand Banks, after your return."

"From where? What is to be my part of your plan—regarding your proposed use of said ship?"

"A man, down on his luck and in need of employment, will make himself known to you. His name—Ayden. You will treat him same as any other with no scut work or harsh command spared him. Although I understand he might be put to good use down in galley stores."

The man nodded again, then grinned, accepting the sudden change in both his and his two son's future. He stuck out his hand, a single shake sealing the arrangement made. Then he was off, his steps a bit lighter as he did so, despite the additional weight carried as he slipped into the night.

Harold used the time between dismissal of the men and impending arrival of those he'd come in search of to make final preparations, finishing just before dawn. Once completed, he took a walk outside, staying in the shadows. He followed the outer walls, finding a small well alongside one side of the hall. It was located several paces from a small side door that opened into the large hall's dining area. He used a ladle, hanging from a nail, to pull a cup of sweet water to his lips from a bucket lowered and raised, the water at a level two body lengths below the opening.

A slope led away to a small marsh below, a thin sliver of moon revealing a hint of still water reflecting between thick tufts of alder and tall rushes, sprinkled about with rafts of ducks in quiet mutter. A tranquil scene, he thought, as he went back inside and lugged a case of wine from the storage room, setting it down on a long shelf in the main hall just beyond the large entry door.

Harold placed a dozen bottles of wine in a row atop the lower shelf, wiping dust from their necks with his sleeve. The other tables in the room were left topped with wooden chests containing boxed silverware and several crates of dishware. A slight risk, he thought, if the man he'd seen standing guard the night before was the first inside, but one he needed to assume, wanting the storage room left undisturbed for as long as possible. Once he'd finished setting up, he made his way inside the confined space, wedging the door shut then sitting in the large chair, his feet stretched out, hands in his lap, his mood serene.

Harold sighed, knowing he was where he needed to be, ready to do what was required. Then he touched his father's carved pipe, secured in his coat pocket, ready for one last fill of its smoke-stained briarwood bowl. He pulled a flint from his pocket, setting it down beside a candle, near to hand. He stared at it, ready to light it when needed to fire the fragrant leaf he'd already tucked in the bowl of the pipe, with several pulls of air to glow the bowl. Turned into the perfect foil to thwart the well-laid plans of men who would be seated in the hall in close gather. Then he settled in, ready to wait out the day through to dusk, when the secretive cabal would return to the hall, under the watchful eye of a man he was most eager to make the acquaintance of. Aware, in his heart of hearts that he would be a man with no name. Middle-aged. Tall. Thin. With a web of scars on cheek and neck.

⸙⸙⸙

George made shame-filled approach to Nathan, hat in hand, eyes lowered in embarrassment for his behavior the night before.

"I was in a boorish mood last night and need to make my heartfelt apologies. Which I will do now, in private, and again, once we are assembled in full. You are worthy of my respect and deserving of my support. Your council on how best to move forward, made with compelling insight, and a willingness to go against what must be done to secure our mutual investments—cold-hearted as those steps are to be, is why you are a man we've come to count on—these past few years."

Nathan nodded, accepting the large man's words as sincere, knowing they were offered in some measure of fear, with the unnamed man in over-watch, as ever, hovering in the doorway, ready to provide deadly response to any outward treat, should need arise. "Think nothing of it my friend, in all things equestrian. We are well met and hale in our partnership, as always. My ego is of sufficient size to stand a bit of ribald humor at its expense."

A host of men began making their way straight to where a fine array of wine had been arranged by several servers arriving early to prepare for their guest's great thirst. Nathan joined them, raising his glass to shouts of acclamation aimed in his direction. He smiled, satisfied at having gained the trust of the company of like-minded men, though he felt a small quiver of uneasiness from something in the air he could not identify.

Nathan made a call to order now that all members had arrived and availed themselves of refreshment. He ushered the crowd into a small meeting room where privacy would be assured, several matters of serious consequence needing to be discussed, then voted on. Potential issues in the plan having come to light, in need of pointed solutions, found. Both here in the colonies and back in England, reaching all the way into the heart of Scotland's southern realm.

He faced the gathered men, taking a moment to settle his emotions, then began to speak. "We are met this day—to discuss and give our yea or nay to the next phase of our plan. One ripe with potential to produce substantial financial returns for our persuasive efforts—along with a measure of substantial investments made to date." Nathan paused, eying George who was standing by the back wall, arms on his chest. He received a nod of the large man's head, and continued, his tone sober. "There is another matter needing your input—to follow. Approval sought for recovery of information with potential for disturbing the—the sensibilities of friends in high places—men vital to our cause."

The assembled group began to murmur amongst themselves as they contemplated the last part of Nathan's opening address, several turning to look at a man dressed in resplendent clothing, overflowing the confines of a chair placed to one side of the speaker's lectern. Alfred tilted his head, acknowledging them, then returned to a study of his fingernails as his stomach rumbled, result of a bit too much wine and not enough food. He was looking forward to the meal to be delivered from the two inns by a small army of servers with platters piled high, entering the hall under the watchful eyes of their chief of security. The thin man vigilant and deadly, responsible for directing acts of retribution ordered, punishing those seeking to interfere with a plan put in place decades ago.

Nathan continued running through various permutations of the plan, listing the options for an immediate response to activities likely to unfold in Boston, and beyond. A thorough list of responsibilities for each man present spelled out, based on this reaction made if that event were to occur. Once finished, he closed the meeting book, a plain leather-bound volume with a list of names, signed in red. "Are there any calls for changes to be made to our portion of the plan, for or against?" No one raised a voice or hand. "Then we are agreed. The publications will be made and distributed within the week, ahead."

Nathan paused, needing another moment to steel himself before moving on.

"We have—another subject in need of a vote. Hard work, indeed—though deemed necessary to promote and protect our cause." Alfred sniffed, catching Nathan's ear, along with another nod of support from George, his approval given before the meeting had begun, while still sober. A state he had remained in, as if in regard of the seriousness of what must come next.

"We are in peril of being exposed, in part, by pages of a document covered with names, dates of clandestine meetings, transfer of monies in and out of commercial and government accounts, and the like. Details that would be—difficult to explain away with words in print, or while standing before a magistrate, should it go so far—which it will not, I can assure you. Steps are already in place to alleviate the immediacy of the threat. Others—in readiness to prevent rise of another. Requiring—a purge of sorts. Repugnant, in consideration by those with weaker resolve. Any of those wishing to leave until we are finished in our discussion of it, are invited to make their leave to the outer chamber."

Several men stood and departed, willing to drink the gander's sauce, but having no taste for its meat. Once they had cleared the room, Nathan began laying out the details of a plan intended to eliminate the uncle of a man who was as close to him as if family. As well the man himself, ensuring recovery of the document described to select members of the cabal by the personal valet of William Pitt.

⚜ ⚜ ⚜

The clock announced the midnight hour with twelve precise strikes of hammer on bell, then resumed its steady cadence of tick and tock. The wind in Bristol was in a frenzied whip, the shutters thudding against the thick stone walls of Thomas's small manor. He watched as the flickering light from coals in the fireplace brightened, air moving with a hushed sigh through the small salon.

Thomas was sitting in a huddled perch in an overstuffed chair, his legs wrapped in a thick wool blanket, feeling the cold despite the heat from the flames. A sound from the kitchen caught his attention, his hands clutching at his lap, sliding beneath the concealing layer of woven cloth, heart leaping to his throat. His nerves were in flux, his emotions bordering on an uneasy fear, as if a fat rodent in a room full of hungry cats. His wife, still weak from a recent illness, was being attended to by a full-time housekeeper, the rest of the household staff let go of. No longer any need for preparation of parties or dinners, their social life let to fade, with Thomas pulling back from any association with men involved in the cut-throat world of commerce.

Thomas leaned forward, reaching for his cane, intending to go and make certain the kitchen door was secured. Aware such things had been let slip in the past few months, his mind wandering now and then. A hand reached out, pressing him back into the chair.

"Your wife?" The voice was barely a whisper.

Thomas swallowed, his eyes gleaming, his voice trembling. "I knew —knew you would come."

"Upstairs, I would imagine." The man knelt in front of Thomas, his face revealed, without scars, Thomas's eyes narrowing in confusion.

"You are not who I—was expecting. Another man, with many-"

The man reached out, squeezing the older man's cheeks between fingers carved from stone. "She is upstairs—your wife?"

Thomas forced a nod, his face released. The man nodded, a shadow slipping past him moving toward the stairway, as if dark water made to flow in reverse as he climbed the stairway. Thomas closed his eyes and made a final farewell to the woman he'd married and made three children with, with twice that number of grandchildren now added. His eyes widened in thought of any actions taken in their regard.

"You saw me burn the papers. I made certain of it."

"Papers burnt are not necessarily papers in print—with other copies made. We know there are more than one set. Your nephew in hold of one or more, no doubt."

"Never! I was the one who did the research. Me, alone. He bade me burn them, which I did, realizing what had been stumbled on. Years have passed since then, with no mention ever made of the information gleaned. I swear it!"

The man returned from his upstairs visit, knife in hand, the blade dripping blood, the housekeeper behind, a grim look on her face. He came over, the honed blade held out, waiting for a signal to begin his work of finding out the truth, one slice at a time.

"There—in the cabinet. A false panel inside. The other copies are there." Thomas's voice faltered, his body slumping forward, head angled down. The kneeling man reached out and lifted him back upright, gripping his thinning hair. A click of a hammer being cocked widened his eyes, a shot ringing out, the ball exiting through the top of the older man's head, a jagged hole gouged through the center of the man's clutched hand.

It was early evening. The sound of voices in a muted muttering of words and laughter vibrated the thick storage room door as the gathered host had made a rapid vote before disbanding. Regathered in a throng around tables laden with food in plenty, filling their plates, the servers sent away before the meeting had begun. The wine was in full and copious flow, eventually requiring resupply. A chore performed by the man with no name, happily so, his wallet stuffed with promissory notes drawn on the Bank of England under an assumed name.

He pushed open the storeroom door and stepped inside, stopping as he noted the man in the chair a few paces away, a pistol in his lap, finger on the trigger, the hammer at half-cock. His eyes went wide as his mind made a quick association with who he was staring at. "You— cannot be here." His confusion turned into a confident smile, one hand outstretched, waving to draw the man's attention while his other hand slipped behind him, fingers on the handle of a small caliber pistol tucked in his belt. "And yet—here you are, with promise of a large purse earned for so little time spent in search of you."

Harold shrugged. "You have placed the cart to the fore of the horse, my adversary in common, seeing we have unfinished business to conclude. The untimely death of my father, for one—at your hands. It would seem a place for the start of our conversation, and not its end." Harold held the pistol out, angled up, aiming at the other man's chest.

"You are as described by a dying man. Every detail—clearly etched in my mind. Only your name left in the shadows, still. But of no real concern. Your death is enough for me." Harold nodded. "The door pressed fully shut if you will. I promise you opportunity of a fair chance given for you to retain hold on your life—once we've finished our discussion."

Harold waited until the other man leaned back, forcing the door closed, then he reached in his pocket with one hand and pulled out his father's pipe, clamping it between his teeth. He lifted a small candle from the arm of the chair that he'd sparked into life when the hall had begun to fill with people. He held it to the bowl, bringing it to a red glow, setting the candle down beside him on the floor.

"One has to be careful—the wood dry. Would not want it to catch fire. A fine building such as this—gone to ashes."

The unnamed man stared, his fingers grasping the handle of his pistol, ready for a moment of distraction to pull it out and fire. "You have my attention—and curiosity. Would you be willing to oblige my asking a question or two?" He received a nod in reply and eased his stance. "How did you find this place?"

Harold smiled, never once taking his eyes off the hired assassin. "With the assistance of friends—in low places."

"Letting you know as to the coming and goings of the men gathered outside, no doubt."

"Your mistake, that. Both in regularity of schedule and loyalty to the locale."

The man nodded. "Agreed. Though I was constant in my warnings against such a thing."

"Their mistake, paying out for services poorly performed. In your not being able to convince them of potential threat—or force an agreement to use of alternate sites."

The thin man didn't not answer, his eyes as cold as those of a snake contemplating how to get its prey headfirst into its mouth. "Your plan is to kill me. Then what? Reload your piece a dozen times and more, hoping those—" He tossed his head back slightly, "Buffoons stay their flight so you can eradicate their little club?"

"No. Only one shot needed. You—the primary target. Now make

good your next question, as our friends outside will soon grow restless in their thirst."

"How did your father—while under my careful watch, his ribs broken, death hovering on the edge of each rasping breath—how did he—" The man grinned. "In his pocket. His hand. No doubt writing you a note. It must have been. The only way—with myself making sure to ease his pain before taking my leave."

Harold nodded, his eyes cold, wondering when the man would make his move and bring out the pistol from behind him, knowing he would be carrying one there. He altered his breathing, staying relaxed, trusting his battle-hardened instincts to let him know when to act, no sign of such an action in the man's eyes, yet.

The unnamed man nodded. "You have the floor—and the weapon. Your move—if we are still in agreement of fair play—not that I have or would ever offer the same in return. No morals, see. Only greed and skill—with one honing the other to a razor's—"

The man's reach for his pistol was a blur. Harold lifting, bringing to full cock, and aiming before the man could get his own pulled around. The barrel of Harold's pistol a dark hole centered directly between the man's light-colored eyes, causing him to lower his own, letting it hang at his side. Awareness on his face of having lost. Harold, pipe still locked between his teeth, drew in a deep breath, bringing the bowl back to full glow. He reached up, removing it, holding it below the arm of the chair, a smile on his lips.

"You still have an opportunity to earn your money. To avoid what will be a bonny blow to come." A thin line of smoke rose from the side of chair, creating a sparking trail as it reached the floor and began to creep across the floor, chewing up a length of fuse running to the edge of the closed basement door. "Time enough to decide if my life is worth more to you than those of your owners, gathered just outside the door. A decision you must make quickly. A single shot to be made. Me, or the fuse—connected to four large kegs of powder, with bags of lead balls piled atop, just beneath the floorboards out there." Harold pulled the trigger of his pistol, the clack of flint to metal striker producing no shot, the gun neither primed nor loaded.

The unnamed man glanced at the spit of sparks as the fuse burned closer to the sealed opening. He aimed at it as Harold rose from the chair, rushing forward. The ball fired, striking the floor just ahead of the smoke, a spray of wood splinters severing the fuse, preventing an explosion. The man's arm was caught and pulled, tossing him through the air, crashing against the spiked legs of the chair, his ribs cracking when it refused to slide away from point of impact.

Harold looked at him as he reached the door/ "Two fuses, my unnamed friend — not one. Say hello to the Devil when you meet him." Harold opened the storeroom door, passing between the assembled men as he dashed toward the side exit, passing George, sitting at a table, looking up in shock, his mouth full of food with a large glass of wine in his meaty hand. Nathan, sitting beside a short, obese man in white clothing, reacted in surprise, his eyes going wide, none of them capable of movement, rooted in place by his sudden and unexpected appearance. Nathan quickly recovered, giving Harold a slow nod of understanding, his head bowing in recognition of what was about to transpire.

Harold was quickly out the door, slamming it shut behind him as he ran over and threw himself feet first into the small well, hands clasped to the rope of the bucket, having lowered it earlier in the day, submerged to his chin as the eruption occurred, a thump of vibration coming through the walls of the well, several stones knocked loose from above, falling past his head. The cold water drove a gasp of air from his lungs, the water shivering with ripples as rocks continued to tumble in from the shattered edge of the well, followed by the pattering sounds of pieces of wood and torn bodies of men falling back to the ground.

Harold gathered himself and climbed out of the narrow opening, the stink of gunpowder and scent of viscera greeting him in a viscous drift. There was no sound of gasps of pain or dying breaths from anyone left alive after the massive explosion. Harold the sole survivor, due to the sheltered confines of the well. He turned away, his mind numbed by shock, knowing he'd caused his friends deaths, looking up as a flight of startled ducks winged past, shocked into nocturnal flight by the flash of light and rumble of noise.

A hand clutched his ankle, fingers in an iron grip, the unnamed man lying on the ground, his body rent by lead shot, one arm missing, the bones exposed. He mouthed words from bloodless lips on a face white with shock. Harold knelt beside his broken body, listening to his final words.

"My name — I owe it — to you."

Harold shook his head. "I prefer you remain a stranger. And though you do not deserve the gift I am about to provide, it is on my father's behalf I grant it." He reached down, covering the man's nose and mouth, holding his hand in place for a count of four hundred and twenty of his own heartbeats. A soldier's gift, given those, friend or foe, left writhing in great pain while hovering at the threshold of death's door. Then he stood up, ignoring the smoking hole in the ground with lumps of bodies strewn about the edges, missing arms, legs and heads. He stumbled downhill, heading for the marsh to hide his trail, feeling no remorse for the deaths of Nathan and George. One, a printer turned profiteer. The other, a brother turned betrayer of oaths sworn, then set aside.

CHAPTER NINETEEN
HIGHLAND CROFT
AUTUMN, 1774

The manor had been stuffed full of people. Husbands, and wives with children in tow as Thomas's daughter's and extended family had come to take the air, invited by Eira on learning of their father and mother's deaths in the fire that burned their home to the ground. Their bodies gone to ashes in the heat, buried beneath the collapse of stone walls.

The change in locale after the funerals had been a change for the better with Eira's grand nieces and nephews in constant roam about the hills. Sinclair's children had been kept busy providing constant oversight with Marion taking the lead, her air of authority not to be questioned. The innovative games she came up with presented constant challenges to all. Meghan, encouraged by her sister to stay out of the way, had taken to spending more of her free time with Aaron, teaching the older children to use snares. Aaron taking her on short hunts in between, the smaller bow, deadly in her capable hands, educating her in the art of approach, stalk, and kill from beneath ghillie suits, the strips of tattered cloth adjusted in color to match field grass or highland brush.

Aaron was near a man now, full-grown in height, with shoulders and legs heavily muscled. Amenable in being tasked to made frequent forays to the croft and mill spring with low-land relatives in trail, young and old, eager to help gather wild grain growing in out of way places, threshing it, leaving it to dry it in the sun, before grinding it into flour. Dark-skinned loaves of bread the result, flavored with fresh churned butter, locally procured preserves, and honey. Or used to sop up gravy dipped from a thick rabbit or sage grouse stew.

All had enjoyed the two-month retreat, their faces streaming with tears when it came time to leave, with promises made of a return for Christmas celebration, if winter weather would allow. The manor house was left feeling empty, its windows open, letting a sigh of unseasonably warm fall air to sigh through the hushed interior. Closed up tight again against the chill of night, the repaired shutters ready for a sudden gale to pound upon the walls, warning of what was to come.

Sinclair had been able to forget, if only for an hour here or there, the loss of her husband. His whereabouts unknown, with no letter home in the three months since his departure. The thought of him lost or injured, or worse, was a deep wound healed during the day by the work of keeping home and hearth together while in constant move. Torn open each night as she lay in their bed, recalling the angry words used in sending him away. Left to cope on her own, Eira in a steady fade. Her once bright-blue eyes now softened in hue, with hands no longer capable of kneading dough. Though she's still had strength enough to hold books while Thomas's youngest grandchildren had perched in her lap, eyes wide in fascination at the stories she read to them, her Scottish accent a pleasant diversion.

"Gran Uncle Shaun is here!" Meghan tossed the comment at her mother as she exited the manor, leaping down the front steps, hair bound up by a blue ribbon, her hands holding down the sides of the dress she had on. She was always excited to see the older man, his angular body in a lofty pose on horseback, reminding her of her father, familiar to her eyes.

Shaun pulled up, a flash of pain crossing his face as he slid from his horse, a black steed of great height and breadth, standing several hands above those more commonly seen in the high places. "There's my lassie, with sunset hair and sun-kissed eyes!" He closed the distance to Meghan, a slight limp in his once firm gait, his hair gone over to silver with threads of reddish-brown. As handsome as ever, his eyes still as blue.

Meghan gave him a quick hug, then stepped back, looking up at him. "You are to stay?"

"Aye—if your mother will allow it. The ride is—a bit longer each time, made." He watched as Meghan grabbed the reins of his mount, leading it away to the stable, the large beast whickering as it nuzzled her shoulder. Sinclair came up, giving him a kiss on his cheek. Shaun looked around, his eyes searching for Aaron, the lad just turned fifteen years of age, a man of the clan in full. "Your son—is he not about?"

"Gone to the mountains, up beyond the croft. Spotted stags there, a few days ago. Hunting for meat, not horns, as I reminded him 'fore he left." Sinclair laughed, the sound twisting Shaun's heart. "Had to threaten to tie Meghan up and toss her in the cellar, lest she sneak out and try to join him there."

"Perhaps I should go up and check on him?"

"He'll be fine—and you're saddle worn, in need of a drink and hot meal. And the weather's drawn down nigh to the ground, with rain in prospect. Better to stay the night and next day or so here with us. Our Aaron knows the high places and has sense enough to bend his course back to the croft when called for. I've lost my worries on that account, though I do hold a concern as to his lack of interest in chase of—fairer game."

Shaun grinned. "I will make certain to bring a bonny lass with me next time I visit. A gran niece—with no blood tie to your own. An image of you, or close enow—the boy not likely to be turned from the mountains by any less a woman than was his own Da."

Sinclair rose to her toes and kissed Shaun on his other cheek, noting his skin was red from the ride up, the wind in steady rise with the temperature starting to drop. When she stepped back, she lowered her voice, hands clasped in front of her stomach. "Still no word?"

"Nae." Shaun shook his head. "I've eyes and ears at all the ports. No sign of him—yet." The look in Sinclair's eyes tugged at his heart. "There has been a rumor going 'round." He paused, feeling her stare. "Of an event in Pennsylvania colony, though no telling by whose hand it was instigated. The locals eagerly spreading the story, carried back here on the wind in ship's sails, though my inquiries to the local publishing houses have been ignored. Still—" Shaun hesitated, looking down at the ground, a shiver trembling through him as a whip of wind tugged at his cloak.

Sinclair tightened her voice. "I swear I will find Meghan's bow and spit you if you don't reveal—"

Shaun raised his hands in surrender. "An explosion—in a small town outside the port of Philadelphia. A building left in ruins. A dozen men or more dead. Powder and shot, made to erupt from below with no damage done to any townspeople. Only those in attend. All gone to meet their maker." He paused, lowering his eyes slightly, continuing before she could demand more from him. "Your friend—Harold's own brother, or brother in arms, I suppose—among the men who were lost."

Sinclair blanched, her face going white as the blood drained away. She felt her knees buckle, Shaun reaching to hold her up, his arm firm about her waist, waiting until she recovered. Sinclair shook her head, the tie in hair had come undone, her hair twisted by the wind. "It could not have been—could not have anything to do with Harold. He would never—never allow any harm to come to George."

"Nae. I had that sense of it myself. Most likely tales spun from tales, shared around glasses of spirits by bored men."

Sinclair recovered her senses. "Come in and warm yourself. Your hands are like ice. There's tea and fresh bread from Gran Ma's mill—fresh ground."

"The lad got it working?"

"Aye. Replaced the wooden gears, having to craft new ones by hand, taking him a week of steady effort.: She paused. "His mind a grand tool, as are his hands."

Shaun walked beside Sinclair as they made their way back to the manor, Meghan slipping past them on the path, racing to the manor. As they moved toward it, Shaun compared the length of Sinclair's stride to his own and thought, as he had since the first time he'd laid eyes on her, of how much a beauty she was, still. Her will as much an asset as were her looks. More, he added, knowing the idea of her in his arms had never been in play, aware he would never be a good match for her.

He frowned, worried for her future should his nephew fail to turn up. The event as described being exactly the thing Harold had been planning to do, in thoughts shared freely with himself. His nephew aware he'd never interfere with an Englander going about the killing of his own kind.

When the two of them finally reached the manor door, a loud squeal of delight cut through the air as Marion dashed down the steps and leaped into Shaun's arms for his hug and a circled dance as his hip ground in protest, his will rising up, denying the pain.

Aaron held the arrow at full draw, a strain on his forearm until his fingers relaxed, the string let slip with nary a sound as the honed-edged arrowhead buried itself behind a young bull's shoulder, the fletched feathers from a red grouse disappearing as the point drove through and out the other side. The stag's lungs cleaved through, with blood pouring from its mouth as it tried to bleat in alarm. The other red deer made a swift departure, their stricken comrade left behind, its knees bending as it fell forward, head stretched out, breath easing to a stop as its heart grew still.

The successful huntsman rose from beneath his cover, a shrug of one shoulder releasing the cloak. His body was bare beneath a light mist in the air, having made the stalk the way his forefathers had done it. Extra clothing a detriment to silent movement, increasing chance of detection from rustle of cloth or its scent released. He'd rubbed himself near raw with coarse grass and dirt, fully committed to a fair chase to be made. Proud, as he stared at the animal, that he'd once again made himself part of the land, inside and out.

Aaron went over and knelt on the icy ground, gazing at the open eyes of the fat animal, knowing it would be three trips down and back to get the meat hung in the stable at the croft. His thick legged mountain horse could make the haul from there to the manor below. He considered using it now, rejecting the thought, taking note of small rocks dotting the ground. No need to risk a broken leg to the trusting animal, he thought to himself, with enough death dealt for one day. He reached down and tugged a twist of grass free from the earth, placing it in the deer's open mouth. "I thank ye, brother deer—for your life, fairly given. Fairly taken—in turn." Then he grasped the small rack, rolling the animal onto its side, reaching for his knife.

A group of fourteen men in dark clothing made a slow climb along a well-traveled path. They'd made their leave, two days before, from Bargrennan, a large inland town at the pinched head of a narrow, coastal strait. They'd arrived there a week earlier, showing up in small groups of two and three, after making landfall at a small port named Wigtown, known as a smuggler's haven with few questions asked of strangers met. Their leader, a man of solid build and medium height, stared up at the rise of land, his face a stony mask.

They were in search of a known man, one who'd thwarted plans for a well-financed incite of an uprising in Boston, capitol city of the Massachusetts colony. A man rumored to have been in the company of a handful of other men, unknown themselves, all making a quick dissolve into a wilderness retreat, their trail gone cold.

"I feel eyes—in the hills about." A whip-thin man, standing close behind, spoke out while removing a worn, tri-cornered hat. He closed one nostril with a finger, clearing his nose with a snort. Repeating the maneuver for the other one. The larger man pursed his lips in disgust.

"You're too much a woman in worry. We're to find and finish one man, not an army. We've the weapons to see it through—and been half-paid to seeing it done."

"Still—the hills here-about are known to have eyes. Many a red-coat fool found their end while marching this very ground. My father —one of 'em."

"You're to shut your mouth and lean into the climb, same as the others. Or I'll have your heart on the point of my dirk, taking your share of the payment, too."

The group of fourteen men continued toward the edge of a rise, each one feeling the same weight of observing eyes from above.

A rider came up from out of the shadows of the night, straight on to the door of the manor, his horse in a lather of white sweat. The one aboard, a young boy of fourteen summers, was near his end, his face white with cold, cloak and kilt soaked through. He slid from the saddle, falling into Shaun's arms who carried him inside, placing him in a chair in the kitchen, before going back outside to care for the horse. Sinclair and Eira tended to the boy with dry towels, his feet placed in a tub of hot water to soak, with warm broth slowly spooned into his mouth by Eira, the boy's hands near frozen through from his ride in the freezing rain.

"The daft fool will be lucky to escape with his life, out and about on a night such as this." Shaun was back from caring for the exhausted mount, knowing it might not survive the night. He was speaking in a low voice, pride for the lad dripping from each word, despite their hard edge.

Sinclair leaned in, her face a twist of anxiety. "Did he say anything to you, when you bore him inside? Was there anything said about—"

"Nae, lass. Another matter altogether—though it may have some relate to actions taken by your man."

Shaun pulled Sinclair out of the heat of the kitchen, the fireplace brought to a blaze. "We are in threat of having visitors arriving in our valley—from away. Hard men, over two handfuls in number. Careful to conceal themselves, this day passed, moving in close formation, staying well away from traveled roads, using local paths. Spotted by the lad, soon as they reached the first heights, below." He paused, rubbing one hand along the line of his jaw. "Near killing himself and horse to give us fair warning. Bloody fool! One of my own create— coming from a croft a long way from here."

"I should go and fetch Aaron. He'll be waiting the storm out at the croft house above."

"The lads a' right where he is. Time enow to gather my thoughts and see where those on the march are aimed for—whether pointed here, or some other holding in the valley below."

"Here." Sinclair clutched the cameo hanging beneath her dress. "I feel it—in my bones."

"Aye, child. I feel it too." Shaun cocked an ear, hearing the wind rise as the storm stiffened, promising two days or more of wilding weather with threat of floods at every crossing. He knew his options were limited and hung his head, staring at the floor. "We can send the boy back down to look them over in the morning. If he dinna come to a fever during the night."

"I'll go." Sinclair looked back into the kitchen, watching Eira using a fire-warmed towel to wipe the boy's chest, arms and legs, his wet clothes removed. "He's near dead from fatigue and exposure."

"It's to be him, or me, Sinclair. No other choice left us. You're needed here. Just pray the boy's lungs prove clear by morning—while we wait on your own boy's arrival."

❦❦❦

The wind was in a steady howl, unabated as the hours passed. Sinclair sitting up, keeping watch on the young man, his name Allyn, his face having found some color, his breathing clear. A soft voice from behind pulled her around. Marion, clad in a nightdress, a doll in her arm, her face wet with tears. "I went to find Meghan. I thought I heard father's footsteps outside my door. I was frightened."

"It's okay. Go and have her tuck you in. Now run—"

"Nae. She's gone. Gone off. To be with Aaron—heading up to the croft."

Sinclair reached out, taking Marion by her shoulders, her fingers squeezing in fear. "Are you certain?"

Marion twisted, trying to free herself. "Left a note." She held it out, Shaun having been roused by her voice, taking it from her as he came into the great room, reading it then looking at Sinclair. "She's been gone since just after I arrived. Before the rider came. Says she's gone to let Aaron know I'm here, taking an oiled cloth and food enough for two. Went by mare—the stocky young gray."

Sinclair pulled Marion in, giving her a hug, comforting her as she began to whine in a fearful complaint, her daughter's tearful words echoing her own feeling of dread.

The door of the croft house opened before Meghan drew near, Aaron standing in the doorway, hand on the handle, watching as she rode up, guided by the light of the lantern he held out to one side.

"Had a feeling you'd be showing up—eventually." Aaron stepped outside, taking the reins, helping his sister to dismount, her legs stiff from the chill air, her hair spilling out from beneath an oil-cloth cloak, her legs soaked through beneath the pants she had on, as was the head, neck and tail of the small mare, who let out a snort of displeasure, having been forced from its warm stall to make the steep ride through lowering clouds, turning over to a rain-soaked night. "Can ya walk?"

Meghan nodded, moving her feet in a slow shuffle, making her way inside the cramped hovel. Aaron removing his shirt and tossed it onto the small bed before leaving to lead the horse to the stable, warmed by the body heat of his large mount and the short-framed, stocky mountain horse. The three animals nickered greetings while he gave the mare a quick rubdown, checking its hooves for sign of embedded stones or splits in its hooves, the trail a mix of small rocks and shards of granite stones. After the mare was settled in, he ran through the wind-driven rain, closing on the front door of the croft. Once there, he hesitated, knocking in warning, knowing his sister would be changing into a set of his dry clothes. When given her okay to come inside, he yanked the door open, the heat of the fire, built to a blaze, beckoned his hands as he reached toward its warmth.

"You've no shirt on!" Meghan stared at her brother.

"Skin dries faster than linen—or wool." Aaron pointed to the table. "There's stew in the pot, still warm. You're welcome to it."

Meghan finished tying a wool blanket around her shoulders, her brother's shirt too large in the neck to adequately cover her shoulders and upper chest. She sat at the small table and jabbed a piece of a dried biscuit into a metal pot, chewing it with gusto, knowing Aaron had not been long back from his hunt. The meal in wait most likely his, and barely touched.

"I brought food." She eyed a pack on the floor, left near the stove. "Enow for us both." She started to take another bite, then stopped. "Gran Uncle Shaun is here. Or rather, there. Wanted to come let you know. And to help bring down your kill."

Aaron opened a small leather sack and removed two loaves of fresh bread, a wedge of cheese, and handful of dried herbs. His sister's voice was a mumble made round bites of fresh deer meat, half chewed. "Figured—you'd have—meat waiting here. Was right. It's so—oh my God. So good."

"Watch your language. The weather is in a murky brew enow without invoke of his righteous wrath." Aaron gave his sister a hard look. "You snuck out, no doubt leaving a note to cover for your misbehaving."

"I had the right to come."

"On what standing?"

"Out of concern for my brother! The only man left me."

Aaron softened his stance, seeing the hurt in his sister's blue eyes. "Don't be saying that. He'll be here. Soon."

"He's dead, Aaron. I can feel it—in here." She raised a hand and clutched her chest, a cameo in her hand, gift from their Da, one made for each daughter. "And no hope in wishing it otherwise—nothing to change what is." Meghan tried to put on a brave face, failing, her lips trembling, tears in her eyes. "Best we get to figuring on how we're to cope, with him gone. Mother, Marion, and Gran Ma in need of us to care for them."

Aaron stepped closer, hands on the table, leaning down and looking his sister in the eyes. "Our mother is more than capable of what needs doing. Stronger than both of us together—and I won't hear anything different. Do ya ken, sister-mine? Answer me yes, or you'll be sleeping in the stable tonight."

Meghan lowered her eyes, sniffing from the cold ride and the heat within the small house, causing her nose to run. "Yes. I meant no real suggest otherwise. I just—" She lowered her head, tears dripping, carefully aimed to one side of the pot of stew Aaron had placed in front of her.

"Those false drops will work on Gran Uncle Shaun—but not me. So, button up and bear the load. You'll be needing to go tend your mount, once you finish with the half-a-deer you've just eaten. And you'll be leaving my shirt here, my back turned to you when you leave and on your return. Because—"

Meghan grinned. "Skin dries quicker than linen. Or wool."

Aaron nodded, wondering if she was right. If what he'd seen in his vision had been but a false wish, and not seen true, with his father a ghost, returning to haunt the wee croft house. "Aye, dear sister-mine— or wool."

CHAPTER TWENTY

HIGHLAND MANOR APPROACH

LATE AUTUMN, 1774

A thick scud of cloud raced by overhead, curling around the slopes of steep hills in a steady rise from the lowlands, left far below. The wind had increased, with harsh slaps to the face, edges of loose clothing made to flutter, bodies cold from the damp air, without sting of rain, for now. Men, in a twisted column, were making their way uphill in a grumble of hunger, matched with angry murmuring of voices, their fingers counting the coins already in pocket, measuring the effort needed to continue the climb against potential risk of making a stand and calling it quit. Each, with eyes on the next in line, wondering how many might be persuaded to join in a mutiny.

The leader of the group could feel the points of the men's eyes. Knives in his back, letting him know something would be required of him and soon, to beat back the weaker men, securing his position as titular head of the pack of wolves, disguised as men. He called a halt, turning around with pistol in hand, fully cocked, aiming it at the face of the man coming along behind. The sound of its discharge a thud of noise, felt in the dense air as much as heard. The man's eyes went wide in shock as he fell back, arms to the sides, left staring up at the sky, his expression frozen in place, as if searching for the reason why.

"He just made suggest that we should abandon our quest to find the man we have been hired to remove. Having made it before, during the night. Hopeful he would find support from others who were of a like mind." Another pistol appeared, halfcocked, but pointed in the general direction of the rest of the men, prepared to dispel another round should anyone waver and run. "Are there any among you—with disagreement in finishing what we've already been half paid to do? Knowing our names will be added to a list of dead men left standing, waiting for a visit by unnamed men should we fail to complete our mission?"

No one moved as much as an inch, the smoking crater punched through the dead man's forehead indicating their leader's quality of aim, and willingness to pull a trigger, again.

The man nodded. "Good. Then we will move onward, my friends— into the scut and rain above. Sooner into the fight—the sooner done, I always say."

⸙ ⸙ ⸙

Allyn's breathing had eased, coming clear with no sound of a rattle, his color back on the cusp of rose-pink cheeks. Along with improved appetite: soup, fried cakes, and a rasher of cured pork in the process of being inhaled. Marion was kept busy, bringing him food and warm tea, while regaling him with a litany of questions asked, his answers cut off as she moved on to a new topic.

Shaun let out a sigh, knowing a bridge had been crossed, one the lad could easily have fallen from, if failing to reach the haven of the manor with the horse coming up lame. A frown crossed his sleep-deprived face as he considered the number of men heading their way, and how few they were in hoping to repel what promised to be deadly incursion. He cursed beneath his breath, heading outside to look at the sky, murky, with bands of rain continuing to fall in the valley approach below. He was angry at his nephew, knowing the approaching group was most likely due to his having meddled in the affairs of men with no conscience. Money their only goal, and the power it provided them.

He measuring the force of the wind, listening to the lowing of cows in the upper pasture where near a hundred head had been assembled for fattening up on sweet hay and a mix of grains, to be driven to markets down below in a fortnight. His hands tightened into fists as he gauged the likelihood of this being his final fight. Not in fear, his fate foretold years earlier, his death described with blood on his hands, and lips, dying on his feet. He didn't mind the ending, like so many of his kin had faced in struggles against the English throughout a dozen generations and more. But the thought of what would happen to the women inside the manor, young and old, curdled his stomach, determined if the end seemed nigh, he would take their lives himself, saving them from the worst of what men could do, when released to their inner beasts.

He felt Sinclair's approach, scenting the faint floral scent of her hair as she stopped alongside him, silent, waiting for him to answer the question poised on her beautiful lips. His answer ready. That it would be two days, at best, before any hope of reaching and returning with men enough to even the odds. Dozens of crossings in flood, too great a risk in sending the lad across, eager as he would be to go. Aaron, and his refugee sister, locked away at the croft house while a raging wind forced them to hunker down, for this day at least. With no reason to hurry down, Meghan having left before Allyn arrived, unable to inform her brother of the danger to those below.

"I should go—and try to reach them." Sinclair was in wet-weather gear, a shroud about her shoulders and face. Her hair was a thick spring of black curls, lying in glistening twists alongside her pale cheeks. Her eyes found his, with the firm express of a mother's will to brave all to get her children home. Shaun ached at the sight of her, feeling her strength of will enveloping him, joined with his own, seeing in her a woman in the full bloom of life.

"Try you might—and fail. The climb impossible to make in such as this. Leaving me one less here, to do what must be done." He took Sinclair by her elbow, leading her into the lee side of the manor where the sound from the red-haired beasts with needle sharp horns rumbled through the sodden air. He stopped, turning to look into the valley, his eyes narrowed in thought then looked at Sinclair, a thin smile on his lips, a glimmer of hope in his eyes. "We need to move the stock—from the rounding enclosure to the approach below. The whole lot of them. Now!"

"Now?" Sinclair stared back, her expression swinging from questioning his sanity to trying to understand his change of mood. She glanced at the doorway, making certain Marion and Eira were nowhere around, then lowered her voice. "To do what? Is it to do with the men in approach?"

Shaun nodded, taking her hands, squeezing, feeling the warmth of her skin. "It'll be left to us to make the stand. Allyn, you—and I."

"Three—against how many? He said there were a dozen or more."

"Against five, if we wait on them here. Better odds if we meet them in the Pinch."

Sinclair narrowed her eyes. "The stock." She dared a smile, seeing in her mind's eyes the shaggy beasts, pouring through the gorge. Reaching the Pinch, a narrow pass between steep rock walls running over two hundred paces, ending in a snaking path barely three paces wide, filled with sharp twists and turns. "You mean to catch them at the Squeeze."

"Aye, lass—with a hundred more added to our number, against. Armed with horn and hoof, and hunger in their bellies, too." Shaun gave her a small bow of head, his love for her as clear as he'd ever dared to show. "If you will allow me the honor, Lady Sinclair of Manor Knutt—of inviting you to the dance, my dear."

She noted his look of affection, knowing how he felt, had always felt since their first introduction. A feeling she could imagine rising to meet, if she were truly left alone in a word without the man who'd crossed through a war-torn wilderness, then crossing an unforgiving ocean to find her, his eyes gazing at her with recognition and love, so many years ago.

"I should like that very much—kind sir."

Aaron woke to a shadowed room, the small window shuttered and barred. He eased out from beneath a thick wool blanket flung over the top of the small bed he'd shared fully clothed with Meghan during the night. He listened to the wind, noting it had fallen off to a soft howl against the corner posts. He got up and added a measure of wood to the stove: a slate box built around a metal door, opening the draft to heat a kettle and pan. One for brewing of tea, the other for reheat of fried cakes along with eggs, with dried herbs stirred in.

Meghan sat up, yawning, her hair in a tangle of gold-red tresses, their glow undiminished by the low light. "The storm—has passed."

"Nae. Only a lull. It will brew up again, half-morning on."

"Should we head back down, then—before?"

Aaron shrugged, his wide shoulders rising. "Are ya so ready to face the wrath of our dear mother—on account of your willful disobey?"

Meghan pursed her lips. "No."

"The whipping will nae be worse if delayed until later in the day. She knows you're here and safe, so she'll abide it a while longer. We'll break our fast and head home later if the weather clears. Or in the morn, should it remain in howl aboot our heads." Aaron listened to the sound of his sister's musical laughter. "Speaking of which, I'll go in fetch the pitchfork from the stable so you can comb your tangles."

Meghan stuck out her tongue, a soft smile on her face, adoring her brother for his calm spirit. His limitless love of family, and absolute kindness of spirit. She knew in her heart some lass somewhere was even now already in rise, waiting to be found by him. No doubt prac- ticing the feminine arts of beguile and attract, looking to steal his heart away. Taking him from her. From all of them, the thought glistening her eyes.

"Are you well, sister-mine?"

"Aye, my dear brother. Never been better—in ever and all my days."

"The fooking muck is in clog 'bout my sodding boots! With the mealy biscuits gone damp." A large man in black garb, a perfect match to his mood, straightened up, cleaning the mud from his boots on a tuft of coarse grass. "With a climb ahead promising little reward for the risk of a broken leg, or worse." He spat, his full lips parted between thick clumps of black hair on upper lip and cheeks, with an overly full beard matted by grime from the arduous trek made since leaving Bargrennan. He was paired with another man, the two of them sent on a side mission, ordered to check on a hide-away in the hills above the valley approach to their assigned destination. Their source of information having met them in the town below, passing on the lay of land, secret trails, and details about the manor and small croft with gristmill, tucked away in the hills above.

The other man was of a slighter build, with wide-set eyes in a face wearing signs of hard use. His expression was open as he gazed up at the heights, hidden beneath a blanket of clouds, seeing himself able to make a life there. "We are removed from having to face the demon and his minions at the manor. Spared from the murder and mayhem certain to follow, with the same pay all around. This climb being the easier road taken—if you ask me."

"Didn't."

"Noted." The smaller man shrugged, continuing to lead the way up the increased angle of the rise, its top almost close enough to reach out and touch, the clouds racing by, just overhead.

Shaun and Allyn, a child of his own issue, born to one of a dozen and more croft-wives spread throughout clan valleys, were on horseback, out in front of the herd of shaggy-haired cows, the animals protesting with a steady barrage of loud bellowing and tossing of their wide heads. Sinclair was in trail, keeping the beasts moving in a slow, steady march forward. Allyn had made a quick scout to a hidden lookout tucked alongside one wall of the Pinch, leaving his mount hidden as he crawled to the stone hide where generations of ancestors had lain in wait, eyes watching for English troops, or any other invaders intent on disturbing their highland home.

Once he'd seen the thin string of men approaching the narrow gorge, he'd waited until they were fully committed to the far end of the trap, then made a dash to the horse given him, urging it to full speed, racing to inform the man he knew as his gran uncle, that the trap was baited, ready to be sprung.

Shaun leaned over, getting the report, then he raised one hand, signaling Sinclair to stop. Allyn cantered over to the lead cow, calling to it in a soft song, lulling it to lower its head and begin cropping the grass alongside the narrow upper approach, his mount doing the same.

Sinclair came riding up, stopping beside Shaun, her eyebrows raised in question. He leaned back, trying to ease the ache in his back and lower legs. "We need them nearer our end than the other. With no way for them to climb free — the walls too sheer."

"What — what if we're wrong?" Sinclair had a pained look on her face. "What if they're just seeking —"

Shaun shook his head. "What do ya guts tell ya? Mine are singing a song of fire, blood, and worse things to come. Worse than ya can imagine." He shut his eyes, lowering his voice. "Far worse."

Sinclair took a deep breath, letting it out slowly, creating a trail of fog that slipped away through the cold air. "Mine as well, though of a — lesser note than yours." She glanced down into the gorge. "It would seem we have — little choice."

"The ordering of it lies on my shoulders, lass, not your'n. I have the lead and will make the decision plain when it comes time for it. So, don't fash yourself — and make certain to stay clear once it's over. I'll have the boy come back for you, telling him it's to protect you. Not that you'll be in any danger — but there are things no woman or young boy should ever see. Or man, neither — truth be told."

Shaun tugged his horse to one side, waving for the boy to circle half-way 'round, joining the two of them at the rear of the restless throng of long-haired beasts. Once he was in place, Shaun raised his voice and shouted the clan battle-cry, echoed by the boy. "I waed, I gore, ac anrhydedd. Boed i'n byrdwn fod yn wir. Bydd ein calonnau'n gryf. Ein buddugoliaeth, yn ogoneddus, yn ogystal â'n marwolaethau, wrth amddiffyn kith, perthynas — a Clan!"

Sinclair joined in, having heard the cry half-a-hundred times and more at family gatherings, her words in English, honoring her two adopted fathers and the one lying beneath a sentinel oak. "To blood, gore, and honor. May our thrust be true. Our hearts be strong. Our victory, glorious, as too our deaths, in defense of kith, kin—and Clan!"

They urged their horses forward, crowding the heels of a sea of red-coated animals, their bawls of anger filling the hills with a tidal wave of energy, moving ahead in a thundering rush.

☙☙☙

Aaron looked back, checking on his sisters pace, her longbow carried unstrung as their Da had taught him long ago, the lesson handed down. A quiver of arrows was strapped across her shoulder, his own in his hand with broadheads made for the killing of stags, with any small game found along the path to be Meghan's for the taking. He shook his head, wishing to have left his bow behind, bringing it with him to placate his imaginative sibling who wanted to emulate the folk tale of a man known as the Hood, and his lady faire. Their ghillie suits were slung across their backs in case of a need to do a low crawl to get close to rabbits, coming out to feed in the small meadows, just past the Gran Ma's Spring.

It had been Meghan's idea while they were at their morning meal, to go to Gran's Mill and grind grain enough from sealed casks left in store, milling up a bag of wheat flour as a gift to their mother, helping reduce, to some measure, the number of lashes to be administered.

She'd looked at Aaron, pleading with him. "Why won't you offer to do the striking? I'd rather feel your love in my pain, than her anger."

"Neither of our parents have ever laid a hand on any of us in anger. Only in firm attendance to our need for—physical guidance. You, more than Marion and myself, for certain. And only when richly deserved."

"Then I should be wealthier by far than the two of you, as if one. Always left standing in front of the mirror, looking back over my shoulder to see how well financed I am."

Aaron chuckled, cleaning their dishes with a rub of sand and rinse of spring water. "You do seem to draw their attention more than seems reasonable—though none have stepped forward claiming to have been born with that trait."

The bowl Meghan had just emptied of fare narrowly missed Aaron's head, leaving him with a wide grin on his face as he leaned down and picked it up.

⁂

A faint vibration through air and surface of the trail was the first indication of trouble, the eleven men remaining of the party moving in a weary line, steep ledges to either side concentrating the noise. The leader came to a stop, hands on his weapons, looking ahead, the narrow path impossible to climb out of.

"Thunder no doubt." His new second in command was standing at his side. The leader shook his head. "No. I think not. More the sound of riders, come to check on us, if we've been spotted. Passing through to the lowlands behind us, if not."

"Leaving us to do what?"

The leader turned and gave the man a wry grin. "Purses are where you find them. Coin cares not the hand that warmed it, previously. We'll form a line here, three abreast, those with pistols to the front. Men with knives ready to move in once we have them in a muddle of beasts in panic, loose reins in their hands."

The other man called the men forward, arranging them as directed. The front line knelt, the next one standing, with three men positioned to the sides, ready with knives in their hands, all with looks of violence in their eyes. The two men leaders moved to the rear, ready to pitch in where needed.

⁂

Sinclair had fallen back, her small-framed horse no match for the two stallions to either side of the heaving backs of stampeding animals in full stride. Their cries of frustration filled the gorge with a milling of grunts and moans, with large hooves pounding the ground. She watched as Shaun and Allyn leaned in toward the shaggy beasts, keeping the herd in a tight compress, sharp-tipped horns mere inches from their thighs. They waved their arms, voices tight with excitement.

It was a mood Sinclair could not share, aware, far too aware, of what was to happen next. She slowed her pace, aware she was no longer needed, the fate of the men on both sides left hanging in the balance.

A sharp turn of a final corner was made, whatever lay ahead hidden from Shaun's view by the heads of the leading cattle raising up, their bodies seeming to be slowed by some unseen blockage. He waved Allyn back, pointing to where they'd last seen Sinclair. The boy spun his mount about, knowing his duty, racing to gather her in and make for the highland field, Shaun to keep the pressure on, his voice calling out, inciting the herd as they charged ahead.

The leader swallowed his smile, prepared for the shock in the eyes of the approaching riders as they were met by a hail of lead. Instead, his own grew wide in disbelief at what came into view. As if a painting, each detail frozen in place. Moist, red noses and fear-laden brown eyes, tips of horns in a polished gleam, hooves in pose above the gorge floor, no sound falling into his stunned mind's ear, impossible for him to accept the fate about to befall his men. And him.

The moment passed, the mass of men swallowed by a sea of one hundred, one-ton panicked beasts in thrust, then leap, then slide. Handfuls going down in a rough tumble, others managing to fight their way clear, continuing their flight. The compressed knot of men was pressed beneath the heaving carpet, lives extinguished from jam of hoof, strike of horn, their flesh torn, bones crushed. No one left standing as the whirl of red haired animals flowed away, two dozen down in broken legged thrashing, bodies heaving as they tried to stand, falling again, their immense weight creating a thick paste of blood, viscera and splintered bone, all that remained of men who'd gone to meet their maker. Their stories having come to a rare, and relatively sudden end.

Shaun slipped from his saddle, reins in hand, the stallion ignoring the slaughter, starting a search for grass, its hopes soon dashed, none to be found. There were no cries of pain or calls for mercy from the men, unrecognizable, their clothing barely able to hold their shattered bodies together. Shaun stepped between several clumps of commingled corpses of cow and men. Animals, and lesser beasts he whispered to himself, for he knew them to be such. He'd a moments view of them before the beasts had run them down, standing in line abreast, pistols aimed, letting him know they were skilled practitioners of the lethal arts.

He turned to go, brought to a halt by the sound of a groan coming from the furthest end of the gore painted floor of stone. "My back. Legs—broken—I think. Are you there?" The man's eyes were closed, his skin gone pale from blood-loss and shock. Shaun went over and knelt, his hand on the butt of his pistol, ready should the man be less injured than he appeared, his legs a twist of torn cloth, stained red. His flesh rent in places with raw-edged wounds, white bone exposed. His upper body, bleeding from a hole in his lung.

"Yes. What are we to do next? Are we still to find the one we came in search of?"

"He's here. This—is one—one of his—his stratagems."

Shaun had made count of the bodies as close as could be done, coming up with eleven or twelve, some legs and arms torn from torsos, strew about or trapped beneath red-haired mounds. He leaned down. "The other men? Where are they? Should we go to them?"

"Sent—to the fooking—croft house. Two men—sent—there. Damn —the pain. It comes again. End it for me! I beg it of you—the soldier's gift."

Shaun ignored the dying man's pleas. "And what of the one who is to pay us, when finished? Where are we to meet?"

"The town. Back down—Barg—"

"Bargrennan."

"At—the inn. Man—all in white. The—" There was a short moment of silence, Shaun starting to rise, thinking the other had passed. Then the battered man forced his eyes open, though unable to bring them into focus. He drew in a final breath, letting it out, forming his final words. "Fooking—prig—bastard!"

Shaun lowered his hand, using his knife, making certain of the man's death. His eyes hardened into a solemn stare. He would need get Sinclair and Allyn heading back toward the manor to seal the shutters and bar the doors. With himself away to the croft in case the other two had managed to reach it, to try and prevent what might already have been done there. Leaving them free to turn their attention toward the manor, planning to join their cohorts, believing them well on the way there.

He stood up and limped to his horse, mounting it with difficulty, feeling every one of his sixty and four years as he nudged the large steed into a gallop.

⚘⚘⚘

Gran Ma's mill door was sealed. Aaron tugged to make certain the latch had dropped into place, preventing any mice an east entry. Meghan held a small bag of flour cradled to her chest, as if new born babe. Aaron knew if he but blinked, it would soon be so, his sister's destiny to step away from her bow and the hunt, as her body called her to other paths. Their days of togetherness soon to end as one young man or another would arrive and end up sweeping her away, leaving him in chase of highland stags, alone.

"Ready?" He got her nod and turned to follow, the wind beginning to build once more, a driving rain soon to follow. The mountains above seemed to be hunkering down, waiting for the worst that late Autumn weather would bring their way.

⚘⚘⚘

The smaller of the two men touched the slate wall of the stove. "Warm, still. He's been gone two hours or so—no longer."

"We'll head down, then. Join the others in the frolic." The large man grinned, his beady eyes bright in anticipation. "Heard there are three lovelies to be found there, or more. Two of them of an age, though barely." He smirked, his tongue running along the chapped lines of his thick lips.

The smaller man kept a look of disgust from his face, with effort. "And you're one to bring them into full flower, I suppose."

"Would be a pleasure for them, to have it done by me. Before slitting of their throats."

The smaller man shook his head, wondering for the fifth time the past hour how he'd come to be there. The men he'd shared campfires with for a week and two days were not the type he'd have willingly joined, had his need for coin not intervened. "It's the man we've come for. Papers, too. The house to be burnt, if they're not found. Nothing was said about killing anyone else. Especially women—young or old."

"Wasn't nothing said against it, neither." The larger man grinned, then wiped his nose, eyes looking at the ground. The discussion came to an end as they noting a line of tracks leading away, a horse's neigh pulling their attention to a small stable. "Might be we are in too great a haste in taking our leave. If he's on foot, we might soon have him in hand. The reward doubled if we catch him ourselves." The other man followed, pistol in hand, half-cocked, finger light on the trigger.

⸷⸷⸷

Sinclair stared at Shaun, his words faint in her ears. He noted her look, reaching out and pinching her cheek, bringing her to full attention. "Maybe three—but two for certain. You will need to go with Allyn and make ready at the manor. There's guns enow to load and position, firing slots well placed to give cover to the windows and doors. Eira can help reload. Marion too. You'll be safe there."

"And what of my children? Do you fear they may already be dead?"

"Hush now, lass. No need in thinking that. Fasten your thoughts on getting to the manor and making ready."

Sinclair could see Shaun's intent, his eyes glancing to a nearby pass that lead direct to the croft house, over a steep and dangerous ascent. She also knew that was where she needed to go. Now. Not a moment longer spent waiting.

"You'll be taking us there." She looked at Shaun. "To the manor—making certain it's clear?"

"Aye." Shaun lowered his eyes, staring at his hands, holding the stallion's reins. Sinclair nodded, then walked several steps away, stopping to gaze down toward the Pinch, her hands shaking as she pulled out the silver locket, holding it pressed to her lips. She tugged it, hard enough to part the thin chain, then let it drop to the ground. Turning around, she made her way toward her small mount, stopping beside Shaun's long-legged stallion. Then she reached for the missing cameo, looking to either side, her gasp of concern drawing the other's attention. "My locket! The one from my own dear Da! It was about my neck but a moment ago." Both boy and man dismounted, going over and scouring the grass in search of it. Sinclair slipped onto Shaun's mount, grabbing the reins, jamming her heels in, her feet clinging to its side, too short to reach the stirrups, away before they could stop her.

The boy leaped back aboard his own mount, ready to follow, stopping when Shaun yelled. "To the manor, lad. Prepare as best ya can. Make your shots, if needed, straight into the heart of any who show."

Shaun shook his head, hoping against hope to catch Sinclair before she reached the end of the pass, wishing her to fall from the horse and break an ankle along the trail, stopping her from riding into the danger he sensed lay ahead.

Aaron called out to his sister. "Drop it."

Meghan stopped, turning her head and looking back at Aaron. His bow was strung, arrow to the nock, another clenched between the fingers of his hand on the riser. She scanned the sides of the path to see what had caught his attention, a shadow of fear in her heart should it turn out to be a wild boar, though none should this high up.

"The flour. Drop it on the path. Hard—splitting it open."

"I will not!"

"Now." His tone heightened her sense of uneasiness as she raised the bag and threw it down, flour spraying out to all sides. Two hours of hard work, wasted. Her hands went to the bow slung on her back, making it ready for the large bladed arrow he pulled from his quiver and handed her. "Come." His second order was softer than the first as he moved back toward the Gran Ma's mill with herself close behind.

⸭⸭⸭

The large horse was in danger of faltering, its breath squeezed from its lungs in a shuddering suck and release, stumbling on a surface of loose rock. Sinclair leaned ahead, her voice in its ear, urging it up and over the last few paces of steep rise. Once they reached the top, she could see into the narrow valley, spotting the croft house below. She caught notes of smoke in the whip of wind, starting to build. Swore she could scent her children there, just ahead. Close by. She nudged the horse into a downhill angle, her hands loose on the reins, ready to slip from its wide back and make a rush to the door of the small house.

⸭⸭⸭

The two men stopped to stare at the flour spilled in center of the path they'd been following. The smaller one reached down, dipping the tip of a finger in it, raising it to his nose, then tasting it with a flick of tongue.

"Flour. Wheat."

The other man scoffed. "Flour? All the way up here?"

"Must be a mill nearby. It's not long from the grind."

"Where?" The large man looked at him, shaking his head. "We've seen no fookin' water."

The smaller man pointed. "There. In the fold up ahead—a hundred paces on." The other man squinted, then turned his head and spat, hitting the small mound of flour dead center. "Bollocks. Fookin' bollocks, this whole mess of shite!"

"In for a pence—in for a pound. Come on with your sad self—the raping will just have to wait."

⸭⸭⸭

Aaron took up station slightly above and to one side of Meghan, who was tucking her grass suit in around her, huddled down behind a cleft rock, making sure her arrow was in place, her fingers ready for the draw. He leaned down, kissing her forehead. "You must wait for my signal, no matter what your feisty self tells ya to do. Or you'll face something far worse than a lashing from Ma. Understand. Release on my signal. Watch for my arrow. Aim where it strikes." He started to pull away. Meghan reached out, grasping his wrist.

"Wait—what will it be? The target?" She hesitated, trying to swallow her fear. "Is it a—a boar?"

Aaron smiled, his love for her fully expressed. "If our luck holds—yes. But if not—" He watched her eyes widen, followed by a slight nod. "The one I mark will be yours. If there are two—load again and do the same."

"And if three—or more?"

"We slink away like frightened rabbits, our cotton tails tucked tight." He held up his hand, finger pointed. "I'll be just there." Then he was gone, moving a few paces away, leaving her feeling more alone than she'd ever felt before.

$$\text{\ding{120}\,\ding{120}\,\ding{120}}$$

Sinclair stood in the open, frustrated. No one had been in the house, Aaron's two horses and Meghan's mare in the stables, the large stallion whinnying in distress, lunging about as if signaling danger. Sinclair reached for the reins of the mount who'd given its all to get her there, then let them drop, knowing it would not survive another journey made.

She pulled a pistol from her waist, starting in a loping run along the winding path leading to Gran Ma's mill. They are there, she told herself. There is where I will find my children. To gather them up and bring them home.

$$\text{\ding{120}\,\ding{120}\,\ding{120}}$$

The mill door slammed open with a kick of the large man's booted heel. The interior was dark, with shadowed corners and recesses beneath a large table that held a light dusting of flour. The small man probed the edges with his pistol in aim, sensing no one was hiding there, the place empty, though in recent use.

"Well?" The large man stood just outside, his eyes scanning both sides of the trail they'd come in on.

"No one *here*. Keep your eyes in swing. Someone was here. Two of them, tracks in the dust on the floor. One a man. The other smaller. His woman, most like."

"Here for more than a grind of flour, I expect." Another hawk and spit came through the light mist of rain as the small man stepped back outside. "Your thoughts—are they always so crude? Fastened on the pleasures of the flesh? Or rather, their torture—based on recent comments, made."

The wind had risen to a howl at the top of the ridge, the air heavy, starting to spit sleet. He cut his gaze to the end of the path, a small run of water there falling away into an open field, gone fallow. The large man shrugged. "I'm no different than are most men. Take my pleasures where I find 'em."

The small man started to reply, then stepped to one side, pistol in his hand as a clattering of a rock on the path drew their attention toward it. The large man stepped aside, the two of them side by side as they focused their attention on the bend of grass and rock-lined slope. A woman, her face pale, came into view with a focused look on her face, moving at a quick pace, pistol in hand, hair unstrung, appearing to be on the verge of collapse.

Meghan felt her body shoved from the side by a gust of wind. The sky seeming to be angry at the ground, reaching out to slap it with ghostly hands. Too windy by far for any hope of an arrow aimed true, her mind wondering what had raised the hackles of her brother's honed instincts. What might appear below. The answer arriving as two men turned the far corner. She started to look for Aaron, then remembered his advice and stayed firmly locked in the spot he'd picked for her, determined to follow his lead.

Aaron knew they were in trouble, noting the pistol held in each man's hands. He'd learned to count on his instincts at moments like these, when several large stags were closing in, the death of one hovering in the balance. The men, moved like animals, cautious in their movements, scouring every inch of soil, grass, and sheltering rocks, ready to fire at the slightest motion seeming out of place. He remained in a frozen pose, hoping his sister was doing the same, watching as the two moved past, one into the mill, the other left standing outside the door.

The smaller man came back out, convincing Aaron to stay hidden until they left. Then he would gather Meghan up and make their escape through one of the high passes. His plan was torn to pieces when he saw their mother come into view, his instinct's rising once more, sensing blood was in the offing. More than willing to sacrifice his own, if it would deliver his mother and sister from the evil waiting below. A slap of wind hit his face from the side, funneled by the narrow path, steep hills to either side, channeling its raw energy. The thought of what he would need to do dragged a silent curse from between the compressed lines of his cold lips.

The large man grinned, his eyes lighting up with excitement. "A man's prayers—have just been answered." The sound of his voice brought the woman in approach to a halt. "Your weapon, miss, set down at your feet if you will. Then step this way." He paused, seeing her freeze in place. "We have what you came in search of—in here— inside the mill." He motioned to Sinclair, waiting for her to comply, the wind easing, the sound of his words louder in the angled pocket of path and hills. "I said, lower your weapon—"

"I heard you, assassin. The first time." Sinclair raised her pistol, using two hands, the weight of it causing her hands to tremble. "Let them come to me, unharmed—and you may leave with your lives."

"Our lives?" The big man grinned, started to reply when the smaller man leaned over, whispering in his ear, staying behind his bulk, his back to the narrow doorway. "Them—more than one out there, watching us where we stand. Care must be—"

The other man snorted. "I will not ask again. Your weapon—placed on the ground—then come forward. We'll release them once you disarm yourself—not before."

Sinclair knew she was without leverage in the deadly debate. No way clear for her or her children, if indeed they were inside. A small movement from one side almost drew her eye, her neck held firm, denying the least flicker of an eye. She felt the lowering of the wind from behind and knew her children were there, beside her. Arrows readied. One target only, the large man blocking the other. She half-cocked the weapon, ready to fire, if only to distract if nothing more, the distance too far for any hope of an accurate shot.

The small man pulled the large man to one side, stepping out and making a dart forward, covering the ground at speed as he watched the woman pull the trigger, the weapon failing to fire, left at half-cock. He saw her eyes widen in fear as she looked down and tried to remedy her error. He had the barrel of her pistol in his hand before she could react, wrenching it from her grasp, the butt used in a swift blow against the side of her head. Only to stun, and not kill, her knees folding as his arm circled her waist, guiding her to the ground. Then he pulled a knife from the top of one boot, raising it up for anyone in overwatch to see.

"She will die, if you do not rise and show yourselves."

A soft hiss of a man's voice came from behind. "She will not die, my pistol aimed at your head." The voice was gravel-thick, the words followed by the touch of metal to the back of his head. "I've come too far to be with her again—to let you or any army get in my way." Harold reached out, taking the knife from the man's hand, slipping it into the top of his own boot. "Your friend—has grown silent, his lungs filling with blood from two shafts, well placed."

The small man stared over, seeing a pinch of feathers from the ends of two arrows centered to each side of the other man's chest, his body on the ground, arms outstretched. "I am dead."

"Yes. Seems likely. Now stand and go to your friend. Do not turn around, and I promise you—I will make your death a quick one." Once the man had complied, Harold lifted Sinclair into his arms and checked her pulse, fingers on her wrist as he gazed into her eyes. The pupils were clear, no sign of concuss, the beating of her heart strong, steady.

She reached up grasping his forearm, looking over at the man kneeling by his partner, her gray eyes blinking as she recovered her wits, tears beginning to stream down her pale cheeks, as beautiful to Harold's eyes as the first time he seen her. "You—have returned."

Harold could not reply, his throat constricted, heart skipping a beat. A sigh of air, followed by another split the air as two shafts were released, with impact coming a moment in between. The small man clutched his chest, his partner's pistol flung to one side as he spun in a half-circle, his body collapsing in a puddle. Left looking up, gasping his final breaths, his face with a shocked expression and staring eyes.

The ground from the side of the draw rose up, revealing two of Harold's children, clad in suits of grass. One of them quickly shed as Meghan came toward him in a blur. She flung herself into his outstretched arm, clutching him, her thick hair a cushion for his tear-streaked face.

Aaron recovered the ghillie suit and dropped bow, then went to check on the two men, gently poking them in the eye with the tip of an arrow, the same as if they were downed stags, though he felt a moment of shame in the comparison. He replaced the shaft and unstrung both bows, taking his time, in no hurry to join the others. His mood was dour, without sense of accomplishment or pride from having saved his family. No real sense of anything, his mind focused on the routine of caring for his gear as he leaned down and began to work the shafts loose from the two men's flesh.

His father's voice reached out to him, a thin vibration in his ears gone numb. A sudden blow to his cheek brought a flood of pain, closely followed by the heaving of his lungs, his knees folding, pressing into the blood-stained ground as his stomach emptied itself of all he'd eaten that day.

Tears streamed down his cheeks, rubbed raw by the stiff breeze and icy rain, his nose in a steady run as he felt his Da's hand on his neck, firm fingers stroking through his hair. Soft-edged words filtering into his ears as he began to fall into a shadowed abyss.

"Let it come through you, son. Let it come through you—then out,

releasing as much as you can let go of. It'll help you later—believe me."
Harold reached out and closed the slain men's eyes, knowing the sight
of them would never leave his son. That he was now marked in the
same way those who'd been the cause of, or witness to, violent death
would always be, with a permanent stain left upon his soul. Then
Harold turned his head and watched Sinclair holding Meghan, the two
of them coming over in a steady shuffle, falling to their knees, their
arms flung across Aaron's broad back, sheltering him from the wind,
rain, and his pain.

CHAPTER TWENTY-ONE

HIGHLAND MANOR

AUTUMN, 1774

The weather had cleared, turning cold, with frost painting the ground in morning shadows, the sun scrubbing it away by mid-day. The roundup of wary-eyes cows had been made. Meat from those lost in the stampede left hanging to dry for winter feed, the bulk of it to be provided to a host of families in the lower places where Clan Scott held sway. Shaun had taken control of the cleaning up of the carnage at the Pinch, making several stop-on-byes to check in on everyone, nudging Harold with a bottle shared between the two of them, distracting the younger man's thoughts with a wry smile as he regaled him with tales of men known in common, most having passed on, gone to a place where only toasts made to their memories could ever find them again.

The manor and family had returned to a false appearance of normalcy, each member in quiet reflection on a host of questions that remained unanswered. Other than sweet Marion, eager as ever to climb into her father's lap, then out again, returning with one thing or another that caught her eye, collected since he'd left, nigh on three months before.

"And this is a paw from a large grouse—that I snatched!"

"Snared." Meghan stood beside her father, her hand on her sister's shoulder. "And it's a foot—not a paw."

"A foot—from one that I snared." Marion looked up, a smile of thanks on her face, closing her eyes as Meghan leaned down, kissing her forehead. "So—I will need to show you how to do that. How to snag—to snare one. Aaron showed us how to do it the first time, but now I am as good—almost as good as him." Marion twisted her head around, looking over at her brother, who was leaning against one side of the doorway of the great-room. Aaron returned a nod, forcing a thin grimace of a smile into place before turning around and walking away.

Sinclair was busy at work with Eira in the kitchen. She looked over as Aaron walked in and stopped to hug his Grand Ma, laying his head on her shoulder as she lifted her arms, threading his shoulders in a warm embrace, her hands raised to keep from getting flour on his shirt. Sinclair glanced over, her own hands busy with rolling out fresh dough, her heart going out to her son, knowing nothing could be done to relieve him of his depressive state. Harold had tried to explain it, unable to find the words, his eyes drifting away, voice fading to a sigh as he relived silent memories of his own, both recent and old.

"I'm off the croft—tomorrow." Aaron came over to his mother, towering above her shoulder. "The stags will be through the rut, and I'll be looking to take a young bull—for the meat."

Sinclair started to tell him they had food enough and more in hang, stopping when Eira caught her eye with a slow shake of her head. "Yes, son. The deer will make for a pleasant change in fare."

"Alone." His eyes stared into hers, though Sinclair knew her boy was not there, still trapped behind a wall \made of something she could barely touch, and never fully understand. She watched with a mother's desperation as he slowly turned and walked away.

"It's his Da he's in need of, child. No one else able to do what needs being done. Was the same for Harry when he returned from the colonies. His Da the only one he could unburden himself to."

Sinclair looked over at Eira, noting her bone-white hair, the blue of her eyes faded to a lighter shade, reflecting the light from candlelit walls, age and recent events having bleached the color from her. The price paid for a life lived as best one could manage it, she thought, with her adopted mother having done it better than most. She stood up and went over, giving Eira a warm hug, holding her close, drinking in her scent.

Eira pulled back, wiping her eyes, ignoring the smear of flour left behind on one cheek. "He's in a seethe of anger, now his Da's returned. The burden of caring for us all, too long in carry. One he is unable to let go of. Added to by the killing of two men—at his hand."

"And Meghan's—as well."

"On his command. The killing blow, his—both times."

"I'll talk to him."

"You'll need to do more than that, dear daughter. This family has been torn to tatters, with only sweet Marion escaping the damage done. It's in your hands, the sewing of it back together again. As wife, mother—and matron of the family Knutt."

Harold stood in the doorway of the bedroom, one he had shared with his wife, before. Unable to find a way to return to it, uncertain how to bridge the gap between the night he'd left and the fateful day of his return. There now, bidden by her invitation.

"Come in, husband." Sinclair was in a nightdress, her hair a thick fall of bonny curls gleaming beneath the wash of light from two candles in stands beside the bed she was sitting on. She watched as Harold made a hesitant approach, letting him reach the side of the bed before lifting a single finger, stopping him. Then she stood up, reaching out and cupping his cheeks between her hands, his skin cool to her touch. "You will be leaving us—on the morrow."

Harold remained still, as if a statue carved from flesh and bone. The candlelight danced in his eyes, reflecting from two depthless wells of blue, revealing his inner pain.

"To the croft, where you will make your home like your Gran Da did—two generations ago. While I will remain here—same as your

Grand Ma did herself." Sinclair stood up, her fingers touching the back of his head, untying a white strip of linen, freshly washed, as was himself. His scent filled her lungs, creating a need for his embrace. Her eyes narrowed as her voice thickened to a throaty murmur. "I will be widow to all who will hear it said, and make repeat of it down every draw, through every valley and wood, from here to the coast—and beyond." She ran her fingers through his unbound hair, encouraging it to fall across his broad shoulders, now shot through with strands of silvered-gray. "Then I will be wed. Again. When the time is right." Her fingers found the first button of his shirt, poised beneath his chin as a slight quiver began to build. "Not to you—but to your uncle. To Shaun."

A second button fell open to her touch, her lips trembling as her husband's eyes widened. "Not in body nor spirit—in name only—which I will take as mine." She saw tears spring from his eyes, waited for them to fall, then leaned in and kissed them away, his cheeks left glistening in the wavering light from the candles. "You will never have me again—as your loving wife." She rose up on her toes, pressing her mouth against his ear, her words dropping to a whisper. "Never again—after this last night together has passed." She paused, her own heart breaking as she forced herself to continue.

"I will lie with you this night—then die you must. Returning to me as a stranger met—living on high, away from sight of family and friends." She undid three more buttons, exposing his chest: white scars scattered between a layer of dark hair. "There." Her finger pressed against his flesh, feeling his heartbeat. "There is where I will come to you—when night falls. To lie with you as your lover—only. To hold your seed when your strength is spent. To eat, drink, and dance with you. But only as your lover—never again as your spouse." Her fingers were on his belt, releasing it, finding the buttons, and undoing them, one by one, until undone, his pants sliding down thighs as strong as the horse he'd rode in on that day at the croft. Finding Shaun's large stallion in near-death fatigue. The other steed, small mare and rugged mountain horse in the small barn, letting him know his two children were there, somewhere in the area.

"You will never again—as my husband—have the touch of these

beneath your hands." Sinclair placed his hands on her breasts, having slipped the tie in front, releasing them to his gaze, a gasp of pain and pleasure slipping between his clenched teeth as he squeezed with fingers formed of iron. "You will never—again—feel my lips on yours —as your wife." She found his mouth, her lips parting as her hand slipped down, finding him, her passion rising as he grew firm, her fingers in eager coax.

Sinclair reached out and pulled him down atop her, the bed sagging as it cradled their bodies. "Never again—as your spouse—wed—to have you—here." She sighed, his length slipping inside her as she clasped his lower back, her fingers clenching, releasing, then clenching again. "You will never—ever—again—have me as open to you as a wife. As I am now." Her moans became louder, beyond her ability to speak past them. The need for his touch, too long unmet. Her body tossing reason aside as the candles beside the bed flickered, their light casting entwined shadows onto the wall.

⸙⸙⸙

The small stag was dressed out, the cavity of its body held open with a stick to help it cool, though the air was barely above freezing. Aaron wiped blood from his hands with a careless drag through the coarse grass, gone over to brown beneath the steady approach of winter. He dried them on the stag's hide, using the residual heat of the slain beast to warm them, then gathered his bow and quiver. He tossed the ghillie suit over his shoulder then carefully descended a steep ridge to where the mountain horse was browsing, fruitlessly grazing the sparse ground to either side, as far as its tether would allow.

His father was standing there, gently stroking the stocky animal's neck, his voice soft as he spoke to it. Aaron nodded, then released the tether from its tie to a stunted tree. "You needn't have come."

"Was not my choice, alone—was added in with the concerns of your Ma and Gran Ma."

Aaron shrugged. "The two of them have the right to worry over me."

"Meaning to say—I don't."

Aaron turned away, leading the horse uphill. His father's voice caught up to him. "How large—the bull?"

"Was not a rack I went in search of—only meat."

Harold strengthened his voice, the wind rising, filled with the sting of icy rain. "How large?"

Aaron stopped, looking at the ground, his lips set in a firm line. "More than I'd planned on—by half."

"The animal—will it not be over-burdened?"

Aaron turned around, his face set in stone. "Are you offering to lend your back to the hauling down of it?"

Harold didn't bother to reply, knowing his son still considered him as no more to him than a stranger. He waited until Aaron retied the long lead, then leaned into the slope, following him up the steep hill.

☙☙☙

The meat was hanging in the stable, the day having turned over to night as they'd finished up, the hours of daylight eaten up by the decreased angle of the sun in the sky. The air was heavy with dampness, promising frost on the ground by morning. Harold stood in the doorway of the croft house, neither fully in nor out as heat flowed out around him, thick with the rich scent of a venison stew. He called out to his son, sitting at the table, back to him. "I'll be in the stable, using the tack room as my bed. Then head back first thing in the morning."

Aaron nodded, locked in a sullen mood with no more than a handful of words exchanged during the long haul down. He turned his head, hearing the door close as his father strode away. He opened his mouth to call him back, then shut it again as he started to form the words, bowing his head, the heat of the fire in the stove creating a heavy fatigue. He turned down the damper, watching as the stew came to a slow boil, a soft curse on his lips.

The whole world had gone upside down, he thought to himself. Nothing right in taste or feel. His only refuge, his Gran Ma, who never asked anything in return. Offering her shoulder, without useless attempts made to try and explain what he couldn't define for himself: how the eyes of the dead men were always there, staring back at him wherever he looked. Watching him from the eyes of the stag, as the arrow was released, unblinking as the shaft penetrated its side and punctured both lungs.

They were still there, even now, even here where he'd hoped to be free of them. In front of him as he stared at the boot-stamped dirt floor. Blue, he whispered to himself, those of the smaller man, gazing up as if able to see what lay on the other side. A person's life, ended by his hand, taking it from him in choosing to release of a bowstring, leading to dire and unrecoverable circumstances, no matter the cause or justification made. He watched as tears fell to the floor, soaking into the soil like drops of blood, robbed of its color.

The sound of his son's voice pulled Harold from a dream. One where he was young again, in a backyard test of will with Jackie, each delivering strokes of wooden sabers as they battled, cheeks and knuckles at risk. Blows landing with bruising effect on forearms raised as shields formed of muscle and bone. The contests ending short of any real damage, himself the arbiter of truce offered, or asked. Their two faces covered in a sheen of sweat and crooked smiles. Only a game, played between two brothers in a moment of shared admiration for each ones skill and will.

"Father—"

Harold was through the door of the tack room in a blur, the tone of his son's voice indicating dire need. He found Aaron leaning against the stall, the smaller horse hanging its head over the stall wall, its muzzle snuffing the young man's hair. Harold went over and took his full bodied son into his arms, feeling the shudder of unbound emotions. No words were needed, Harold understanding the need for release, having felt it himself, many years ago and far away.

"There is no shed of it. No—no place I can look and not see the—the sight of it. Always there before me."

Harold was sitting in a small chair, hands clasped between his knees, in support of his son's halting attempt to get it said. The stove of the croft house was in a low glow with tea steeping in a kettle, keeping the house warm.

Aaron looked up, his eyes full of tears. "How—I mean—you've been there so many times. Why is it so easy for you—for you and Gran Uncle Shaun—when the two of you share your stories—the memories of those you've served with. When speaking of the men lost, or— killed." Aaron looked up, his face open to his grief. "Why is it nae the same as the taking of a stag's life? Is one death greater—or less than t'other?"

"They are much the same, Aaron—with man and stag. Each clinging to life as long as they are able to—no matter if it be a man or beast."

"Then it is me with no stomach for it—when nae a beast."

Harold squeezed his son's broad shoulders, a match to his own, feeling a man's body wrapped round a boy's heart and soul. "I would wish the answer to be left there Aaron—if only to protect you from yourself, in knowing who you are. Your spirit—your will pulled from the same bank of clay as was mine—and your two Grand Da's. With all our fingers pressed firmly into the making of who you are, from every side."

Aaron straightened up, staring at his father. "My mother's—Da? I had thought him a person of letters, with a genteel disposition. A Lord —a man of politics."

Harold released his son and stood up, going to the door and opening it, checking the direction of wind in the grass while listening for any sound of discontent from the animals in the stable. He closed it then turned around, leaning against it and taking a deep breath, releasing it with a drawn out sigh. "Not that one, son. But your mother's real father. The man who formed her from his own flesh and blood, passed down to you." Harold looked at Aaron, no longer able to find the young boy who'd come running, tossing himself into his arms, laughing with unbound joy on his and his mother's return from the colonies. "It's the reason we went, your mother and I, to the colonies when you were still a child. Taking her to where I placed her father—so she could know of him from the press of hand to his grave."

Harold went over and lifted a thick wool blanket from a wooden chest. He touched it with the tip of his boot. "It's all in here. All my journals—from that day, and before. From when I first left Bristol for the war in the colonies. My own story, here—along with his and many others. Your story too, or the beginning of it—for now." He looked at his son, watching Aaron's eyes widening as the roots of his ancestry came into full flower.

"His name?"

"Robert—Robert Scott. Born into a small croft in the north of England, close to the border."

"Does that mean he was—of the same clan as us?"

"Most likely, aye. As you are—on both sides. That's why you've been allowed to live here, for the greater part of the year. Why you're to go to the same university I attended, next year."

"You served together—in the war against the French. You mentioned you buried him. Were the one to bury him. Where?"

"In the western reaches beyond the Pennsylvania colony. Atop a high place, with a grand view. Looking east—toward his home. As near as I could get to bringing him here, burdened as I was at the time, facing his demise—and in quiet consideration of my own."

Aaron stood up and came over, touching the toe of his boot to the wooden chest. It was made of hardwood, with thick metal bands and two solid brass latches. He looked at his father with light-colored eyes, a match to his mothers. "Am I—am I allowed to read them?"

Harold didn't hesitate. "Aye, son—as I said, they're part of your story, too. With your own words to add—in time. If you choose it."

"My—Gran Da—Robert. You've written his story down in there as well?"

Harold nodded. "Along with many others. Of those I fought with— and against. People I met and fell in love with—before I found your dear Mother. Some who were lost to me. Each one—a dagger to my heart. One of them—more than all the rest, combined." Harold let his tears flow as he gazed at the boy who'd become a man as tall and broad as himself. "Bravery—one's ability to face up to the realities of life—to the taking of it from another person's desperate grasp—is a burden you will carry for as many days and nights as you are left with. Your own measure to make, the justification of it. Same as your dear sweet mother had to do—with what she went through with Gran Uncle Shaun in the Pinch."

Harold stopped, his eyes taking on a distant look, one Aaron recognized, having seen it many times before. "It's easier—what you did—for both you and your sister. Easier when killing to defend your family against evil men with hard eyes. Easier than the taking of a soldier's life—approaching from the other side of the field. Someone with similar upbringing, parents filled with expectations of a long life for their child. Worshipping the same God, at times. The same church—same need for friends and family."

Harold paused, collecting himself. "The same expression in their eyes when you lean down and close them, of a person no different than you, knowing it was your ball, or knife, or bayonet—or arrow, that's taken all from him. All their days in stretch, their laughter and joy, aches and pains. That's the rock you can never crawl out from under. The first one, a heavier burden than the rest, and never forgotten. Like the first kill of an animal. First fight with someone outside your—clan. First kiss. First love. First heartache, when love is lost to you through no fault of your own. The first of many miseries borne, coming from the loss of people close to you—due to difficult decisions having to be made—to try and right a wrong."

Aaron opened his mouth, realizing his father was talking about the reason for having left his family behind. As he started to ask, the door swung open: Meghan standing there with tears on her freckled face. She flung herself into her father's arms as he turned toward her, leaving Aaron to close the door then come over, laying his hand on her shoulder.

"Gran Ma said you were up here. That Ma sent you away. I called her a lying bitch! I struck her. I took her favorite vase and—and smashed it on the floor. Told her she was a liar." Meghan pulled back, her eyes red from the cold rain. "Da—tell it true—that you're coming home. You're coming back to us—back to me." She collapsed, her strength spent. Aaron helped his father carry her to the small bed and cover her with a thick wool blanket, the stove vent opened, allowing the fire to build. Harold held Meghan's hand while she shook her head in grief, adrift in a fog of misery, knowing from the look in her Da's eyes that her Gran Ma had told it true. Her breath came in shuddering sobs, her chest aching, feeling as if her heart was about to burst.

Daylight slipped through the small window of the house, left partway opened so Meghan would know afternoon had found its way to the small valley in the shouldered draw. She stretched, feeling rested, having had her first real sleep since the chaos at the mill and later events, each taking a toll. Made to cross between emotions of horror, to joy, then back again at the thought of her father being banished from the manor home. Now that she'd had a chance to recover, Meghan was certain she'd discovered how to work things to her advantage. Confident in her well-honed skill at manipulation, practicing with young boys hanging around the manor fields, seeking work.

Meghan poured herself a cup of warm tea, then shoved a biscuit in her mouth as she opened the door and stepped out into the sunlight. The air was crisp. The weather cool, and dry, the storm from the night before having passed. She could hear her Da in the stable, mucking it out, a barrow standing by the door, half-filled. She walked over, smiling, eager to let both brother and father know of her plan. When she entered the stable, the stalls were empty, Aaron's sturdy horse no longer there, with her father's bay standing in the paddock enclosure. Her own sweet little mare was nowhere in sight. Meghan turned to one side, watching as her father came out from behind the building, shovel in hand.

"My brother—has left?"

"Good morning to you, daughter." Harold leaned the shovel against a fencepost. "Aaron headed back with the meat from the stag, leaving before sunrise, no doubt giving it a wave as they passed each other by." Harold wiped his brow with the back of his forearm, finished with the chore. He grabbed the handles of the over-filled barrow and started to wheel it away, aware the day would come when such a thing would prove more difficult to attend to. The stable left framing a single horse or large bull, he supposed, in a reflection of his own Grand Da from what seemed to have been an age ago.

"Where's my horse? Did Aaron take it with him? She's not his to take—"

"Go, and *look* for it, child. Starting from where you left it last night, standing in the rain. It shouldn't have wandered too far."

Meghan pursed her lips, wanting to assign blame to someone else, shrugging as she accepted the responsibility, heading off to find a high point from where to spot it in the brush-lined slopes.

Harold could see his daughter's thoughts as if reading them in a book, knowing she was set to a path she would not be easily moved from. Stubborn, brilliant, firm in body and mind, and absolutely stunning in form, with a radiant glow of love flowing from her, matched by knife-sharp anger. And fully his, as she'd been since her first draw of air. Now on the cusp of being a woman, and unaware of what lay in store for her. Her plan no doubt to visit him every day or so. One doomed to failure as her uphill treks would dwindle away as young men with hearts in their throat and flowers in their hands tried to coax her away, leaving him with another hole to fill. His only salvation: the increase of visits by a woman no longer his to call wife. With longer stays in between. Until, when enough time had passed for him to be no longer be considered a threat to men in far off places, he would take his family in hand and head to the colonies, once the flames of the impending war for independence flared up, burning bright for a while before dying down, as he knew they would.

The sound of hoofbeats caught his ears as he upended the barrow, adding to a pile of future loam. Of shite turned into seeds, he thought with a smile, same as it has always been, remembering the old man who'd given him a vision, come true. He hadn't returned as husband and father. His wife left a widow with a fatherless brood, just as his Gran Da had told him on a morning much like this one was promising to become.

Harold watched as his daughter came on in a full gallop, the mare coming to a sliding stop, Meghan dismounting with a throaty laugh as she ran toward him then struck a pose, hands on her hips, just starting to swell, with a crooked smile on rose-colored lips 'neath sky-blue eyes. Her hair was in a loose formed twist of burnished copper and gold, backlit by the sun, looking so much like her namesake, it caused him to lose his breath. So aptly named, he whispered as she walked toward him. Madonna—standing in the sun.

The End of Book Two

ABOUT THE AUTHOR

M. Daniel Smith is a writer of fiction, with interest in producing series covering various genres including historical fiction (Legacy's Road) speculative psychological (*Coalescence*) historical/sci-fi (*A Soul, Between*) and an upcoming murder mystery (*The Cross*).

His writing encompasses relationships between a diverse group of characters that are real to life, gritty at times, intelligent and feisty, helping to connect the reader emotionally to people that are difficult to let go of. (Thus, the series presentation)

Raised in a blue-collar environment, he spent hours in front of his mother's extensive library, reading novels, exposed to every genre of literary works, from family sagas on through to sci-fi, military histories, and the like.

Now retired, able to write full time, he fills his days with the words sent him by the characters who show up, compelling the telling of their stories, allowing readers an intimate look into their motives, desires, joys—and moments of pain. His own thoughts, beliefs, and experiences, garnered from a life lived full, are liberally sprinkled throughout his writing.

Daniel can be reached at mdanielsmith@aol.com, or at PO Box 49, Phippsburg, ME 04562. His website is: www.bayledgespress.com.

www.ingramcontent.com/pod-product-compliance
Lightning Source LLC
Chambersburg PA
CBHW030922210726
48290CB00007B/2033